P9-AON-624

LANA'S WAR

Also by Anita Abriel and available from Center Point Large Print:

The Light After the War

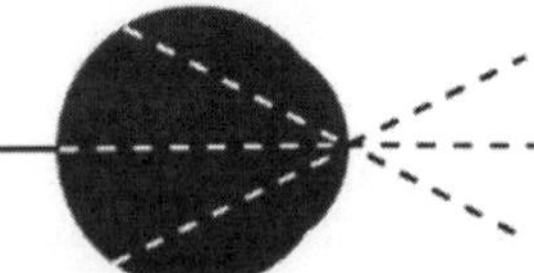

This Large Print Book carries the Seal of Approval of N.A.V.H.

LANA'S WAR

Anita Abriel

Center Point Large Print
Thorndike, Maine

This Center Point Large Print edition
is published in the year 2021 by arrangement with
Atria Books, a division of Simon & Schuster, Inc.

The text of this Large Print edition is unabridged.
In other aspects, this book may vary
from the original edition.
Printed in the United States of America
on permanent paper.
Set in 16-point Times New Roman type.

ISBN: 978-1-64358-842-1

The Library of Congress has cataloged this record
under Library of Congress Control Number: 2020950551

To my mother

Chapter One

PARIS, JULY 1943

Lana Hartmann hurried down the Boulevard Saint-Germain to St. Catherine's school, where Frederic taught piano. For once, the signs of the occupation—the slick German cars cruising down the boulevards, the Parisians crammed into buses, the endless lines of people waiting hours for a stick of butter—didn't bother her. She was wildly, irrationally happy.

If it was possible, she was happier than the day she and Frederic had married in the autumn of 1941. Everyone said they were crazy: Who gets married when Europe is at war? Her wedding gown was an old party dress, and her shoes were made of rubber. But when she faced Frederic in the office at city hall, she felt as elegant as a princess.

Her hand went instinctively to her stomach. She couldn't wait to tell Frederic her news. It was the worst possible time to have a baby; they couldn't even afford an extra loaf from the corner patisserie. But Hitler and his army couldn't take away the velvet sheen of a baby's cheek, the sweet smell of breast milk on its breath.

Lana froze at the sight of a German truck that was parked in front of the convent. The sight of any truck emblazoned with the red and black swastika filled her with dread. The Germans usually left the nuns alone. With rising concern, she walked around the stone building and noticed Frederic standing in the music room talking to two Gestapo officers. She crouched down so the top of her head couldn't be seen from inside and listened through the open window. If she raised her chin, she could just see Frederic facing the two men.

"Your papers, please," the older officer said. He was in his thirties with a widow's peak and dark eyes.

Frederic produced his papers, and the officer examined them carefully.

"Frederic Hartmann?" He looked at Frederic quizzically. "Hartmann doesn't sound French."

"My mother is French and my father is of German descent. . . ." Frederic stammered.

Frederic developed a slight stutter when he was nervous that Lana had always found endearing. It took him ages to get out the five words *Lana, will you marry me?* She had waited with delight for him to finish the sentence.

"You are from the north, from Lille?" the officer prompted.

"I came to Paris to study music at the university."

“You must have been quite the musical protégé to come all the way to Paris.” The officer pointed to Frederic’s ring. “And you are married.”

“My wife is a student too; she’s going to be a chemist.”

“An upstanding young couple.” The officer handed Frederic his papers. “The rumors must be wrong.”

“Rumors?” Frederic gulped. Lana could see his Adam’s apple bobbing on his neck.

“There is a rumor that several Jewish children are attending St. Catherine’s convent, studying music.” His eyes narrowed. “I must have been misinformed.”

“Yes, you must be,” Frederic answered. This time his voice was stronger. As if he knew he had to vanquish his own fears to protect the children. “There are no Jewish children here.”

“Then you won’t mind if Gunther looks around.” The officer waved at the younger man.

“I’d be happy to take you to the children,” Frederic said. “They are with Sister Catherine studying geography.”

“You and I will stay here.” The officer glanced at the piano. “You can play some Wagner for me. One of the things I miss about Germany is hearing my beloved Wagner.”

Frederic sat stiffly at the piano. Lana held her breath. Frederic refused to play Wagner these days. How could he play music by Hitler’s favorite composer when Hitler was intent on wiping out all the Jews in Europe? And Wagner himself was known for despising Jews.

There was the sound of voices, and the younger officer appeared in the doorway. Lana craned her neck even farther to look into the room and saw four dark-haired children. Two she recognized: Ida and Sophie Rosenberg were Jewish sisters. Their father had been shot by the Gestapo for arguing with a German officer. His wife had been in labor, and the officer wouldn't let them pass without their papers. By the time the girls' father went back to their flat to retrieve them it would have been too late to get to the hospital. There was a scuffle, and Sophie and Ida's father was killed.

"These children were hiding in the laundry room." The officer pushed them into the room. "Sister Claudette was with them."

Lana could see his pistol gleaming in its holster, and she put her hand over her mouth. She couldn't make a sound; it would only cause more trouble if anyone discovered her.

"You mustn't blame Sister Claudette or any of the nuns in the convent for having Jewish children," Frederic said. "It's my fault; these children are so talented it would be a crime if they couldn't study piano."

Frederic looked at the children, and Lana remembered the first time she saw his brown eyes and knew instinctively that he was kind as well as handsome.

"I understand your dilemma," the older officer said pleasantly. "The German army has been in Paris for three years, and the French still don't appreciate how much we support the arts. We brought the Berliner Philharmonicker to perform at the Paris Opera. We hold German music festivals and art shows all the time." The benevolent expression disappeared. "But it is a greater crime to allow Jewish children to attend school when it is strictly forbidden. Everyone makes mistakes, Frederic Hartmann." He lingered on his last name. "I will escort the children home to their parents and warn them it must never happen again."

The younger officer's grip tightened on Sophie, and she let out a small yelp.

"I'll take them," Frederic volunteered.

"That won't be necessary," the older man said. "We have a truck waiting out front."

Lana saw Frederic take in the gleaming pistol. "It's an easy walk from here." Frederic reached for his hat. "It will feel good to get some air."

"Is your wife pretty?" the officer asked.

"My wife?" Frederic said, surprised. "Yes, she's beautiful."

"And you would like to see her again."

The color drained from Frederic's cheeks, and his hands fell to his sides. "Yes, of course."

"Then you will stay here while we take the children," the officer instructed. He moved the children toward the door when a muffled sound came from the grand piano.

The officer stopped.

"Open the piano." He took out his pistol and waved it at Frederic.

"Why would I open the piano, there's nothing inside," Frederic stammered.

"Do as I say or these children will see your blood splattered all over the floor."

Lana watched Frederic fumble with the piano lid. A small face appeared, and Lana recognized Esther Cohen. She was six years old. Her father had been Frederic's music professor before he was sent to a labor camp. Her mother worked two jobs, so Frederic sometimes brought her to school with him.

"Please don't hurt her," Frederic begged. "The sound of your boots scared her. I told her to get in the piano."

"Hand me the child." The officer pointed his gun at Esther.

"I'll take responsibility for her." Frederic held her in his arms. "She isn't doing any harm. She's an innocent child."

"Give me the child now," the officer barked.

Frederic tried to put Esther behind his back, but the younger officer grabbed her. Esther screamed, and Frederic lunged for her. Then the other officer fired his pistol. The shot made a sound that seemed to bounce off the walls of the music room and pierce Lana's heart.

Lana stood on tiptoe and saw Esther dissolve into sobs and was relieved that she was alive. But then she peered closer and saw Frederic's body splayed over the piano seat. Blood seeped from his chest and the worn rug turned red.

Lana sat on a bench in the Place du Panthéon opposite the Sorbonne. Her teeth chattered; she couldn't stop shivering. She wasn't ready to go home yet, to see Frederic's music books and his photographs. Frederic loved taking photographs. He said even with the war there would be times they would want to remember: a weekend bicycle ride to the country that resulted in finding fresh vegetables and a whole carton of eggs; the kitchen table set with their one good tablecloth and a plate of mushroom omelets. Whenever Lana looked at the photo she could taste the fluffy yellow of the yolk and the olive oil used in the pan.

Frederic was too serious to be an optimist. He wasn't like the students who sat around the cafés and proclaimed the Allied army would recover and push the Germans out of Paris. But she loved his seriousness. He was serious about his music and about their marriage, and he would have been serious about the baby. He would have checked hourly to make sure her chest was rising and falling when she slept.

She would miss his gentle manner and the way he made her feel loved and cherished. Only a few hours ago, this had been the happiest day of her life. She couldn't wait to tell Frederic about the baby. How would she carry on without having him to talk to? Ever since they'd met, she had told him everything. She remembered when he had first approached her. All the students in the chemistry department knew one another. But Frederic didn't tag along to any of the boisterous study sessions that often ended with someone taking out a bottle of schnapps. So she was surprised when he slid onto a bench beside her as if they were friends.

SEPTEMBER 1940

The Germans had occupied Paris for three months. For the most part Lana tried to ignore them. Although rationing had begun, she could still get a café crème from the patisserie near campus. And if she walked quickly, she barely heard the soldiers whistling at her from their seats at the outdoor cafés.

She was sitting in the park, a textbook in her lap.

"Do you mind if I sit down?" A male voice interrupted her studying. Lana looked up to see a man in his twenties with dark brown hair.

"I recognize you. You're Lana Antanova," he said before she could answer.

"How do you know my name?" she asked.

"You're in my chemistry class. I looked you up on the class list," he replied. His eyes sparkled when he smiled. "You wear crêpe dresses, and you always know the right answers."

He took a bag of raisins out of his sack and offered it to her.

"I didn't think anyone noticed what I wear," Lana commented. She had seen him walking around between classes. He had always been alone. Could he be flirting with her?

"My mother works at a dress store in Lille," he explained. "When I was younger she'd take me to work. I learned to appreciate colors and fabrics."

"My mother lent me the dress; we're the same size." Lana ate a handful of raisins. "I like wearing something pretty, especially with all the Germans in their drab uniforms. It might sound frivolous, but I've always believed beauty makes you happy. I used to visit the Louvre every weekend." She sighed. "But now that *Venus de Milo* and the *Mona Lisa* are hidden, it's like attending a wake."

"I don't think beauty is frivolous," Frederic said earnestly. "I'm studying to be a pianist. Music fills up my head and here." He pointed to his heart.

Lana closed her book and paid more attention. None of the other boys in her class understood her. They all thought girls in pretty dresses didn't belong in the laboratory.

"I'm going to open a cosmetics company so when women look in the mirror, they're happy. I'll have a store on the Champs-Élysées with my name in gold letters over the window."

"I wish I had a head for business. I'm only taking chemistry to please my father. He said if I was coming all the way to Paris to attend the conservatory I also had to take classes at the university that were useful. He doesn't believe music is a real career."

"Chemistry isn't useful unless you want to be a chemist." Lana laughed.

"It was either chemistry or engineering, and I'm even worse at technical drawing."

"I can help you study chemistry," Lana offered.

"Would you?" He brightened. "I can't afford to pay you, but I have tickets to a student concert on Saturday night. Perhaps afterward we could get something to eat."

Was Frederic asking her on a date? She wondered if she wanted to date him. She knew so little about him. But there was no reason to turn him down. His eyes were kind, and there were so few opportunities to enjoy herself.

"All right," she said, and handed him the bag of raisins. "I would like that very much."

• • •

On Saturday, Lana stood in front of the mirror at her dressing table and adjusted the buttons on her dress. The school week had seemed to drag on forever.

She did a small turn and studied the blue dress and matching cape. Was it too elegant to wear to a student concert? But Frederic complimented her dresses, and the color brought out her eyes.

Lana and her mother had moved into the apartment on Avenue Montaigne three years ago, when her mother had married Count Jacques Delacroix. Lana had delighted in the interior: a living room with red velvet walls and parquet floors like something out of Proust. Her own room with a wrought iron balcony overlooked the courtyard. And her mother had a closet just for her newly purchased ball gowns. For most of Lana's childhood she had recycled the few dresses she'd brought from Russia until they had to be held together with clothespins.

But since the war began, she felt guilty for having thick rugs under her feet when Jews who had lost their homes slept in doorways. How could she appreciate the fireplaces in almost every room when all of Paris worried about having enough coal for the winter?

Her mother reminded her that the apartment had been in Jacques's family for decades, which hadn't made life under occupation easier. Their cook quit when her husband was sent to the front. Her mother presented her coupons at the shops like everyone else. The kitchen occupied a whole floor, but its cupboards were practically empty.

Lana appraised her dress one last time and walked to the hallway. Her mother and Jacques were away in Biarritz, and the rooms were silent. She felt a twinge of guilt for inviting Frederic without her mother's permission. But they would only be there for a minute. Frederic was just a school friend.

There was a knock at the door, and Lana answered it. Frederic towered over her even though she had on heels. He wore a blazer with patched elbows and held a small bunch of daisies.

"For me?" she said. "I didn't know you could buy fresh flowers in Paris unless you're a German general."

"They're from my landlady's garden." He glanced around the entry and noticed the crystal chandelier. "I thought I must have the wrong apartment. The mailbox said *Comte Delacroix*."

"That's my mother's husband," Lana said. "Please come in while I put the flowers in water."

When she returned with a vase, she found Frederic examining the artwork.

"Is that a Salvador Dalí?" He looked up.

"The count wrapped up all the valuable artwork and stashed it in the country." Lana nodded. "He replaced them with a few modern pieces in case a nosy German gains entrance and wonders why the frames are empty."

Frederic opened his mouth to say something and then closed it. Lana glanced at the grandfather clock and gathered her purse.

"We should probably go, I don't want to make us late."

Frederic was quiet on the walk to the theater, and Lana thought he was nervous. But he hardly said anything at intermission too, and when it was over, he stood awkwardly outside the auditorium.

"I think I'm coming down with a fever, perhaps I should take you home."

Her hand went to his forehead the way her mother always checked if she had a temperature.

"You feel perfectly cool."

"I have something, I wouldn't want to get you sick." He shuffled his feet. "We could have dinner another night."

They walked silently to the apartment. Lana's heels clicked along the pavement. She wondered what had changed since last week and then considered the start of their date.

"You think because I live in a fancy apartment, we shouldn't be together. Is that why you don't want to have dinner?" she demanded, hardly pausing to let him speak. "But my life wasn't always like this. For most of my life, we had nothing. My parents were both members of the

Russian nobility. My father was killed by the Bolsheviks, and I was born in a refugee camp.

"My mother did anything for us to survive: took in sewing, worked at a Citroën automobile factory. She met her husband when she worked in the cloakroom at the Ritz. Jacques asked her out for three months, but she refused because she didn't have a good dress." Lana's eyes flashed. "The first time he proposed she turned him down; she wouldn't marry without being certain she was in love."

Lana finished, and her eyes dropped to the ground. She had never spoken to a man like that before, but she couldn't let him walk away without knowing her history. His hand touched her shoulder, and she looked up.

"I know a place where we can get veal cutlets if you're still hungry," Frederic offered.

"Veal cutlets." Lana's mouth watered. Her mother hadn't been able to find veal cutlets at the butcher since July.

"A friend has a restaurant in Le Marais. He gets veal on the black market. He wraps the cutlets inside a lettuce leaf for his favorite customers, and no one is the wiser."

Lana imagined a juicy veal cutlet brushed with oil and sprinkled with basil.

"A whole veal cutlet?" she breathed.

"We might have to share one, but we can each have our own dessert," Frederic said, and his smile was as bright as the lampposts lighting the sidewalk.

Lana sat on the bench in the Place du Panthéon and rubbed a bloodstain on her skirt. The shock of the afternoon had left her exhausted and her thoughts jumbled together.

For three years, they had lived in fear, but the fear was somewhat removed: like a gossamer curtain that separated the stage from the audience. Of course Lana had witnessed things that left her shaking: when she went to her mother's one day and found the Levins' apartment on the second floor empty. No one knew where they had gone, but Lana discovered Madame Levin's toy poodle trembling in their coat closet and was certain they had been sent to a labor camp.

Last year, Avram in her geometry class never returned from summer vacation. Lana learned from a professor that Avram was one of the five thousand Jews rounded up by French police and sent to Drancy. From there they were put on trains to one of the camps in the east.

But now the abstract fear had become something that happened to her. The misery was so thick and deep it threatened to overpower her. It would be easy to let it take its course, to sit on this bench forever and simply stop living.

She noticed a new bloodstain on her skirt before the pain even started. The spot spread between her legs, and she stood up and shakily walked the five blocks to their flat.

The knot that had been in her stomach since she had hid outside the convent became a knife piercing her flesh. She climbed three flights of stairs like a blind person led by a sense of the familiar. Then she sunk to the floor and slid to the bathroom.

It was only hours later, when the cramps subsided and she had somehow managed to heat up a hot-water bottle that she let herself acknowledge what had happened. The Gestapo officers hadn't just shot Frederic, they had also murdered Frederic's child.

Chapter Two

PARIS, OCTOBER 1943

Lana stood in the convent kitchen and sliced a rutabaga. These days, it seemed the only thing she did was slice vegetables. In the three months since Frederic died and she lost the baby, it was one of the few ways of dulling the pain. She was slowly pulling herself out of her grief. The first two months had been a blur of whole days spent sleeping, coupled with nights when sleep wouldn't come. She lay hunched on Frederic's side of the bed and pictured the Gestapo officer's gleaming pistol and Frederic lying in a pool of blood on the piano seat.

Her mother visited every day, and her landlady kept an eye on her at night, and Sister Therese brought flowers from the convent's garden. Eventually, Lana began getting dressed and venturing outside. Shopkeepers who didn't know what happened waved gaily as if she and Frederic had been on vacation. Monsieur Gaston, who owned the bakery, had scraped up ingredients to make a *pain au chocolat* because he remembered it was their anniversary.

Lana returned to the university in the new term, but she took only one class. Even turning the pages of her textbook was difficult. She was like the patients in the military hospitals who had gone off to war whole and healthy and now struggled to feed themselves. Slicing vegetables was easier. She didn't have to solve chemistry equations or interact with classmates.

"Lana, you shouldn't spend all your time in our kitchen." Sister Therese entered the room. She placed a bucket of potatoes on the counter and took out a peeler.

"You're saying that because you don't like my cooking." Lana laughed. "I only had rationing coupons for rutabaga. But the vendor gave me a new recipe: dice the rutabaga and stir it into vegetable bouillon. He said it's delicious."

"Rutabaga stopped being delicious months ago." Sister Therese grimaced. "When the war is over, I never want to eat rutabaga again. Even if it is accompanying sirloin tips and served in the dining room of the Hôtel de Crillon."

"I think you're right." Lana stared despondently at the yellow vegetable. Rutabaga was the only thing that grew plentifully in wartime. They had it almost every meal. "I'd give a week of my life to turn this rutabaga into a crêpe."

"I forgot what a crêpe tastes like," Sister Therese said.

"A crêpe filled with raspberries and fresh crème and dusted with powdered sugar," Lana said dreamily, recalling the first months of their marriage when it was possible to find a restaurant that served crêpes. She and Frederic didn't mind the growing lack of food on the shelves with the promise of sweet crêpes once a week. The memory dissolved, and she stabbed the rutabaga with a knife.

"Be careful, you'll slice your finger." Sister Therese watched her. "You spend all morning in class, and then you come here and help with the children until nighttime. When do you have time to cook your own dinner or see people?"

"There's no one I want to see." Lana grunted. "I like being here, I feel useful."

"We are grateful for everything you do." Sister Therese nodded. "I know it hasn't been long since Frederic died, but you mustn't forget that you're alive."

"What if I don't want to live?" Lana returned. "The Gestapo took everything, I couldn't even save my baby."

"It's not your fault that you lost the baby," Sister Therese countered.

"You can't understand what it's like to lose everything."

Sister Therese's eyes dimmed, and she bowed her head. Her expression was filled with grief.

"Three nuns at our sister convent in Lyon were stabbed by Gestapo officers for harboring Jewish refugees," Sister Therese said quietly.

"I'm sorry, you're right," Lana said. "Everyone

in France has experienced loss. At least here I don't have to think. It's easier to slice rutabaga than to imagine life without Frederic."

"What if I knew a way you can help others survive?" Sister Therese looked up from the potatoes. "And avenge Frederic's death at the same time."

Lana stopped. She turned to stare at Sister Therese.

"What are you saying?" she asked.

"Certain people come to nuns and tell us things. People who despise the Nazis."

"Like what?"

"I was approached by a man who had heard of you. He would like to meet you."

"A man wants to meet me?" Lana repeated.

"If I tell you more, I'm putting you in danger."

Lana remembered the way the Gestapo officer was so friendly to Frederic and then mocked him. She recalled Esther's frightened eyes when she was discovered in the piano.

"I would like to meet this man," she said.

"Are you sure? Once you do, your life will never be the same."

Lana wiped the knife with the sleeve of her dress. "I'm perfectly sure. Please tell me where."

Lana looked from the piece of paper that Sister Therese had given her to the coffee shop across the street. The address matched the one on the paper. But the sign above the door read SOLDATENKAFFEE MADELEINE. The sign used to read CAFÉ MADELEINE; the Germans had taken it over like they took over everything in Paris.

Sister Therese must have given her the wrong address. Why would this man ask to meet her at a café that was favored by German soldiers?

She locked eyes with a young soldier whose cheeks were covered with acne and wondered how he could fight in Hitler's army. How could boys who wrote letters home to their mothers turn into men like the Gestapo officer who shot Frederic?

A man sitting at a table in the back picked up his book. Lana strained to see the cover. Sister Therese said her contact was about thirty-five and would be reading Thomas Mann.

The man had dark hair and wore a navy coat.

"Madame Hartmann, I'm Henri," he said when she approached the table. "Thank you for coming. Please sit down."

"Call me Lana." Lana pulled out the chair. "I thought I was in the wrong place."

"You mean why would I ask you to meet in a café frequented by German officers? It's quiet now, and no one will hear us. It doesn't get busy until later in the day." The man grinned. His smile made his face somehow older. His forehead wrinkled, and the lines around his mouth were more pronounced. “In this game, it’s all about perception. If I run into any German soldiers who walk by the window in a different setting they’ll remember they saw me at a café that’s popular with Germans and think we’re old friends. But no one will overhear us; we’re quite safe.”

“I see,” Lana said, glancing around warily. The tables were almost empty.

It still made her nervous. A German officer could come in and sit at the table beside them. And how could she trust a complete stranger? But Sister Therese was one of her dear friends, and she had confidence in her judgment.

“I took the liberty of ordering you a café crème.” He pointed to the cup. “I didn’t want to be interrupted by a waiter; they have the biggest ears in Paris.”

“Thank you.” Lana took a sip and waited for him to continue.

“How much do you know about the Drancy internment camp?” He leaned forward.

“I’ve read about it,” Lana said.

The first Jews were rounded up in 1941 and taken to Drancy, northeast of Paris. It was supposed to be temporary, but they were kept there for weeks without adequate food or water. Lana had read about the terrible conditions. Eighty people slept in a room. Some died in their beds, and the others were too weak to move them.

“Up until early this year the camp was run by

the French, but in July the Gestapo took over." He looked at Lana. "The Gestapo thought the French were moving too slowly and wanted to be sure all the occupants were exterminated. Mothers were separated from their children and sent to labor camps in the east. The children were made to wait alone for weeks before they were sent there too. Then they were gassed on arrival. The SS officer who was put in charge is someone you'll recognize." He paused. "His name is Alois Brunner."

She didn't know the name. Her expression was blank.

"Until recently Brunner was here in Paris. He's the SS officer who killed your husband," Henri clarified.

"I see." Lana's cheeks felt hot, and she worried she might faint.

"Three weeks ago Brunner was sent to the South of France. The Riviera was taken over by the Germans in September, and the coastline is full of Jews who escaped persecution in Austria and Germany." He sipped his coffee. "It's Brunner's job to fix that."

"What do you mean?" Lana's eyes widened.

"Under the Italian occupation, the Jews on the Riviera were mainly left alone. Mussolini himself had a Jewish mistress, and he refused to turn Jews over to the French police. But all that changed last month when the Germans took control. We've learned that Brunner plans on rounding up every Jew between Marseille and Monaco and putting them on trains to Drancy and then to the camps."

"But what can I do?" Lana wondered. She ran her fingers over the rim of her café crème. "I live in Paris."

"I'm getting to that," he said calmly.

He picked up his coffee cup and sipped it slowly. His brow was furrowed, and he sat upright in his chair.

"Until now the French Riviera has been a pleasant oasis for people of many nationalities. The casinos are thriving, and there are nightclubs and promenades with elegant shops. It attracts an eclectic mix of residents, including a group of White Russians."

"White Russians?" Lana repeated.

"Members of the Russian nobility, like Tatiana Antanova, who fled Russia during the revolution. Some of them left with jewels they turned into cash, allowing them to live in villas and throw parties. Parties that German officers, including Alois Brunner, attend."

How did Henri know her mother's name? Lana talked about her mother's heritage with Sister Therese. Perhaps she had told him.

"I take it you know about my mother," she said. The blood pulsed through her veins. "The Bolsheviks took everything she had; she left without a penny. She would never become friendly with Germans, people who think nothing of killing children. Of course she misses imperial Russia; her family lived there for centuries. But she's married to a French count, and she's happy. Paris is her home now, and she despises the Germans as much as anyone."

Henri was silent for a long time. "Now I can see why Sister Therese recommended you. At first I was afraid you were too young and inexperienced for this kind of work, but Sister Therese said you'd be perfect. She was right, you have the fire needed to be successful without buckling under pressure."

The air rushed out of Lana's lungs, and she sat back in her chair. "I don't understand."

"There are many White Russians who feel the same about Hitler as your mother. After all, the Russian nobility ruled Russia for centuries. They hope to return, and they don't want Russia to be overrun by Germans." He stopped. "But others feel differently. They think the Germans will help get rid of Stalin and then they can take back what's rightfully theirs.

"Your job would be to take up residence in the French Riviera and become part of the latter group." He looked at Lana approvingly. "A beautiful blond descendant of Russian nobility in Nice to escape wartime Paris and have a good time."

Lana tried to imagine attending parties in seaside villas and playing the roulette wheel at the casinos. She had never been to the Riviera. What would it be like to be alone in a strange place? And Frederic had been dead for only three months. It would be difficult to pretend to enjoy herself when she missed him so much.

"I don't know anyone on the French Riviera," she said. "Where would I live? What would I do?"

It would be difficult living away from her mother. And leaving Paris would mean never seeing any of the places she and Frederic enjoyed: the public gardens and the quaint streets in Le Marais. She didn't want to miss her class at the university or stop going to the convent.

"All you have to do is say you're Lana Antanova and you'll be accepted. Leave the rest to us. You'll live with our contact there: His name is Guy Pascal. He's a Swiss industrialist with a splendid villa above Nice."

"You want me to live with a man I've never met?" She gaped.

He chuckled, and his eyes sparkled. "There are worse covers in the French Resistance. Guy is thirty-two and he's handsome and charming. You will be his lover."

Lana gulped. She couldn't be a man's mistress. Frederic had been dead for a short time. She still thought about him every day.

Henri leaned forward and smiled encouragingly. "Don't worry, it will only be for show. Guy is a perfect gentleman, and he's serious about his work."

"How would we say that we met?" Lana queried. "I was a married woman. My husband died so recently."

"You will say that you and Guy met on holiday years ago. You bumped into Guy again after your husband's death, and the spark was rekindled." Henri studied Lana appreciatively. "You're too young and pretty to spend the rest of your life alone."

The thought of sitting across from a strange man at the breakfast table made Lana's stomach turn. But she couldn't continue to spend the war slicing rutabaga in the convent's kitchen. She had an opportunity to help, to avenge Frederic's senseless death. It wasn't just Frederic, it was Esther and Sophie and Ida and the other Jewish children at the convent. Her baby. There had to be a way to stop all the death. Here was her chance to help the children survive.

"Why should I trust you?" Lana asked. "You're asking me to change my life, and I don't know anything about you."

Henri looked at her levelly. He nodded and sat back in his chair.

"The war affects all of us. My mother is half-Jewish." He paused. "She was sent to one of the camps from Drancy six months ago when Alois Brunner was in charge. I'm like you in a way. I want to get rid of Brunner and help as many Jews at the same time."

"I see," Lana whispered.

"You could save a lot of Jews, Lana."

She guessed that Henri was a member of the French Resistance. She had heard how they blew up railways and performed all kinds of dangerous acts. And she often wondered how people could be so brave. Now she understood. It was easier to risk your life if you had lost the reason to live. But what if she failed? She could put other people's lives in danger.

"But what would I be doing?" she wondered. "I don't know anything about explosives, and I've never carried a gun."

"You wouldn't have to do anything like that. It's better if you don't know too much until you agree and until you arrive, but I promise you'll find it easy. The important thing is to become part of the social set. Guy will tell you everything you need to know."

"Can I give my answer tomorrow?" she asked.

"Of course. Give Sister Therese your answer." He nodded.

A few German soldiers walked in and approached the counter.

"It'll be best we don't see each other again. Though I've enjoyed this immensely. It's not often that I have the pleasure of drinking coffee with an accomplished young Russian countess." He leaned back in his chair. "I'm confident Countess Lana Antanova will be a welcome addition to the social set of the French Riviera."

Lana walked down Avenue Montaigne toward her mother's apartment. Her mother had begged Lana to move in when Frederic died, but she kept putting it off. It was silly: she couldn't afford their rent, and Frederic would have wanted her to be more comfortable, surrounded by her loved ones. But she wasn't ready to leave behind their life.

She spent the afternoon in the Tuileries, debating Henri's offer. Lana was the last person to become some kind of spy for the French Resistance: she almost never told a lie. And could she leave Paris? Leave her mother and professors and the nuns?

But when she thought of Alois Brunner, she felt as icy cold as his pistol. What if she could stop him from doing to others what he did to Frederic? And perhaps it would distract her from the pain of losing the baby. It seemed better than waking up every morning and wishing the day were already over.

Her mother was having tea in the living room when Lana arrived. At forty-five she could pass for Lana's sister. Tatiana claimed she owed her smooth skin to applying olive oil to her face before bed. The rationing of olive oil was one of the great frustrations of the occupation.

"Lana, I'm glad you're here." Her mother opened her purse and produced a pair of leather gloves. "I got you these gloves; they'll keep you warm all winter."

"Where did you get them?" Lana asked.

Only Germans could afford gloves. They had become a luxury, and they were rationed as strictly as butter.

"It doesn't matter. I found some sugar, as well." Her mother took out a bag of sugar tied with a string. "Jacques will be thrilled. He can't get used to coffee without milk and sugar."

"But you must have used all your rationing coupons for the week. I was going to give you some of mine."

"You have to keep yours; you're too thin. I don't mind going without certain things; I've dropped a whole dress size." Her mother laughed. "But Jacques gets irritable when he's hungry."

"You still didn't tell me where you got the gloves," Lana said.

Her mother smiled mischievously, and Lana gasped.

"Don't tell me you bought them on the black market! People have been shot for that."

"I know a Russian who is very discreet," Tatiana confided. "We meet under the Arc de

Triomphe. I give him a few pieces of silverware in exchange for whatever he has. Next week he's bringing a side of lamb."

"You can't put yourself in danger so Jacques can eat a lamb cutlet."

"It isn't just for Jacques," she said evasively. "Sergei has eggs and bread that I get for others."

"For who?" Lana demanded.

Tatiana stirred her tea as if she wasn't sure if she should continue. "Do you remember the Lippmans? We shared a room when you were young. Gilda's husband was sent to a labor camp in 1942, and she's afraid to leave the house. I try to get enough to feed her and her daughters."

"You never said anything," Lana said, absorbing the information.

"I didn't want to put you and Frederic in danger." She shrugged. "How can I sit back and let the Germans treat Paris as if it were a holiday destination when behind doors, families fear for their lives?" Her voice brightened. "The Arc de Triomphe is the perfect meeting place. No one is going to suspect two Russians chatting in the middle of the day under a German swastika."

"It seems I'm the only one in Paris not disobeying the Germans." Lana poured a cup of tea. They reused every tea bag until the tea was just flavored hot water. But the weather was turning cold, and it was pleasant to hold a warm cup.

"What do you mean?" Tatiana asked.

Lana had debated telling her mother about Henri's offer. Lana was Tatiana's only child; what if something happened to her? And Tatiana's name would come up at parties; Lana couldn't put her mother at risk without consulting her.

"I met a man for coffee today."

"A man?" Her mother raised her eyebrows.

"Sister Therese set it up. He's a member of the French Resistance. He wants me to move to Nice and help stop the Germans."

Her mother started, and the teacup clattered on its saucer.

"He asked you to be a spy?"

"He didn't say exactly. A number of White Russians live on the French Riviera. Some are friendly with the Germans. He wants me to attend parties and become part of the social scene. My contact will tell me what I'll be doing when I arrive."

"That's even worse!" Tatiana's voice was sharp. "You could be asked to do something very dangerous."

"The black market is dangerous," Lana retorted.

"That's hardly the same thing." Tatiana scoffed. "You're talking about being a *spy*. I'm a mature woman; I can make my own decisions. You're a young widow whose husband was murdered before her eyes. That man is taking advantage of you. If you're caught you'll be shot on the spot."

“I won’t be caught,” Lana said with more certainty than she felt. “They have a contact in Nice, a Swiss industrialist named Guy Pascal who I’ll stay with. I’ll be a young woman escaping the drudgery of occupied Paris to have fun on the French Riviera.”

“You’d live with a strange man?” Tatiana said in alarm.

“There are more dangerous things than living with a man,” Lana insisted. “Guy is in the Resistance too.”

“What about your degree? You’ve been studying for almost four years,” Tatiana reminded her. “You’ve worked so hard. You can’t give it up.”

“I only have one semester left. I’m going to finish my degree; I just need a break.” Her mother’s questions made her only more determined to accept Henri’s offer. “This might be the perfect thing. The chance to do something important.”

“You’d be trusting people you’ve never met with your life,” Tatiana implored.

“I feel so helpless since Frederic died. I can’t concentrate on my class at university, and the only useful thing I do is slice vegetables at the convent. I have to find a way to make a difference. If I can save one Jewish child it will be worth it,” Lana tried to explain. “The Germans are intent on wiping out the next generation of

Jews. I can't wait out the war in Paris and let innocent children like Esther Cohen be locked up in Drancy or sent away."

Tatiana stood up and walked over to Lana.

"When your father and I were married we had everything. Then Nicolai was murdered and I didn't have time to feel sorry for myself. You were born, and I had to make a new life for us in Paris. Even though every day was a struggle, I felt so blessed. You'd look at me with those big blue eyes, and I had everything I needed. I understand how you feel. Nothing is more important than saving the children." She hugged Lana. "I'm proud of you; just be careful. You may be a woman, but you're my child. I couldn't live in a world where you do not."

Lana pulled her coat tighter as she walked along Rue de Passy. Her mother had asked her to stay for dinner, but Lana knew there wasn't enough vegetable stew to feed all three of them.

The sixteenth arrondissement was almost deserted except for a few old women out walking their dogs. Many of the great houses were shuttered, and their occupants had fled. Lana wondered if any of the houses were occupied by German officers and pushed the thought away. The sixteenth arrondissement had always been her favorite part of Paris, and she didn't want to picture Germans trampling over oriental carpets or dripping water in marble bathrooms that were centuries old.

She and Frederic used to love strolling through the neighborhood. Sometimes they'd imagine what it would be like to live in one of the grand *hôtels particuliers*. Frederic would have a music room with a Steinway piano, and Lana would have a home office, where she'd hang photos of her lipsticks and perfumes.

She stopped under the oak tree where Frederic had proposed on a springtime afternoon when they had been dating for six months. She plucked a rose from the bush nearby and inhaled deeply. The scent brought the memory rushing back, and she closed her eyes and remembered the giddy feeling of exploring Paris after the long, cold winter.

APRIL 1941

The first winter of the occupation was behind them, and the short days and a coal shortage had been replaced by weeks of glorious warm weather. The Eiffel Tower gleamed under the sun, and roses bloomed on the sidewalks and in the public gardens.

Frederic and Lana spent almost every moment together. They couldn't do the things couples did before the war: the cinema played mostly German films, the theater was too expensive, museums displayed swastikas, and even the bookstores had replaced their stock with books written in German.

Lana didn't mind too much. It gave her the chance to show Frederic the parts of Paris that managed to retain their charm under the shadow of the occupation. Montmartre teemed with actors because the Germans loved going to the cabaret. The *grands boulevards* retained their beauty even though Germans crowded the outdoor cafés.

That afternoon, Frederic used his ration card to buy a bag of dried fruit they shared as they strolled past ivy-covered mansions. Iron gates hid fountains and stone statues.

"My mother and I used to come here when I was a child," Lana said, holding Frederic's hand. "The estates reminded her of growing up in Russia. Her parents owned a dacha in the country with twenty bedrooms and a private lake."

"What would your life have been like if the revolution hadn't happened?" Frederic asked curiously.

"Probably terribly boring." Lana laughed. "My mother said she went to university to escape marrying a Russian prince. She was eighteen; she wasn't ready for her life to be over."

"Marriage doesn't mean that your life is over," Frederic said.

"I suppose not." Lana shrugged. "But you have to do some living first. In Russia, noblewomen often had ten children. It's hard to enjoy life when you're waddling around like a duck."

"But if you fall in love, then marriage is the best thing in the world," Frederic persisted. "And there's nothing more fun than children. My sister has two little boys. I love being an uncle."

Lana noticed Frederic fiddling with the bag of dried fruit. His cheeks were red.

"Being in love is wonderful," she agreed.

"Then so is marriage. It means you found the person you want to share things with and you're confident it will last forever." He looked at Lana, and his expression was serious. "I never imagined it would happen to me so soon, but I wouldn't change it."

"What are you saying?" Lana asked. Did Frederic want to spend his life with her? A shiver of anticipation ran through her, and she looked at Frederic expectantly.

"I wasn't going to say anything." He sounded sheepish, and Lana was suddenly embarrassed. Had she steered the conversation toward marriage? She was barely twenty-two; it was too soon to think about a wedding.

"But now that we're talking about marriage I have to speak," Frederic continued. "My parents have been married for thirty years, and they're still in love. There's a war on and we don't know what the future holds, but I've never been happier and I hope you feel the same."

They stopped under an oak tree, and the sun

glinted through the leaves. Frederic moved closer, and she could smell his cologne.

"I have no right asking this question. I'm still a student, and even when I become a pianist will there be anywhere to perform? The Germans could occupy Paris for years." His hand went to Lana's cheek. "But I love you. You're the most wonderful girl I've ever met, and . . ."

"And what?" Lana sucked in her breath. She was afraid if she moved she would break the spell.

"I want to spend the rest of my life making you happy." He dropped to his knee and took Lana's hand. He swallowed, and his voice stammered. "Lana, will you marry me?"

It took Frederic a full minute to get out the proposal, but it didn't take Lana any time to decide. Her heart already felt enmeshed with Frederic's, as if they were two pieces of thread woven in the same cloth.

"Yes, I'll marry you." She nodded.

He glanced down at her bare hand.

"I don't have a ring!" Frederic exclaimed, and Lana was afraid he'd take back the question. He took the string off the bag of dried fruit and tied it into a knot.

"I'll write to my mother and ask her to send my grandmother's ring," he promised, slipping it around her finger.

"It's perfect." Lana felt almost giddy. She reached up to kiss him.

"I love you more than anything," he whispered.

"I love you too," Lana said, and her heart bubbled up with happiness.

Lana strolled along the Rue de Passy and twisted the wedding band on her finger. It was still impossible to believe that Frederic was dead, that she wouldn't go home and find him hunched over his sheet music.

A woman holding the hand of a little girl emerged from behind a gate. The girl wore a felt coat, and her hair was tied with a ribbon. Lana's hand went to her flat stomach. She couldn't help but envy the woman. The sight of the mother and daughter made her wonder now if she would ever have a child of her own.

"Frederic, I saw you murdered, and then I couldn't save our baby," she said aloud. "But I promise I will make you proud. Other children will live because of what I lost." She bit back a tear and walked determinedly down the sidewalk. "It's a small way I can repay you for the joy you brought me."

Even if she never had a son or daughter, she would do everything possible to help Jewish children during the war. The next day Lana would tell Sister Therese that she was accepting Henri's offer. Then she would pack her suitcase and board the train to the French Riviera.

Chapter Three

NICE, NOVEMBER 1943

Lana looked out at the silver-gray lavender fields from the window of the train. In the distance she could see small towns and villages. The afternoon sun glinted off church spires and clusters of pine trees. It seemed impossible to imagine that bombs were falling on most of Europe.

Every day for the last week she had told herself she couldn't go through with it. She was a young widow grieving her husband. She was a university student who wanted to become a chemist. The last thing she would ever be was a spy in the French Resistance.

But when she said goodbye to Sister Therese at the convent, the children hugged her and she knew she was doing the right thing.

Pulling out of the Gare de Lyon with her mother and Jacques waving on the platform had been even harder than she imagined. Her mother insisted on giving her a suitcase of dresses, including a ruby cocktail dress and yellow sheath. Lana hadn't wanted to take her mother's favorite gowns, but Tatiana reminded her that there was nowhere to wear them but the line at the butcher. Paris and the north were in occupied

France, controlled by the Germans, and the rules were stricter than in the south, which was ruled by the Vichy regime.

Lana turned the page of her book and tried to ignore the German soldiers crowded into the train car. They had been everywhere at the station in Paris, drinking espresso and buying souvenirs to take back to Berlin.

"Do you mind if I join you?" a male voice asked. "All the other seats are taken."

The man was about thirty. He wore an expensive-looking suit and clutched a newspaper.

"Please." She motioned to the seat next to her.

"*Anna Karenina*?" He noticed her book and frowned. "Isn't that a little serious for the French Riviera?"

"My mother recommended it," Lana said.

"It's great literature, but it might seem a little grim when you're sitting at a café on the Boulevard de la Croisette." He took out a cigarette case and offered her a cigarette. "Do you visit the Riviera often?"

Lana didn't smoke, but Henri said it was one of the things she should learn to do. Sister Therese had given her a letter from Henri with instructions on how to behave: always accept a man's offer of a cigarette because it made a good conversation starter; wear perfume because it made men stand a little closer and become more inclined to share their secrets.

“This is my first visit.” She accepted the cigarette. “What about you?”

This was an opportunity to practice flirting before she arrived on the Riviera. One of Henri’s suggestions was to follow up a question with one of her own. She held the cigarette carefully and thought she may as well practice so she’d be prepared when she arrived in Nice.

“My family owns a villa in Menton.” He lit her cigarette. “We’ve been holidaying here since I was twenty.”

“I’ve heard the Riviera is beautiful,” Lana said, trying to inhale without choking.

“It’s even better than you can imagine,” he said, and his smile was boyish. “It was Queen Victoria’s favorite destination in the last twenty years of her life. When she was dying she famously proclaimed: ‘If only I was in Nice, I’d get better.’ There’s a statue of her in front of the Hôtel Excelsior, you’ll have to see it.” His smile faded. “You won’t find many Brits or Americans on the Riviera now. The war chased them away.”

Lana took in the man’s accent, his manner of dress, the mention of Queen Victoria.

“Then why are you here?” she asked.

“I happened to be in Menton in 1940, right before Dunkirk. After that it wasn’t safe to travel to England by boat, and I couldn’t find anyone to fly a plane, so I stayed.” He shrugged. “I’m glad I did. Rationing is so strict in England, and the climate on the Riviera is milder." He stabbed his cigarette into the ashtray. "Enough about me. Where are you headed?"

Lana gulped. She didn't want to give a stranger too many details.

"A villa in Cap Ferrat." She waved her hand. "It belongs to a family friend."

"You must come from a well-connected family." He whistled. "That's where all the American movie stars built homes. Where I live in Menton is a bit further removed. We aren't on the party circuit."

"I haven't heard of Menton," Lana said.

"That's because it's quite boring. Our most exciting event is the annual Lemon Festival." He chuckled.

"I was fortunate my parents owned the house and I was able to stay. I told the local authorities that someone needed to care for it, and the young people were off fighting the war. They gave me permission to remain in Menton, and it was fairly tolerable under the Italian occupation. As long as the soldiers had a shot of Campari and a plate of spaghetti at dinner they were happy. The Germans are different. It's like being babysat by a litter of Alsatian puppies. One wrong move and you'll find yourself between very sharp teeth," he joked. He noticed Lana's frightened expression. "You have nothing to worry about, pretty blondes are perfectly safe. You'll have a wonderful time."

Lana watched passengers taking down their suitcases. Outside the window, the lavender fields had been replaced by small towns nestled into the hills.

"I should get ready, we're almost at my stop."

"Here's my card." He reached into his pocket. "If you find yourself in Menton, please look me up."

Lana slipped the card in her purse and waited while he took her suitcases down from the overhead compartment.

"I didn't catch your name," he said, handing her the suitcases.

"Lana Antanova," Lana replied.

"Charles Langford, it's a pleasure to meet you." He pointed to the swath of blue Mediterranean outside the window. "Enjoy yourself, but be careful. There's a reason why they say the Côte d'Azur is magical; no one leaves with their heart intact."

Lana stood under the clock and glanced around the Nice train station. She wanted to go outside and breathe in the sea air, but she worried about missing her contact.

She read the paper Henri had given her again.

> *Guy will meet you at the station at 4:00 p.m. Wait under the clock in the main terminal. Guy will be eating a sandwich wrapped*

in wax paper. He'll offer you half the sanwich.

Lana slid the letter back in her purse. What she would give for that sandwich! She had been too nervous to eat on the train, and now it was well past lunchtime. But she had been waiting for an hour, and there was no sign of Guy.

She noticed a kiosk on the other side of the terminal and was tempted to leave her spot and get something to eat. But she couldn't haul two bags across the station. She decided she would leave them against the wall—it would take only a minute, and she could keep her eye on them the whole time. But when she reached into her purse for her wallet it was gone. She riffled through her suitcases, but it wasn't in there either. Someone must have taken it when she walked through the station.

A young man of about nineteen lounged against the wall. A scarf was tied around his neck, and he wore a beret.

"Are you all right?" He approached her. "You look like you lost something."

"My wallet!" Her eyes were wide. "I had it when I got off the train, but now it's missing."

"I'm afraid it happens all the time," he said somberly. "The pickpockets are some of the most skilled workers on the Riviera."

"How do I get it back?" She glanced around the station. "There must be a policeman."

"The pickpockets work in partnership with the gendarmes," he explained. "They give them a small cut for looking away. The tourists go to the gendarmes to get their wallets back, and the gendarmes shrug and say the tourists should have been more careful."

"I can't do anything without my wallet," Lana said anxiously. "I was supposed to meet someone, but he isn't here. I don't have any way to get to where I'm staying." She sighed. It was obvious that Guy wasn't coming. She would have to get to the villa on her own.

"I drive a taxi. I'll take you," he offered.

"You drive a taxi?" Lana repeated.

Was it possible that he had something to do with her stolen wallet? Was this some kind of test from Guy and Henri? That was ridiculous; she certainly couldn't assume that everyone was part of the Resistance. And she hadn't noticed him when she got off the train.

"What if no one is home?" she wondered. "I won't be able to pay you."

"Then it will be my treat." He picked up one of the suitcases and grinned. "If I don't, you'll think everyone in Nice is as bad as the thieves who stole your wallet." He held out his other hand. "I'm Pierre."

Lana introduced herself and carried the other suitcase. Outside the station, the sky and the ocean were the same shade of cobalt blue. The people milling by wore bright colors, and even the air smelled different. Lana inhaled deeply and decided one day she'd create a perfume that smelled of flowers and the sea.

"Where to?" Pierre asked as they walked.

She opened her purse and was relieved that Henri's note was still inside.

"Villa du Soleil," she read aloud. "Cap Ferrat."

Pierre turned and nodded approvingly.

"Cap Ferrat has the most beautiful homes on the Riviera, you won't be disappointed."

Lana already felt better. The sun warmed her shoulders as they approached a row of taxis.

"How can there be so many taxis?" she wondered, as Pierre opened the door of a rusty old Peugeot. "In Paris, only the Germans have cars. Everyone else crowds on buses."

"The locals on the Riviera have made money off tourists for decades, and during the war it is no different." He stepped on the gas so quickly that Lana was thrown back in her seat. "My father sold his fishing boat a few years ago and bought this car. It's quite profitable. There's always a drunken soldier stumbling out of the casino who needs a ride."

They reached the center of Nice, and Lana pressed her face to the window. Nice was the opposite of Paris's orderly boulevards. Streets bled together, and the taxi sped through alleys that were so narrow, Lana held her breath. Eventually, the scenery began to change. Fruit trees with orange leaves slipped by, and vineyards were laid out in neat rows. The Peugeot climbed into the hills, and Lana's fingers gripped the dashboard. The Mediterranean was far below olive trees that clung to the cliffs.

"Don't look so scared!" Pierre glanced at her. "This car is nimble as a goat. And I've been driving these roads since I was fifteen."

"It's beautiful, but the cliff is so steep." Lana watched the road tumble away in a blur of pink and white flowers.

They stopped in front of a row of villas, and Lana stepped out of the car. The air smelled of honeysuckle. She felt like she could reach up and touch the clouds. Suddenly she had a longing for Frederic that was so overwhelming it weighed on her chest.

"Villa du Soleil." Pierre waved at a yellow villa shaded by palm trees. It had green shutters, and there was a fountain flanked by rosebushes.

Lana went to the door and knocked. There was no answer. She tried again.

"There's no one here," Lana announced, returning to the taxi. She couldn't just sit here and wait. It was getting late, and soon it would get cold. She was about to ask Pierre to take her back to the station when she noticed a young woman with a wide hat and a basket on the other side of the road.

"Are you looking for Guy?" the woman asked as she approached them.

"Yes, he was supposed to pick me up at the train station," Lana replied.

"He went out a few hours ago. He said he had to go to a party."

"A party?" Lana repeated. The fear and uncertainty that had been building since the train arrived in Nice turned into rage. It was one thing for Guy to be delayed with Resistance work. But did he really stand her up to go to a party?

"You look tired and thirsty, why don't we go inside and have a drink?" the woman said, indicating the villa—the one Lana had been unable to enter.

"You have the key to Guy's house?" Lana asked, in surprise. She wondered if they were lovers.

"It's not what you're thinking; I'm not involved with Guy." The woman laughed as if she could read her thoughts. "We're just neighbors. My name is Giselle."

She pointed down the road. "I'm the last one on the right. Villa Grasse." She entered the garden and dug a key out from under a rock. "Up here, we tell one another where we keep our keys in case of emergency."

"It would be nice to go inside and sit down," Lana said gratefully. She turned to Pierre. "I don't know how to pay you."

"I'll take care of that." Giselle reached into her basket and took out a two-hundred-franc note. She handed it to Pierre.

"I can't let you pay for my taxi too," Lana protested.

Giselle couldn't have been much older than Lana, but she had an air of authority combined with a gracefulness that made her seem older. Her French was fluent, but she had an accent that Lana didn't recognize.

"I'll put it on Guy's account." Giselle laughed. "I keep chickens, and he always takes my eggs without paying me."

Lana said goodbye to Pierre and followed Giselle inside. The villa had wide rooms facing an inner courtyard. The floors were dark wood. Heavy drapes covered the windows. A sheet was thrown over a sofa.

"Doesn't Guy live here?" Lana asked. The air felt stale, and there was dust on the coffee table.

"His housekeeper has been away. He says it's easier to live in the kitchen." She guided Lana through the hallway.

The kitchen was the opposite of the front rooms. Late afternoon light flooded through French doors, and the marble counters were spotless. Open shelves held spices, and there was an enamel stove and small refrigerator.

"It's so different from Paris." Lana ran her

hands over the marble. “In Paris, the war is everywhere. The cupboards are empty.”

“We had a fairly easy time until the Germans arrived; now it’s getting harder,” Giselle explained as she took off her hat. “But you can get anything on the black market if you’re willing to pay for it.”

She found a bottle of Scotch under the sink. She filled two glasses with soda water and added one shot to each drink.

“How do you know Guy?” She handed Lana a glass. “I ran into him this morning, and he told me he had a visitor coming but said nothing else.”

“I’m Lana. We met in Switzerland before the war,” she answered, remembering Henri’s instructions. “Guy said I could stay whenever I wanted.”

“You don’t look old enough to have been doing much before the war,” Giselle commented.

“I’m twenty-four. I was on holiday in Montreux with my family.”

“Guy mentioned that he has a château in Lausanne. I asked him why he doesn’t stay in Switzerland, especially with the Germans breathing down our necks,” Giselle said thoughtfully. “He said his business interests on the Riviera don’t take care of themselves. Plus, Switzerland is boring. We still hold parties here. You’ll have to ask him to bring you to some.”

Lana wanted to know more about Giselle. Was she a member of the Resistance too? Or could she be friendly with any of the Germans—one of the people Lana was supposed to get close to?

Giselle finished her drink and put the glass on the counter.

"I should go," Giselle said before Lana could think of a reply. "I'm making fish stew, and I was just picking tomatoes."

"I haven't had fresh vegetables in months," Lana said. She noticed the tomatoes in Giselle's basket.

"Here." Giselle handed her one. "Guy must have some bread and a bottle of olive oil. That's all you need to make dinner."

"Thank you for everything," Lana said. "If you hadn't come along, I don't know what I would have done."

"It's my pleasure." Giselle turned to the door. "I hope you stay awhile. I'm often alone, and it will be nice to have female company."

A few minutes later Lana was slicing the tomato when a man appeared in the doorway. He had dark hair smoothed back and a tan complexion. His eyes were the brightest green Lana had ever seen.

"You must be Lana. I'm Guy." He put a pastry box on the counter. "I went to the train station and ran into Pierre. He told me he drove you to the villa."

"You know Pierre?" Lana put down the knife. She was so embarrassed that she was making herself at home in Guy's kitchen without permission. For a moment she forgot that the reason Giselle had let her into Guy's house was because he had abandoned her at the station.

"Everyone knows Pierre. His father, Louis, was one of the few honest taxi drivers on the Riviera." Guy peeled off his jacket. "Louis was killed two years ago by the French police. Now Pierre drives the taxi, poor kid." Guy poured himself a shot of the Scotch.

Lana pictured Pierre with his jaunty beret, and her stomach tied in a knot. The war that had seemed far away suddenly returned.

"I'm sorry," she said.

"Well, that's why we're here. To get rid of Nazis and end the war." He drank the Scotch, and his face broke into a smile. "Unless you came all the way to Nice to drink my Scotch and eat tomatoes in olive oil."

"You did strand me at the train station." She remembered why she was angry. "If your neighbor Giselle hadn't let me in, I'd be waiting outside or back at the terminal."

"I planned on getting you; I was just a little late," he corrected.

"You went to a party," she retorted.

"Did Giselle tell you that?" He shrugged. "I

didn't mean to miss the train, but sometimes things happen that I can't control."

Lana picked up the knife and went back to slicing the tomato.

"I didn't eat on the train, and someone stole my wallet at the station, and then you weren't home," she said, arranging the tomato on a plate. "I'm very hungry."

"You're angry because you missed lunch?" Guy whistled. "I told Henri I needed someone with ice in her veins. The Germans have been in Nice for only two months and already five hundred Jews have been transported to Drancy and then Auschwitz. SS officers enter the hotels and drag the guests out in their nightgowns. Last week a woman drank the cyanide she kept hidden in her suitcase." Guy's face was hot, and he refilled his glass. "Just yesterday, they made a sweep of the Hôtel Negresco. I watched an old man jump out the window to avoid being taken away. If you're going to give up because you haven't had a meal since breakfast, then you probably should leave now."

Lana's cheeks flushed, and she held back the tears. What was she doing here? And how could she live with someone so rude?

"I didn't think it was too much to ask to keep the arrangement planned." She grabbed her purse. "I didn't intend to be a burden. I'm going to freshen up, and then I'll go."

She walked down the hall to the powder room. The door closed behind her, and she leaned against the vanity. What if Guy was right; what if she wasn't strong enough to be in the Resistance?

Her reflection stared back at her, and she thought about Pierre, about Frederic and the baby. Sister Therese had given her this opportunity, and she couldn't pass it up. Even her mother understood how important it was to help the children. Nothing mattered except making Frederic proud and saving as many Jewish children as she could.

Guy was hovering in the hallway when she opened the door. She started to say something, but he took her hand and led her back to the kitchen.

"I need to apologize." He motioned her to sit down. "I bought a slice of cake to welcome you to Nice."

"I'm not hungry anymore," Lana answered.

"Please, it cost fifty francs on the black market. You won't find such a moist filling on the Côte d'Azur."

"All right." Lana picked up the fork. The first bite was dark and sweet and reminded her of her wedding cake. Lana's mother had made it. They'd all had a slice after the ceremony at the registrar's office.

"Can we start over?" He held out his hand. "I'm Guy Pascal."

“Lana Antanova.” She shook his hand.

“When I didn’t meet you at the station you could have taken the train back to Paris. And when those thieves stole your wallet you could have been stranded at the station, but you figured out a way to get to the villa. And when I wasn’t here you might have been forced to wait outside,” he said. “But instead I find you drinking Scotch and eating tomato with olive oil in my kitchen. I suppose you’re more capable than I’d given you credit for.” He ate a bite of cake. “Henri was right; you’ll be a wonderful spy. I’m sorry for being rude, and I hope you’ll stay.”

The sun was beginning to set outside the window, and the sky was a ribbon of purple and yellow.

“I’ll stay.” She nodded. “As long as you promise not to stand me up again.”

Chapter Four

NICE, NOVEMBER 1943

When Lana woke the next morning, the sun was already high in the sky. A breeze blew through the open window, and the light made patterns on the bedroom wall.

The night before, she had told Guy she was exhausted from traveling and asked if she could go to her room. In truth, she felt uncomfortable sitting alone in the kitchen with him. It was all so foreign—being away from Paris, from her mother, and mostly missing Frederic. She couldn't remember the last time she had eaten dinner with a man who wasn't her husband.

Guy had led her upstairs, and Lana tried to hide her anxiety. What if their bedrooms were next to each other and they had to share a bathroom? But Guy led her to a bedroom at one end of a hall and pointed to his suite at the other end. Lana had her own bathroom. Her door even locked from the inside.

She had been too tired to do anything but strip off her clothes and climb into bed. But this morning she sat against the pillows and admired the furnishings. The bed was covered with a white comforter, and there was a dressing table with an oval mirror in the corner of the room.

A floral rug was flung over the wood floor. The bathroom held a claw-foot tub.

Lana opened the French doors and stepped onto the balcony. The sea was perfectly calm, and the sky was the color of topaz. Below her, the hills were dotted with villas featuring manicured lawns and swimming pools.

A sadness welled up inside her, and she clutched the railing. It seemed impossible that she could inhale the scent of irises and watch fishing boats bob in the water when Frederic would never smell or see anything again.

When they married, they couldn't afford a honeymoon. Now Lana wished they had gone somewhere together: to Biarritz with her mother and Jacques or to Marseille. But they agreed that it could wait until after the war.

Lana touched her stomach and thought how lovely it would have been to travel to the seaside with the baby. They would have built sandcastles, and when he was older Frederic would have taught him to swim.

"Frederic, what would we have named our baby?" she said aloud. She felt better when she talked to him. It made her feel close to him. "If it was a boy, perhaps Aramis like in *The Three Musketeers*. He would have grown up to be so brave. Or Margot for a girl because she would be as precious as a pearl. When she was older, she would have learned to sing and you would have accompanied her on the piano." She gulped and straightened her shoulders. "I would have been so proud."

Somewhere bells chimed, and Lana went inside. She selected a green dress and walked downstairs to the kitchen.

Guy was sitting at the table, eating a plate of eggs. He stood up when Lana entered and moved to the coffeepot.

"Good morning," he greeted her. He wore a collared shirt and slacks. "I hope you like eggs, they're the only thing I know how to cook." He waved at the counter. "I can make a soft-boiled egg or an omelet. And there's coffee, thank God." He handed her a cup. "I stored enough coffee beans in the basement to last if the Germans stay for a decade."

"A soft-boiled egg would be nice, thank you." Lana sat at the table. "I didn't thank you for my room. It's beautiful."

"I love this house. It's so peaceful up here in Cap Ferrat; it's easy to forget what's going on below us in Nice." He dropped an egg into boiling water. "Yesterday an older couple was eating dinner at a restaurant on Boulevard Victor Hugo. There was a group of SS officers at the next table. The husband addressed his wife as Rachel, and the officers dragged them onto the street. They were put on the train to Drancy just for having a Jewish-sounding name."

“Did they ask for their papers?” Lana inquired in shock.

“The Germans in Nice don’t care about papers.” Guy shrugged.

Tears pricked Lana’s eyes, but she blinked them away. She couldn’t start crying every time she heard of the atrocities committed by the Nazis.

“The Germans have commandeered almost every hotel in Nice. The Gestapo are at the Hôtel Negresco, and the German navy occupy the Atlantic, and Alois Brunner and his pack of Jew hunters have taken up residence in the Hôtel Excelsior.” Guy sipped his coffee. “They conduct raids all over Nice to round up the Jews. Twice a week, the prisoners are paraded down the Promenade des Anglais to the train station.”

Guy cracked the egg and threw out the shell. He placed the plate in front of her.

“The SS officers on the Riviera are just like those in Paris; they are determined to enjoy themselves,” he continued. “They feel they’re not treated well at the casinos, and they complain about the service at the restaurants. So they’re happiest at parties.” He paused. “Parties where they receive lots of strokes for doing battle with Stalin and his army. The White Russians see Stalin as the dictator who murdered their czar and destroyed their futures. They’re happy to host. I get invited because Switzerland is a neutral country, but I’m a man, so German officers aren’t likely to share their secrets." He handed her salt and pepper. "That's where you come in. Lana Antanova, daughter of a Russian aristocrat."

"I told Henri that just because my mother is Russian doesn't mean she sympathizes with the Germans. If you think that's why I'm here, you're wrong. I came because—" Lana began, but Guy stopped her.

"I don't care if your mother played blocks with the czar's daughters when she was a toddler or bedded the entire Cossack army when she grew up. The first rule of this business is I don't want to know why you became a member of the Resistance." His voice was sharp. "We all have our reasons, and it's better we keep them to ourselves. You could have a lover in a death camp in Germany, and I couldn't care less. The quickest way to get killed is to know too much, and I intend to sit here eating eggs and drinking coffee long after this war is over."

"I assure you my mother never slept with a Cossack." Lana flushed.

If Henri had told Guy about her mother, would he have told him about Frederic too? She glanced down at her hands and remembered she wasn't wearing her wedding ring.

"But you never know when you're put in a situation where people start asking questions. Not knowing the answers can save a life."

"I see." Lana nodded. Guy was talking about

being tortured. She ate a bite of the egg, but it wobbled in her mouth.

"The second rule is not to get emotionally involved," he went on calmly. "I had an associate early in the war who got too close to another member of the Resistance. They began trading pillow talk." He looked at Lana. "She was caught and interrogated by the Nazis. She collapsed under pressure and revealed her associate's name. He was captured, and they were both hanged."

"I'm sorry," Lana said, and realized she already said those words in the last twenty-four hours.

"The rumor is that they were holding hands when they died." Guy buttered his toast. "The only way to remain safe is to keep your lips sealed."

"We have to be able to trust someone." Lana thought of Henri. She wouldn't be here if she hadn't believed in what he was doing.

"Say you got stuck on the roof of this house. Would you jump, or would you try to find a way inside through a window?"

"I'd try to climb through a window," she said confidently. "If I jumped, I could break my neck."

"Exactly. Trust your instincts and you'll do fine." He stood up. "Now let's go over our story. Henri mentioned that you were married and that your husband died."

Lana looked up abruptly. So Henri had told

Guy about Frederic. But why? She felt at a disadvantage; she knew nothing about Guy.

"Don't look so surprised, Henri only shared it with me because it fits your cover." Guy noticed her concerned expression. "Your reason for being on the Riviera is even more sympathetic. An attractive young widow spending a few months in Nice to get over an unspeakable loss. But we have to be careful. The Germans are suspicious by nature, and it's always possible I'm under surveillance. After all, I'm wealthy and I have a Swiss passport. Why shouldn't I be hiding Jews and then transporting them across the border?"

"Under surveillance here?" Lana put down her fork. The egg seemed to have gotten stuck in her throat.

"There's nothing to worry about, I do a complete sweep of the house and grounds once a week. And I'll show you where I keep the pistol in the hall closet. Just in case you get unwanted visitors when I'm not home."

"Thank you." Lana gulped, resolving not to show Guy her nervousness.

"We met in Montreux in 1938. You were on holiday with your parents."

"I'm only twenty-four," Lana interjected. "I would have been nineteen. Don't you think I would have been too young to capture your attention?"

"I'm only eight years older than you, and I'm sure you were a beauty at nineteen," Guy said reflectively. "It was a brief summer affair. We knew it wouldn't last: you had to go back to university in Paris, and I had business to run in Switzerland. I bumped into you a few weeks ago in Paris after the death of your husband. Our old attraction was rekindled, and I asked you to come stay with me at my villa in Cap Ferrat."

"Frederic died such a short time ago." Lana worried. "Won't people frown that I'm already living with another man?"

Guy glanced at her with a new appreciation. "That's a good question. Perhaps in regular times, but all of Europe is at war. You wanted to escape the dreariness of Paris, and I offered you a solution," he said with a small smile. "I'll be the envy of anyone we meet. I make a trip to Paris, and a few weeks later a beautiful Russian countess arrives to share my bed."

Lana tried to hide her blush. She had been a married woman; she knew all about sex. But it still embarrassed her to discuss it.

"Don't worry, the rules are more relaxed on the Riviera." He noticed her cheeks turning red. "You'll find many members of the social set have questionable morals."

"I suppose that's all right, then." Lana hesitated.

"I'm glad that's settled." Guy put down his coffee cup and walked to the door. He turned around, and his smile was electric. "I have to go into Nice. I'll see you tonight."

Lana glanced at the clock. It was only noon. She thought again about the pistol in the hall closet and Guy's weekly surveillance sweep.

"I don't want to sit here all day. Can I come with you?"

Guy's eyes traveled over her dress as if he was wondering if she would be any trouble.

"I suppose so," he agreed. "But don't ask me any questions in the car. I think up my best ideas when I drive."

Lana wouldn't have tried talking to Guy even if he hadn't discouraged it. He took the turns so abruptly, it made driving with Pierre seem relaxing.

"Where did you learn to drive?" she asked when they reached the center of Nice.

Guy had a convertible, and her hair had flown all over her cheeks.

"Who said anyone taught me?" He grinned. "Driving is like so many things: it's all about trusting your instincts." He noticed two German officers looking at Lana. "I have a meeting, but will you be all right by yourself?"

"Don't worry, I'm used to Germans nodding at me when I walk by. In Paris German officers are everywhere." Lana followed his gaze. For a moment she longed for the way her stomach had lurched when Guy's car rounded a bend. It was better than the loathing she felt when she locked eyes with the officers in their brown uniforms and red armbands.

"If you say so. Meet me here at two p.m." He put on his hat. "Try to stay out of trouble. I don't want to spend the afternoon at the police station. It cost me two bottles of vodka the last time I had to bail someone out."

Lana was about to ask whom he had bailed out, but Guy was already across the street. She turned away from the German officers and strolled along the sidewalk.

Along the promenade lined by palm trees, Lana passed stone buildings with striped canopies. It seemed so incongruous that the Riviera was at war. The shops were open; she passed a menswear store with beautifully tailored suits in the window. But there weren't any tourists licking ice cream cones or taking photos. And the German army trucks parked with the blue of the Mediterranean behind them made it frighteningly real.

The group of German officers moved closer to her, and she wanted to get away. On the corner was a pharmacy. She ducked inside. She had always loved pharmacies. When she was a girl her mother would send her to buy cough syrup or tissues. She'd admire the lipsticks and imagine her own brand displayed at the cash register: silver tubes with the name *LANA* scrawled on the side.

She bought postcards for her mother and Sister Therese and returned to the street. The officers had moved on, and she breathed a sigh of relief. Then, suddenly, she heard quick footsteps, dogs barking. Soldiers called out in German, and Lana heard people scuffling. She turned and saw a woman carrying a basket. A small dog cowered at her feet.

"Open your basket," a soldier snapped.

"But why? I haven't done anything wrong," the woman protested.

"We've been instructed to search anything that looks suspicious," he informed her. "I saw you slip something into the basket."

"Whatever you saw, you're wrong. It's only cod for dinner," the woman answered. "If I open the basket, your uniforms will smell like fish."

"Open it." The soldier poked it with the rifle. "Or I will do it for you."

The woman peeled back the cover, and the soldier peered inside. He reached in and took out a gold chain with a Star of David.

"I'm not Jewish," the woman pleaded. "I found it on the road, and I was going to sell it. My husband is ill and needs medicine. I can go to my house and show you my papers."

"Put it on." The soldier handed it to her.

"You want me to wear it?" The woman's hands trembled.

"Put it on. Now!"

The woman fastened the necklace around her neck, and the soldier stepped back. Then he lifted his rifle and pointed it at the dog. A shot rang out, and the dog fell to the ground.

"That will teach you. Consider it a warning." He ripped the necklace from her neck and slipped it in his pocket. "I'll send the chain without the star to my fräulein in Berlin." He waved the rifle at the woman. "Next time it will be you instead of the dog."

Lana slipped into an archway until the officers were gone. When she emerged, the woman with the basket had disappeared. She noticed a girl of about twelve hiding between two buildings, sobbing.

"Are you all right?" Lana asked.

The girl looked up. She had dark hair and freckles. She wore a cardigan over her dress.

"The dog didn't do anything wrong," the girl said between sobs.

"Where are your parents?" Lana tried again.

"My mother is at home." The girl gulped. "I went for a walk without telling her. I can't stand being stuck at home all the time."

"It's dangerous to be out alone. I'll take you home," Lana said. She couldn't bring her back to Guy's house: she didn't have the keys to his car and he didn't want her to get involved with strangers. But she couldn't leave her here. What if the soldiers returned?

"I don't know you," the girl said cautiously. She took a step forward, and Lana noticed her knobby knees and thin shoulders.

"I'm Lana." She held out her hand. "Come. Your mother must be worried."

The girl took a deep breath as if she was working up all her courage. Then she put her hand in Lana's, and they walked quickly down Rue Droit. They turned into an alley and up a flight of steps.

"Odette!" A woman in her early thirties opened the door. "Where have you been? I was so worried!" She glanced down the stairway and ushered Odette and Lana inside.

Lana looked around the room. The curtains were drawn. There was a worn rug and a brown sofa.

"There was a disturbance. German officers pointed a rifle at a woman and then shot her dog," Lana said. "I brought Odette home."

The woman pulled Odette close and hugged her.

"I told you not to go outside! It's too dangerous to leave the house."

"I can't stay inside forever," Odette said. "It's like being a sardine in a can."

The woman turned to Lana. She was pretty, with Odette's dark curls. "My name is Sylvie. Thank you for bringing Odette home."

"I'm Lana. It was no trouble." Lana nodded.

"You're right. It isn't safe on the streets. German soldiers are everywhere."

"Odette, go upstairs," Sylvie instructed. "And thank Lana for bringing you home."

Odette murmured a thank-you to Lana and climbed the staircase.

"Can I give you something to drink?" Sylvie asked Lana, leading her into the kitchen. "I don't have milk or cream, but I can make coffee."

Lana glanced at the bare kitchen counters and wondered if the fridge was also empty.

"Thank you. A cup of coffee would be nice," Lana said. "Odette must have been so frightened."

"We're Jewish, and Odette knows she isn't allowed outside. She sneaks out anyway, and she refuses to wear her yellow star."

Sylvie put a kettle on the stove. She glanced at Lana, and her face crumpled.

"Odette's father was killed a month ago, and she won't listen to anything I say."

"I'm sorry. That must be terrible for you and Odette," Lana replied.

"Jacob was an assistant pastry chef at the Hôtel Negresco." Sylvie sat opposite Lana and handed her a cup. "Odette and her father were very close. Every morning Odette would make him a flask of coffee to take to work. I sing nights in a cabaret and was usually still asleep when he left. Last month, Jacob forgot his coffee one morning, and

Odette ran after him. A German officer stopped her and asked why she wasn't at school," Sylvie explained. "Odette isn't allowed to go to school because we're Jewish."

Lana pictured the officers on the Boulevard Victor Hugo with their black boots and pistols wedged into their pockets. Odette must have been terrified.

"Odette said she was only giving something to her father," Sylvie continued. "Jacob heard the shouting and turned around. He ran back to Odette and told the officer to leave her alone. The officer pulled out his pistol and pointed it at Odette. I'm sure he only meant to frighten her, but Jacob lunged for it. The gun went off and hit Jacob in the chest."

"And Odette escaped?" Lana asked in horror.

"If only Jacob hadn't acted, perhaps it would have been all right." The anguish was thick in Sylvie's voice. "Odette is twelve years old. Not even Germans would kill a young girl in the middle of the street. But Jacob was a father. His first instinct was to protect his child."

"Oh, poor Odette," Lana breathed.

"She ran home, and I put her in the bath. I was afraid someone would hear her crying." Sylvie twisted her wedding band. "It's been a month, and I don't know what to do with her. I work two jobs."

Lana thought of all the nights her mother

had worked to earn enough for rent and food. But there hadn't been a war, and Tatiana didn't have to worry about Lana being killed for going outside.

"It's impossible to manage by yourself," Lana insisted. "You're doing the best you can."

"Odette thinks if she hadn't taken her father his coffee, he wouldn't be dead," Sylvie said worriedly.

"She's only a child. She'll recover," Lana assured her. "Is there anything I could do to help?"

Sylvie took in Lana's blond hair and classic features and guessed she wasn't Jewish.

"You've already done enough by bringing her home," she said, suddenly wary. "You must have your own troubles, everyone does in a war. Why are you being so kind to strangers? And we're Jewish. You could get in trouble for being here."

"I may not be Jewish, but I've seen a lot of suffering," Lana said slowly. "Religion isn't important. No war should involve women and children."

Sylvie nodded, and her shoulders sagged. She looked at Lana as if she had made up her mind about something.

"No matter what I do, I can't get through to her." Sylvie sighed. "Every day when I go to work, I'm afraid something terrible will happen. Perhaps if you tell her the danger of going outside . . ."

Lana put her cup on the table and walked to the stairs.

"Don't worry, I'd be happy to talk to her."

Upstairs there were low ceilings and a narrow hallway. Lana knocked and waited for Odette to open the door.

"Can I come in?" she asked when Odette's thin face appeared.

Odette nodded, and Lana followed her into the room. The shutters were closed, and there was a desk strewn with books.

"Your mother said it was all right if I came to your room," Lana began awkwardly.

"No one except my mother comes into my room anymore. I don't have any friends because I'm not allowed to go to school." Odette noticed Lana looking at her desk. "I used to do my homework at my desk, but now there's no point. The teachers will never see it."

"You can still study. When I was a child I got the measles and was in bed for a month. I read books and when I went back to school I was ahead of my class."

"I do like to read," Odette acknowledged. "And I like geography. My father and I used to love making maps."

"Your mother told me what happened to your father." Lana perched on the bed.

"My father didn't even need the flask of coffee. There was always a pot of coffee waiting for him at work." Odette's mouth wobbled. "He said my coffee was better than hotel coffee, but he was only trying to make me happy."

"It had nothing to do with you," Lana said. "People die during wartime."

"He didn't have to die," she protested. "My mother keeps telling me I shouldn't go outside, but it's so dark in the house. I feel like I can't breathe."

"You have to do what she asks," Lana urged. "Can you imagine how she'd feel if something happened to you?"

Odette tugged at her braid as if she couldn't decide what to do.

"Sometimes I stand outside her door at night and hear her cry," Odette said. "I don't want to worry her more."

"Then you promise you won't walk around Nice alone?"

Odette stood up and pushed back her slight shoulders. "I'll try, but you can't know what it's like. The birds at the botanical gardens have bigger cages."

Lana said goodbye to Sylvie and Odette and hurried down the street. She found Guy leaning against a lamppost, his eyes scanning the sidewalk.

"There you are." He took her arm and started walking. "I was afraid I was going to have to search all the cafés in Nice."

“I’m sorry I’m late,” she apologized. “I went shopping and lost track of time.”

She couldn’t yet tell him about Sylvie and Odette.

“I don’t see any packages,” he said suspiciously.

“I bought some postcards,” she answered, pulling them out of her purse.

Guy started to say something, but then changed his mind. He opened her car door and waited until she slid into the passenger seat.

“Rule two again: don’t get personally involved with anyone you meet.” He sat in the driver’s seat and started the engine. “Because one day you’ll pay a visit to your new friends and the house will be boarded up and no one will know where they went. You’ll think you don’t really care—after all, you’ve only known them a few weeks. But it will keep gnawing at you like a letter from an old lover you shouldn’t read but do anyway. You’ll make a few inquiries. Somehow word will get round to a German officer you met at a party that Lana Antanova has a Jewish friend, and everything we are trying to do will be thrown into jeopardy.”

The car climbed the steep road to Cap Ferrat, and Lana studied the passing landscape. How did Guy know where she had been? Maybe he’d followed her; maybe something about her manner made her seem guilty. Embarrassment at being found out was replaced by anger. How dare

Guy tell her what to do when they had just met. He was her contact on the Riviera, but he knew nothing about her life in Paris. She was a grown woman, and she was capable of taking care of herself.

"I'm not some innocent ingenue," she snapped when they pulled into the villa's driveway.

Pink chrysanthemums grew on either side of the garage, and water trickled through a fountain.

"In case you forgot, I've come from Paris. Rationing is so strict, I can't remember what it's like not to be hungry. I've watched my fingers turn blue from cold. And I've experienced more death than . . ."

Guy put his hand over her mouth. His palm was smooth, and she looked up in surprise.

"I'm sorry. I shouldn't have barked at you," he soothed her. "You may not understand but someday you'll thank me. I'm only trying to protect you."

Lana instinctively touched her mouth. She fixed her hair in the rearview mirror and stepped out of the car.

"If you don't mind, I'm going up to my room." She turned to Guy, and her eyes flashed. "Maybe I'll read a book. Or would you like to choose what I read? I wouldn't want a German officer barging into the villa and arresting me because he doesn't like *Anna Karenina* by Tolstoy."

Lana ran up the steps before Guy could answer.

She was still upset when she sat down at her dressing table. How could she not help Odette when the whole reason she was on the Riviera was to save the children? Frederic risked his life teaching piano to Jewish children at the convent. And it wasn't just that. Since they met, he always put others before himself. It was one of the things she admired about him. She remembered the first time she stumbled on his actions. For one miserable afternoon, she believed their marriage was in jeopardy.

FEBRUARY 1942

Lana felt despondent. It wasn't just the icy rain that seldom let up or the slush on the streets. Many things dragged Lana's spirits: the nine-o'clock curfew that stopped Lana and Frederic from taking walks; the fear that Frederic would be forced into the Vichy government's compulsory work service; the lack of coffee on supermarket shelves; the German propaganda on the radio.

Lana still tried to make their home life happy. On Saturday nights, she set the table with a white tablecloth and candles and prepared a romantic dinner. Frederic didn't seem to care that the cream-of-potato soup was really pureed cabbage and the wine she poured into their best wineglasses was made of chicory. The cabbage might not taste as good as potatoes, and the chicory was a poor excuse for red wine, but sitting across from each other in the flickering candlelight made them both feel better.

One afternoon, Lana hurried along the Rue de Rivoli. Her neighbor Madame Berte had told her of a delicatessen that kept a supply of chocolate for favored customers. She pictured Frederic's delight when she served melted chocolate over hot porridge.

A black car adorned with a swastika was parked on the street. She averted her eyes and suddenly saw a familiar figure. It was Frederic! His coat collar was pulled up to hide his face as he climbed the steps of an elegant apartment building.

Frederic had told her he was going to rehearse for a student concert. What was he doing in a luxury apartment on the Rue de Rivoli?

She stepped into a covered doorway and waited an hour for Frederic to reappear. Finally the front door opened and Frederic walked outside accompanied by a beautiful blonde wearing expensive-looking boots and a fur coat. They kissed on both cheeks, and then Frederic hurried along the pavement.

Lana stood perfectly still until he disappeared around the corner. Who was that woman, and what was Frederic doing in that apartment? She abandoned her plans for the delicatessen and ran all the way home. The afternoon passed, and

Frederic still hadn't returned. She tried to prepare dinner, but she was too preoccupied.

It was already dark when she heard Frederic's key in the lock. She jumped up from where she had been reading on the sofa and entered the kitchen.

"Lana, I'm sorry I'm late." He put his arms around her waist and kissed her. "The rehearsals dragged on forever."

"You were at rehearsal all this time?" Lana moved away slightly. She grabbed an apron so Frederic couldn't see the expression on her face.

"Where else would I be?" he asked, unwinding his scarf.

Lana tied the apron around her dress and turned to Frederic.

"In an apartment building on the Rue de Rivoli with a beautiful woman in a fur coat."

"You saw me with Elaine?" he gasped.

Lana picked up a knife and started to chop the cabbage.

"I was walking to the delicatessen and saw you enter the building. I know it's hard coming home every night to the same dinner. And we don't make love often enough because it's too cold to be naked." She gulped. "But every day you make me happy, and I thought you felt the same. . . ."

Frederic faced her at the counter. His expression was perplexed.

"You have it all wrong. You make me happier than I've ever been in my life."

Lana put down the knife.

"Then why were you with that woman?"

"I wasn't there to see her, I was there for her daughter."

"Her daughter?" Lana repeated. The woman was in her late thirties. How old was her daughter?

"Vivienne is fourteen and was the most gifted piano student at the academy," Frederic began. "But she's Jewish and not allowed to attend classes. It was my idea to give Vivienne private lessons."

Lana acknowledged this made sense. She marveled at how thoughtful Frederic was. He never considered the harm that could come to him; he only wanted to help others. But Lana had been so worried; he should have told her about Vivienne.

"Why didn't you tell me?" Lana asked.

"I know I'm putting myself in danger. If I told you, you would be in danger too. But I couldn't let Vivienne's talents go to waste," he explained. "You have to hear her play Brahms: it's as if the stars dropped from the sky and landed on the keys."

Frederic was only trying to protect her. He was always thinking of her. It was one of the things she loved about him.

Lana glanced up and saw the anguish in Frederic's eyes. She wiped her hands on her apron and walked over to kiss him.

"Maybe one day I will hear Vivienne play," she whispered. "After the war, she'll play a sold-out performance at the opera house and it will be because of you that she's there."

"You're not angry?" he asked.

"I'm only angry at myself," she said with a little smile, and picked up a rutabaga. "I should have trusted you and kept walking. Then I would have gone to the delicatessen and we'd be eating porridge with melted chocolate instead of stewed cabbage and rutabaga."

He kissed her harder. "I don't care what we eat, as long as I'm sitting across from you at the table."

Lana gazed in the mirror on her dressing table in Guy's villa.

"Frederic, all I want is your courage," she said to her reflection in the glass. "You believed in what you were doing and didn't care about yourself. I must carry on the work you started."

She hated being told what to do by a stranger in Cap Ferrat. Would Frederic have listened to Guy? But she could acknowledge that Guy had a point. German officers could have seen her and Guy together and then followed her to Sylvie's. If German officers interrogated Guy on her whereabouts, how would he answer? She was putting Guy in danger. And she wouldn't be any help to the Resistance if she got herself killed.

She heard footsteps. Guy stood in the hallway, holding a small box.

"If you've come to see what book I'm reading, I haven't chosen it yet," she remarked, defiantly, turning back inside.

"I didn't come for that. I got you something in Nice and forgot to give it to you." He entered the bedroom.

"You bought me something?"

"Well, think of it as a welcome present." He handed her the velvet box. "And to make up for stranding you at the train station."

Lana opened it and revealed a silver charm bracelet.

It was pretty, and for a moment Lana was touched. Then she closed the box. It was too intimate a gift for an almost stranger.

"It's beautiful, but I can't accept it." Lana handed it back.

There was no reason for Guy to be giving her jewelry. She'd never been gifted jewelry by anyone other than Frederic and her mother. Only moments ago Guy had been furious with her.

"We hardly know each other."

"I did a favor for someone, and he gave it to me as a thank-you," Guy said evasively. "You can wear it tonight. Make sure you're ready by eight p.m. Wear something striking: we want to make a good first impression."

"Tonight? Where are we going?" Lana asked.

"We're going where everyone should go when they arrive on the French Riviera. To the Casino de Monte-Carlo in Monaco."

"You said the casinos don't like the Germans," Lana reminded him. German soldiers made the other patrons uncomfortable.

"They may not be completely welcome, but they still go. There aren't many other places to find evening entertainment." He shrugged. "And they'll notice a pretty new face winning at blackjack. With the buzz that a young Russian countess has arrived in Nice, we'll receive dinner invitations."

"I've never played blackjack. How do you know I'll win?"

"You have to give me a little credit." Guy's green eyes twinkled. "I wouldn't be a good Resistance worker if I couldn't fix a game of blackjack."

Chapter Five

NICE, NOVEMBER 1943

Guy went out, announcing that he'd be back to pick her up for the casino. Lana spent the afternoon writing to her mother. It was a challenge to think of what to say without revealing anything that could put them both in danger. She told her about Charles, the Brit she met on the train, and the taxi drive with Pierre, and Giselle and her basket of tomatoes.

Guy hadn't returned from his errands, and Lana felt restless. She walked downstairs and removed the dust covers from the sofas and wiped down the coffee table. She pulled back the drapes and admired the swimming pool and manicured hedges. Henri had said that Guy was a Swiss industrialist with a splendid villa in Cap Ferrat. She wondered why Guy moved to the Riviera from Switzerland. She couldn't ask him. He made it clear that whatever they didn't already know about each other should remain private.

She had only three hours before they left for the Casino de Monte-Carlo and she was filled with a terrible panic. What if Alois Brunner was there? How could she engage in pleasant conversation when she had seen him terrorize little Esther Cohen and turn his gun on Frederic?

Her stomach rumbled, and she entered the kitchen. The fridge was empty except for a bottle of milk and a carton of eggs. Even if Guy knew how to cook, there weren't enough ingredients to prepare a dish. Tomorrow she'd go to the market. But right now she longed for some company and a warm meal. The bottle of olive oil stood on the counter and reminded her of Giselle. Giselle had mentioned she was often alone. She'd clip some of Guy's carnations and go visit her new friend.

Giselle's villa was at the end of a long gravel path. The stone walls were covered with ivy, and a little yellow car was parked in front of the garage.

Lana knocked.

"Lana." Giselle opened the door. She wore slacks and a navy blouse. Her hair was knotted in a bun, and she held a cocktail glass. "What a nice surprise. I was fixing a martini. Would you like one?"

"Yes, thank you." Lana followed her into an entry with parquet floors and tall windows. "I brought flowers from the garden to thank you for yesterday."

Giselle admired the carnations, a mixture of white and pink.

"They're lovely, let me find a vase." Giselle

led her into the living room. There were more parquet floors and gold frames on the walls. Sofas were arranged around an oriental rug, and French doors opened onto the garden.

"What a pretty room; it's so bright and sunny," Lana commented.

Giselle handed her a glass and motioned for her to sit down. "I came to the Riviera for the quality of the light. I like to think I'm an artist. So far, I'm the only buyer of my work." She laughed and waved at the paintings on the wall.

"Those are wonderful." Lana studied a still life of violets. "Are you shown in a gallery?"

"Not yet, but I love to paint." Giselle smiled. "I'm glad you came over. I want to apologize if I was too forward yesterday, I have a habit of being nosy."

"You were a great help; I would have been stranded outside without you."

"I'm glad, but I admit I had an ulterior motive." Giselle peered at Lana. "I was curious about you. Guy has been my neighbor for a year, and he's never brought a woman to his villa."

"Never?" Lana said in surprise. Henri had made Guy out to be some kind of wealthy Swiss playboy.

"I assumed it was because of some tragic love affair in his past, but perhaps he was just waiting for the right woman," Giselle mused. "Don't get me wrong, I'm not interested in him for myself.

Except as an artist's model if I ever tried to paint a portrait. He would make a handsome subject with those tanned cheeks and piercing green eyes."

Lana thought about how Guy's eyes seemed to change colors with his mood. When she was late to meet him in Nice they'd been a dark green, and when he gave her the charm bracelet they became a buttery hazel.

Lana wanted to tell Giselle that she had the wrong idea. But then she remembered her cover as Guy's mistress.

"Guy and I are very fond of each other," she said, hoping she sounded convincing.

"Fond of each other?" Giselle arched her eyebrows. "Guy doesn't seem the type of man who would be happy to have a female guest who is merely a friend."

Lana jiggled her glass. She smiled mysteriously as if she discussed these things every day.

"Well, I wouldn't say we're merely friends," she said, hoping that the insinuation came off convincingly. "He is wonderful company at all times. But I came to the Riviera to escape the war in Paris. It gets very depressing with the rationing and no entertainment."

"One forgets how difficult the war is all over Europe when life on the Riviera hasn't changed quite as much," Giselle agreed, leaning back against the cushions. "Though now that the Germans are here that might be different. The

Gestapo officers who replaced the Italian soldiers are quite intimidating. And I've heard rumors the Germans are going to build barricades on the promenades: one won't be able to see the ocean." She paused and sipped her drink. "Who knows, maybe you and Guy will elope, and after the war you'll stay here forever?"

Lana tried to think of a way to turn the focus on Giselle instead of herself. She didn't want to think of eloping with Guy, especially with her wedding to Frederic still fresh on her mind.

"Are you married?"

Giselle looked up sharply.

"Heavens, no! I gave up on men years ago, I'm happier with my art. Anyway, the Riviera isn't a good place to find a husband these days, unless you're interested in Germans or fishermen." She laughed and stood up. "Why don't I go fix something to eat?" Giselle seemed as eager to change the subject as Lana had been. "Gin makes me starving."

Giselle disappeared into the kitchen, and Lana glanced around the living room. There was a cigar humidor case on the side table that resembled Jacques's favorite humidor. She opened it to reveal the red velvet interior and noticed two sets of initials. She looked closer and read *To HM with love from GSC*.

Giselle appeared, carrying a tray of cheese and crackers and olives, and Lana closed the case.

"I was admiring your humidor," she said hastily. "My stepfather has one just like it."

"The villa came furnished. I haven't changed anything besides the paintings and a few pieces in my bedroom." She put the tray on the coffee table. "A bedroom has to reflect a woman's personality, don't you think? Mine is decorated in silver and blue, so I feel like I'm sleeping on a raft in the middle of the ocean."

They ate cheese and crackers and talked about Nice and Monte Carlo. Lana's mind kept returning to the humidor. It wasn't really a furnishing. *GSC* could easily be Giselle's initials. But who was *HM*? If Giselle had given it to someone, why did she say it came with the villa? And why did she change the subject and talk about her bedroom? There was something in Giselle's body language when Lana had mentioned the humidor case—a tensing in her shoulders, the lines that formed around her mouth—that made Lana uncomfortable.

"This humidor is so attractive." She picked it up. "I wonder where it's from. I'd like to get one for Guy as a present."

Lana was about to turn it over, but Giselle snatched it out of her hands. Giselle crossed the room and slipped it in a desk drawer.

"I shouldn't keep these things on display," Giselle said calmly. "If I break anything, I'll have to pay for it."

She looked at Lana and her expression was unreadable. “I’ll ask the landlord where he purchased it.”

Lana walked to the door. She didn’t want Giselle to think she was suspicious.

“I should go before I eat more cheese and crackers.” Lana smiled. “I have to get ready for the casino, and I won’t be able to zip up my dress.”

“I knew Guy had good taste. His villa is one of the prettiest on the street, and he drives that fun convertible. Now I see he has good taste in female companionship too.” Giselle followed her to the entry. “Most people in our social set are so busy impressing one another, it’s hard to know who they really are. I can already tell that’s not the case with you. I predict we’re going to be great friends.”

Giselle kissed her on both cheeks, and Lana inhaled the scent of musk perfume.

“I’m sure you’re right,” Lana agreed. “I could use a friend too.”

When Lana returned to the villa, she took a bath and selected a dress from the small selection in her closet. Guy was already in the living room when she descended the staircase. He wore a black dinner jacket and bow tie.

He didn’t say anything at her entrance, and she wondered if she had chosen the wrong gown. She wore her mother's black Chanel with the white cuffs. Perhaps she should have chosen something more seductive: the red Balenciaga that had a slit skirt.

"Well," he said finally. "I was wrong to give you the charm bracelet."

She glanced down at her bare wrist.

"I forgot to put it on," she explained, suddenly embarrassed. "I'll go upstairs and get it."

"No, no." He shook his head. His eyes moved slowly over the sheer black fabric and white cuffs. "A silver bracelet wouldn't do you justice. Next time I'll have to do a bigger favor for someone and get you diamonds."

"You like it?" She waved at her dress.

"It's perfect." He filled two glasses with gin and soda water and handed one to her. "The first rule of gambling is never drink and play at the same time. One cocktail now is all you need."

Lana sipped her drink and tried to think of something charming to say. It felt strange to be standing in the living room in formal evening wear, when this morning they had been sharing eggs and toast in the kitchen.

"I've never known a Russian countess before," Guy remarked. "I see them at parties, of course. I'm always impressed how well they speak French."

"The Russian nobility have been speaking French to one another for centuries," Lana replied. "My mother spoke French to me as a child even when we lived in a house full of Russian refugees."

"Ah, yes. Tolstoy wrote about that, didn't he? The Russian nobility spoke French because they believed the Russian language was meant for peasants." He jiggled his glass. "Your mother must have had the classic Russian aristocratic upbringing. Perhaps she had servants and a country estate like in Russian literature?"

Lana's face grew hot, and she put her drink on the bar.

"My parents moved to the country when they married. For a while after the revolution they lived undisturbed, but one day my mother came home and found my father's body hanging from an orange tree," she began. "She fled with nothing but the dress she was wearing and a suitcase. When I was growing up in Paris she took any job that came along so I had clothes and a bed. She did that for me, but so many children have no more security. Hitler has taken that away. If I can be half the hero to children in this war that my mother has been to me, I'll die happy."

Guy was silent, and Lana expected him to rebuke her for talking about her past. Instead, he put his glass down next to hers.

"We should go. You want to get a seat at the blackjack table early." He handed her a velvet cape. "So that every German who enters the casino has a chance to admire your beauty."

• • •

Guy was quiet in the car. He drove so fast, she was afraid he would miss a turn and plunge into the Mediterranean.

A sign announced Monte Carlo. Yachts bobbed in the harbor, hills glinted in the moonlight, and lampposts illuminated the cobblestones. Guy stopped the car in front of a creamy white building with turrets that rose up like those of a fairy-tale castle. Palm trees lined the circular driveway, at the head of which rested a fountain lit from behind.

"Oh, it's beautiful," Lana breathed. She had never seen anything like the casino, even in Paris. A wrought iron canopy covered the entrance, and a red carpet was rolled over the steps. Sports cars hummed on the pavement, and valets in velvet jackets and pantaloons greeted the guests.

"The Casino de Monte-Carlo never disappoints." Guy turned off the engine. "Did you know that residents of Monaco aren't allowed at the gaming tables? The government doesn't want them to lose their money. The casino was conceived by Princess Caroline in 1854 to save Monaco and the House of Grimaldi from bankruptcy." He looked at Lana. "The design might be familiar to you. The present-day casino was built in 1878 by Charles Garnier, the same man who built the Paris opera house."

"Isn't the casino affected by the war?" Lana wondered.

“Monaco is technically a neutral country. Which means they are happy to take the money of anyone who throws it on the roulette table.” Guy took Lana’s arm and guided her up the casino’s steps. “Let’s go inside. We have a big night ahead of us. Countess Lana Antanova is about to make her grand entrance into Riviera society.”

The lobby of the casino reminded Lana of a more decadent version of the Hall of Mirrors at Versailles. Crystal chandeliers hung from the ceiling, and marble columns were painted with naked cherubs. She ran her hands over the wallpaper that glittered as brightly as if it were embedded with precious jewels.

Guy put his hand on her back and led her into the gaming room. Men in dashing dinner jackets and women in elegant evening gowns occupied every table. German officers remained in their brown uniforms. The croupiers wore black bow ties.

Guy pointed to a blackjack table in the corner.

“Sit over there.” He waved at the table and pointed to a croupier. “Jules will take care of you.”

“Everyone is so sophisticated,” Lana noted. “What if I don’t know what to say?”

Guy put his hand on the small of her back and propelled her forward.

“You’re Countess Lana Antanova, of course you’ll know what to say.”

• • •

Lana sat on a velvet-backed stool as the croupier dealt her cards. She looked for Guy, but he had disappeared. Her cards were a queen of diamonds and a seven of hearts and she motioned for another card the way Guy had instructed her in the car. She waited anxiously until the croupier peeled off a three of hearts. Her hand won, and the croupier pushed the chips in her direction. She lost the next round and won the two after that.

A German officer with blond hair sat beside her.

"I've been watching you," he said, and Lana froze.

Guy had asked Jules to fix the table. If the German officer suspected she was cheating he might not want to talk to her.

"You've won almost every round."

"It's purely luck," Lana said blithely. "I hope it doesn't run out. The house often wins if you play long enough."

"I doubt that," the officer responded, and the skin prickled on the back of her neck. But then his features relaxed, and he smiled. "Women like you always seem to win at blackjack. They must teach you how to play at nursery school."

"Women like me?" Lana arched her eyebrows.

"Beautiful blondes who look like they don't have a thought in their head but end up with all the winnings." He waved at the stack of chips in front of her.

Lana wanted to rebuke him for being rude, but she bit her tongue.

"I did spend time at finishing school," she said instead. "We couldn't fill all our days with skiing; sometimes it was too cold to go outside."

"Are you French?" he inquired.

"Russian, but I grew up in Paris." She held out her hand. "Countess Lana Antanova."

"I knew there was something different about you," he offered. "Captain Peter Von Harmon."

Lana instinctively recoiled at his touch, but she kept out her hand.

He brought it to his lips and kissed it. "May I buy you a drink?"

Guy said not to drink, but it would be impolite to refuse. If she wanted to continue the conversation, she had to accept Captain Von Harmon's offer.

"Yes, thank you." Lana nodded.

The waiter brought two glasses of champagne, and Lana held hers in her hand. She tipped it to her lips and pretended to take a sip. She hoped that Captain Von Harmon wouldn't notice that she wasn't actually drinking.

"Are you enjoying the Riviera?" Captain Von Harmon asked. The medals on his lapel gleamed. A red band with a black swastika wrapped around the sleeve of his uniform.

"I just arrived," she answered. "Paris was so dreary; I needed to go somewhere fun."

"I was stationed in Paris last winter," he said, sipping his champagne. "I agree, the weather is even worse than in Berlin, but there is excellent entertainment. The symphony is wonderful, and the cabarets are enjoyable."

"Entertainment is available for handsome German officers but not for French citizens," she said. Too harsh, perhaps, so she adjusted her voice to become coquettish. "Don't get me wrong, Captain Von Harmon. I'm grateful to Hitler. We can live without amusement for a little while if it's for the greater good."

"You're grateful?" he said cautiously.

"My father was murdered by Cossack soldiers in 1918, and my mother barely escaped," she continued. "For twenty-five years we've been waiting to return to Russia: the Russia that was the homeland of the nobility for centuries, not the Russia of the Bolsheviks. We hope Hitler can restore Russia to the way it was before the revolution."

Captain Von Harmon didn't say anything, and Lana's heart pounded. But then he drained his champagne glass and signaled the waiter for another.

"The German army will defeat Stalin," he began. "You would be amazed how close we came to Moscow in 1941; we were in skipping distance of the parliament buildings. And the Battle of Kursk last July was a testament to the German army's strength. Stalin might declare himself the winner, but he's wrong. How could the Russians win when they lost eight hundred thousand men?"

Even though the Russians suffered enormous casualties, Lana knew they had won the Battle of Kursk. Hitler was stopped from reaching Stalingrad and hadn't made any progress since. But she gazed at Captain Von Harmon as if she hung on every word.

"You mustn't worry, Herr Hitler knows what he's doing," he continued. "It's just a matter of time until Stalin and his band of communists are removed and Russia becomes part of the Third Reich. I hope Stalin enjoys his winters in Siberia."

"You have no idea how happy this makes me." Lana leaned back in her chair. "I can relax and enjoy my holiday."

"Perhaps I can show you the Riviera," he suggested. "Where are you staying?"

Lana was about to answer when she saw a group of SS officers enter the casino. The secret police comprised the most select members in the Gestapo. In Paris, the secret police had been even more terrifying than the regular Gestapo. The Gestapo's job was twofold: to keep the peace and get rid of Jews. SS officers reported directly to Himmler; they were free to do whatever they wished to protect Hitler and his government. They were made up of the most loyal Nazis. Just seeing one on the sidewalk in Paris had made her shiver.

She recognized Alois Brunner's dark cowlick across the room. Her head began to swim.

"Are you all right?" he inquired. "You look pale."

Lana gripped the table to keep her balance. What if Brunner joined them? She wasn't ready to greet the man who murdered Frederic. But if she excused herself for no reason, Captain Von Harmon might become suspicious.

She tipped her glass so that a few drops of champagne splashed onto her dress.

"I'm so clumsy." She jumped up. "If you'll excuse me. This dress is silk and it will stain."

Lana hurried toward the ladies' room and collided with a tall man eating a canapé.

"Are you all right?" The man steadied her. He had a British accent and wore a white dinner jacket.

"I'm fine, thank you." She smoothed her hair and rearranged her dress.

"I thought it was you," he said.

She looked up.

"Charles Langford. We met on the train."

She stopped, nearly forgetting about the stain on her dress. Charles Langford lived in the country; he'd suggested he didn't get out much. But here he was, right at the Casino de Monte-Carlo.

"Of course. It's nice to see you," Lana answered. "What are you doing in Monte Carlo? You said the most interesting thing you do is attend the Lemon Festival in Menton."

"You have a good memory." He chuckled. "I came with a friend. And what about you, are you alone?"

Lana thought about Guy. She hadn't seen him in a while. What would he say if he saw her talking to a strange man?

"Not alone," Lana said. "But I can't find my date."

They were standing in a wide hallway with gold-framed paintings on the wall. Couples walked by, and a man who seemed slightly drunk juggled a pile of chips. She looked around for Guy but couldn't find him.

"Well, then, why don't I get a couple of drinks?" Charles suggested. "It's bad manners to leave a lady alone on the floor of the casino."

Lana glanced across the room, where Alois Brunner had joined Captain Von Harmon at the blackjack table. She wasn't prepared to go back and she didn't want to stand in the hall alone.

"A drink would be nice, thank you." She nodded.

"So you're not with the German officer who

looks like a Doberman pinscher," Charles said when he returned from the bar.

"You were watching me?" she inquired.

"Only admiring the beautiful woman winning at cards." He grinned.

"Beginner's luck," she corrected. "And no, Captain Von Harmon isn't my date. He sat next to me. I spilled champagne on my dress and was on my way to the powder room. I should go back soon. He bought me the glass of champagne; it would be rude not to return and finish it."

"That's very wise. He doesn't seem like someone who is used to being brushed off." Charles nodded and looked at Lana. "I see you're not carrying your copy of *Anna Karenina*. Have you been enjoying it at the villa in Cap Ferrat?"

"You have a good memory too." Lana smiled. The champagne warmed her throat, and the knot in her shoulders relaxed. "I haven't done much reading. There's so much to see; the scenery is spectacular."

"I told you it was stunning. And the Riviera isn't all beaches; the Italian Alps are practically at my back door," he replied. "You must come to Menton and see for yourself: snowcapped mountains behind you and the ocean spread out below like a sheet of glass."

"That's a wonderful invitation, I'd love to," Lana answered. She turned and saw Guy striding toward them.

“I found you,” Guy said when he joined them. His forehead was sweaty, and he was scowling.

“I was on the way to the ladies’ room and ran into someone I met on the train.” She turned from Guy to Charles. “Charles, this is Guy Pascal.”

“Pleased to meet you.” Charles shook Guy’s hand. “You look familiar, have we met before?”

“I wouldn’t know. I’m farsighted and too vain to wear glasses in public,” Guy answered. He turned to Lana, his eyes wide. “We have to leave for the villa. I received a message from my housekeeper that your mother called.”

Guy was very obviously lying, but she didn’t know why.

“My mother!” Lana repeated. “Is everything all right?”

“She didn’t say,” Guy said, and turned to Charles. “Thank you for keeping Lana company.”

“It was my pleasure.” Charles nodded. “Perhaps you’ll both come up to Menton. We have many beautiful public gardens. The Serre de la Madone alone is worth the trip.”

But Guy was not listening, and Lana hurried to catch up to him. He retrieved her cape from the coat check, and they walked down the steps of the casino.

“What was that about?” Lana demanded when they were sitting in Guy’s car. The roof was up but the interior was chilly. “Your housekeeper hasn’t been at the house since I arrived, and my mother doesn't have the phone number."

"I needed an excuse to get out of there." Guy gunned the engine. "What were you doing talking to that man?"

"What was I doing?" Lana said hotly. "You deserted me. I'd been chatting with a Gestapo officer and collided with Charles on my way to the ladies' room. Charles caught me. We met on the train here."

"Maybe he tripped you," Guy muttered. "Charles Langford is not to be trusted."

"You know him? You said you'd never met." Lana frowned. "And since when are you farsighted?"

Guy pulled up in front of the harbor and stopped the car. He took a pack of cigarettes out of the glove compartment and offered her one.

"No, thank you." Lana shook her head. "I don't really smoke."

"Neither do I, except at moments like these." He snapped open his lighter. "I left you alone because a Gestapo officer is hardly going to flirt with you if I'm hovering close by. And I've seen Charles Langford at parties. There's a rumor that he's a Nazi sympathizer."

"That's impossible," Lana retorted. "He's British. His family owns a house in Menton."

"Just because he's British doesn't mean he's a supporter of Churchill." Guy brought the cigarette to his lips. "Charles's parents were part of an international set in the 1930s who were known for their Nazi leanings. The Duke of Windsor and Wallis Simpson were frequent guests, along with Hitler's foreign minister, Joachim von Ribbentrop. Back then von Ribbentrop was the German ambassador to Britain." Guy let the information sink in. "Charles's parents held salons featuring German writers and musicians and had a whole wine cellar of German gewürztraminer."

"That was years ago. They couldn't have been certain war was coming. And it wasn't a crime to drink German wines or listen to German composers."

Frederic had adored Wagner. It had caused him pain to stop playing his sonatas.

"There's more." Guy grunted. "In the last three weeks, two groups of Jews were shot attempting to escape over the Maritime Alps. Charles mentioned that his home is right by these Alps." Guy paused meaningfully. "And both times he was seen at parties with SS present the night before the escapees were captured."

Lana looked out at the lights twinkling on the harbor. Yachts shimmered in the moonlight, and behind them Lana could make out the steeple of the Cathédrale de Monaco. How could Jews be shot in cold blood when all around them, there was so much beauty?

"It could have been a coincidence," she said

stubbornly. "It sounds like everyone on the Riviera is either at the casino or at parties. Perhaps there needs to be a new escape route. Even in Paris I've heard of Jews trying to get over the Maritime Alps."

"We in the Resistance are open to your suggestions," Guy retorted, and Lana could see the veins in his neck. "What do you propose? That we steal Hitler's car or send a fighter plane to pick up refugees?"

"There's an ocean in front of us." Lana waved at the harbor. "Why don't they go by boat?"

"Because it's miles to England, and as Charles can tell you, the channel isn't safe," Guy said grudgingly.

"You could sail a small boat to somewhere closer, like Algiers. Then you could take a larger boat to England," Lana suggested. "No one would stop a boat in Algiers. It's full of Allies and Germans. If the Germans torpedoed a boat at night, they might sink one of their own."

The Allies had recently recaptured North Africa from the Germans during Operation Torch. Algiers was teeming with soldiers from both sides. It was an ideal location to sail the boat.

Guy froze with his cigarette in midair. He turned to Lana, and his face was so close, for a moment she thought he was going to kiss her. Then he stubbed the cigarette into the ashtray and started the engine.

"Where are we going?" Lana asked.

"I'm taking you to the villa, and then I'm going into Nice."

"It's the middle of the night." Lana gripped the dashboard. "Can't it wait until morning?"

"Not if we want to save the next group of Jews scheduled to be paraded down the Promenade des Anglais and put on the train to Drancy." He drove faster. "I've been searching for a way to transport the Jews to safety, and this just gave me an idea."

Guy deposited Lana at the villa, and she dropped her cape on a chair in the living room. She ran her fingers over the coffee table and longed for her and Frederic's flat in Paris. Their bedroom had been the size of a bread box, but it had been theirs. Guy's villa contained no personal touches. There were no vases for flowers or paintings other than standard landscapes.

And she missed her mother and Jacques's apartment on the Avenue Montaigne. She missed the scent of her mother's perfume in the entry and the carafe of brandy in the library.

She needed to hear her mother's voice. She picked up the phone and dialed the number.

"Lana, is that you?" Tatiana answered the phone. "I just sat down to write you a letter."

"There's so much to tell you. I . . ." She stopped.

She had to be careful; what if the Germans

tapped the phone? She was about to make an excuse and hang up but that would be worse. A young woman alone in a new place would call her mother for advice. The important thing was to keep the conversation light. She gave her mother a quick description of Guy and the villa.

"I'm glad you're having fun," her mother replied as if they really were discussing Lana's holiday. "It rained all day in Paris and the forecast is predicting snow."

"Then I'm happy I came," Lana said. Her chest constricted, but she made herself keep talking. "Tomorrow I'm going to the market to buy dried fruit and oranges."

"I can just see you sitting on the terrace with a plate of fruit and a cool drink," Tatiana responded. "You have to send photos."

"I will." Lana nodded. "I should go; it's late and I'm tired. I just wanted you to know that I'm having a wonderful time."

"Before you go, why don't you give me your phone number," her mother suggested. "I'd like to be able to reach you."

"My phone number?" Lana repeated.

Was it safe to give her mother her phone number? Her mother knew she was working for the Resistance. She would be careful.

Lana hung up the phone and walked to the French doors. The moon had slipped behind a cloud, and the night was completely black.

She worried again whether the phone was tapped. She replayed the conversation in her mind. If any Germans had been listening, all they would have heard was a young woman and her mother comparing the weather.

It was so peaceful; the only sounds were frogs croaking and the distant hum of a car engine. She breathed in the scented air and gazed at the stars. If only Frederic were there. He would hum a tune, and they'd dance on the patio. She closed the doors and picked up her cape. Then she walked upstairs alone to her bedroom.

Chapter Six

NICE, NOVEMBER 1943

A week after the night at the casino, Lana attended her first dinner party. Guy had dropped her off in Nice to get her hair done at the salon in the Hôtel Atlantic. It was unnerving to sit under the hair dryer while Gestapo officers read newspapers in the hotel lobby. How could she even think about what kind of updo she wanted? But Countess Lana Antanova needed a new hairdo for a dinner party attended by some of the most fashionable people on the Riviera.

She had hardly seen Guy all week. He was gone before she came down for breakfast and disappeared at night. When she asked where he went, he grunted and said he would tell her when he was ready.

Whatever he was doing put him in a better mood. Lana bought fish and vegetables at the market, and on the one night that he was home, they ate dinner on the terrace. Afterward, they moved into the living room, where Guy uncovered the phonograph. They drank sherry and discovered they both liked Charles Trenet and Edith Piaf. It was at moments like that, with the stars glinting down on the garden and the air smelling of orchids, that she felt brave and confident and capable of doing anything.

But then Guy told her stories about the war: In July the head of the Resistance, Jean Moulin, was arrested while he was having tea at a private home in Lyon. Moulin was interrogated and tortured by Klaus Barbie, the Gestapo chief known as the Butcher of Lyon. Moulin attempted suicide and died from his wounds. After Guy finished his story, Lana went upstairs to her room and cried.

And she found it hard to stay at the villa when Guy was gone all the time. She spent a whole day in Grasse with Giselle. At first when Giselle suggested the excursion, Lana refused. She was on the Riviera to stop the deportations, not to enjoy herself. And she didn't trust Giselle completely. Giselle had acted oddly when Lana mentioned the humidor. But she needed to keep busy. And as long as Lana didn't divulge anything about Guy or the Resistance, they could remain friends.

They hopped into Giselle's little yellow car, and Giselle sailed along the road. Everyone on the Riviera drove as if they were competing in the 24 Hours of Le Mans race. Giselle handed her a scarf to protect her hair from the wind, and Lana leaned out the window and tipped her face up to the sun.

The fields around Grasse were filled with

silver-gray lavender. Lana had never smelled air so sweet. They parked in the old town and explored the eleventh-century cathedral and Gourdon Castle.

The best part of the day was visiting the perfumeries. Lana stood in the distillery with its copper stills filled with anise and orris root and imagined her own scent for her cosmetics company: it would be light and fresh with a hint of something Parisian, a seriousness she hadn't found in any of the sample bottles.

They toured Galimard, which was founded in 1747 and had supplied perfume to the court of Louis XV. At Fragonard, they sampled Moment Volé with its famous blend of black currant and raspberry and damask rose. Her favorite perfumery was Maison Molinard. The perfumes were displayed in crystal bottles created by renowned glassmakers: Lalique, Baccarat, and Viard. Lana held the Lalique flask that won the award for the most beautiful bottle at the 1939 World's Fair and remembered the old excitement of being around things she loved.

She knew exactly how she would design her perfume bottles. They would be made of glass in the shape of a rose. As she and Giselle sat at an outdoor café in the Place aux Aires, Lana sketched on a napkin. The lid would be painted a pale pink. The bottle itself would be clear so as not to hide the precious liquid inside. *LANA* would be scrawled on the side in gold letters.

It was only when Giselle remarked about the internment camp near Grasse that the war came careening back. Lana pictured inmates locked behind barbed wire fences, wondering if they would see their homes and families again.

"Thank you for bringing me," Lana said, biting into a crêpe. She hadn't had a crêpe since she and Frederic had visited his friend's restaurant in Le Marais. "I've never been to Provence, the towns are so pretty."

"Aix-en-Provence was the first place I visited when I arrived on the Riviera," Giselle said. "I had heard about artists painting watercolors in the town square and pictured setting up my easel beside them. That's before I learned about Les Milles."

"Les Milles?" Lana inquired.

"It was built as a tile factory and became an internment camp in 1939, ostensibly to house Germans—mostly artists and writers—who had fled before war was announced and were considered a threat to France. It was overcrowded, and the conditions were terrible: people slept on straw, and there was never enough to eat."

"I had no idea," Lana replied, putting down her fork.

"It gets worse." A shadow crossed Giselle's face. "A couple of years ago it started taking in French Jewish families who were waiting for exit visas. The Vichy government didn't know where to put them, so they sent them to Les Milles. Dozens died from starvation and disease. Then last year, all exit visas stopped, so the French police had to find something else to do with them. They couldn't stay at Les Milles forever."

Lana wanted to ask where they were sent, but she was afraid of the answer.

"The Vichy government deported two thousand Jews interned at Les Milles to Auschwitz," Giselle finished. "French police sending French citizens to their deaths. And hundreds of them were children. The Germans had nothing to do with it."

Lana pushed the crêpe aside and shielded her eyes from the sun. How could she sit and enjoy her meal when a year ago Jewish women and children had been marched through this square on their way to their deaths?

Now Lana left the hair salon in the Hôtel Atlantic and entered the pharmacy. She decided she was going to buy presents for Sylvie and Odette. She hadn't been to see them again since the day she brought Odette to her house. Guy was right; it was dangerous to get involved. But the more she thought about it, the more she couldn't stay away. Frederic would have tried to protect Odette, and she had to do the same.

She bought mints for Odette and soaps for

Sylvie. Then she tucked her parcel into her purse and walked briskly through Old Town.

No one answered when Lana knocked, and she wondered if anyone was home. But Sylvie would have taught Odette not to come to the door.

"Odette." She knocked again. "It's Lana."

There was the sound of footsteps and a key turning. The door opened to reveal Odette wearing a navy dress. Her eyes seemed too large for her small face. For a moment Lana wondered what her and Frederic's baby would have looked like at Odette's age. Would she have had curly brown hair like Odette? Frederic had dark hair and brown eyes, and their baby might have inherited those traits.

"What are you doing here?" Odette asked, interrupting her thoughts.

"I brought you presents." Lana held up the bag.

Odette opened the door, and Lana entered the living room. The curtains were closed, and the air smelled faintly of dust.

How different it must have been a month ago when her father was alive. Lana imagined Odette making coffee for him in the mornings and hugging him goodbye. Perhaps he brought home a few treats from the Hôtel Negresco, a pot of honey or a macaron.

"My mother is at work," Odette said, popping a mint in her mouth. "I'm not even allowed to open the drapes. It's worse than being in one of those German prisons you see on a newsreel at the cinema."

"Don't talk like that. The conditions in the prisons are intolerable." She looked at Odette curiously. "When do you go to the cinema?"

"I don't," Odette admitted. "I don't go anywhere anymore. All my friends are gone. Hilda Stein and her parents were taken away months ago. My father said it was because they weren't born in France. He said we were protected. But that's not true since the Germans arrived. Now every Jew in Nice is in danger."

"How do you know so much?" Lana inquired. "You're only twelve years old."

"I used to listen to my parents talk at night." Odette sucked on the mint. "The Italian soldiers weren't bad, but the Germans want to kill all the Jews. A German soldier will shoot you because your nose is too long or your last name is different."

Lana wanted to assure Odette that she was wrong, but Guy had said the same thing. The important thing was that Odette listened to her mother and didn't go outside.

"It's not always going to be like this. As long as you stay inside you're safe," Lana counseled. "The war will end sometime, and life will return to normal."

"Before the Germans arrived I used to go to play with my friend Annalise," Odette went on. "Every Saturday, Annalise's mother used to take us to the market and let us pick out a sweet. But Annalise's mother won't let me see her anymore. It's the same with Dr. Benoit. He hasn't been here in weeks."

"Who's Dr. Benoit?" Lana asked.

"A doctor who used to take me on house calls. I wanted to be a doctor when I grow up, and Dr. Benoit was going to show me how to use a microscope. But I'm not sure I want to be a doctor anymore."

"Why not? Medicine is a wonderful profession."

Odette's mouth turned down at the corners.

"What's the point of making someone well if a soldier is just going to come along and shoot him?"

Lana left Odette's and hurried down the Promenade des Anglais. Guy would be furious if he found out that she had visited Odette in the little house on Rue Droit.

She raised her arm, and a rusty Peugeot pulled next to the curb. A young man wearing a scarf jumped out. Lana recognized Pierre.

"Pierre, what a surprise!" she said. "It's nice to see you again."

"And you, Countess Antanova." He bowed. "Allow me to open your door."

"Thank you." She slid into the passenger seat. "The villa at Cap Ferrat, please."

"Have you been taking in the sights?" Pierre asked as the car nosed onto the main road. "The stairs in Old Town take you to the top of Castle Hill. It has the best view of the bay. And you can't miss the gardens of the monastery in Cimiez; the ruins date back to the Romans."

"No wonder you do well as a taxi driver," Lana said with a small smile. Pierre had such a youthful enthusiasm; being with him made her feel a little better. "You know everything about Nice."

"I am fortunate to live on the most splendid coast in the world." He waved out the window. "It's my privilege to share my knowledge with visitors."

They pulled up in front of the villa, and Lana opened her purse. She handed him a two hundred franc note, but Pierre shook his head.

"Monsieur Pascal already paid me." He gave her back the note.

"What do you mean, he paid you?"

"He asked me to wait for you and drive you back to the villa."

Lana processed what Pierre was saying, and her jaw tightened.

"Guy had you follow me?" she demanded.

"Many taxi drivers in Nice rip off the tourists. A passenger asks to go to the Place Masséna, and the driver winds through the alleys when it is in the center of Nice," Pierre explained. "He was only trying to protect you."

Lana ran up the steps and stormed into the villa. Guy was in the kitchen, polishing a pair of dress shoes.

"There you are, I was beginning to worry." He looked up. "The party is in two hours."

"You were spying on me!" Lana fumed.

"What are you talking about?" Guy asked. He wore a silk robe and slippers, and his hair was wet.

"I put up my hand to call a taxi, and Pierre appeared," Lana said. "He'd been following me all afternoon."

"I told you all the other taxi drivers in Nice are thieves," he commented. "They double the fare for a woman and then they steal her purse while she's checking her makeup in the rearview mirror."

"It's not the taxi drivers you don't trust, it's me," Lana insisted. "You hired Pierre to keep an eye on me."

"Why would I do that? I knew you were getting your hair done. It looks very nice, you should wear it in an updo more often." He looked at her inquisitively. "Unless there's something you're not telling me."

"I bought some things at the pharmacy, and then I came home," Lana muttered. "That's not the point. I've gotten around Paris by myself for years, I don't need a man watching out for me."

"War makes for strange times," Guy said, examining his shoe. "For soldiers it's very straightforward. They sit in a foxhole with bombs exploding around them and they're sure of two things: that the soldiers beside them in the trenches want to kill Germans and not be killed themselves. But the Resistance is different. People often join the Resistance because they've seen things that make them uninterested in living. That's when you have to be careful. If someone doesn't care about dying, he can put everyone else in danger."

Lana wondered if Guy had ever been in battle. He would never tell her. She glanced at the floor so Guy couldn't see her eyes. She remembered standing in the kitchen at the convent and telling Sister Therese she couldn't go on without Frederic and the baby. But then she pictured Odette sucking on the mint. Just knowing Odette gave her life meaning. Odette was only a child, but one day she'd blossom into a young woman. Lana had to try to make Odette's life bearable. And she wouldn't let it be cut short just because Odette happened to be born Jewish.

"I don't know anyone like that," Lana said, her voice cold. "If you don't mind, I'm going to take a bath. I want to look my best so every SS officer at the party spills their secrets to Countess Lana Antanova."

Guy's car pulled up in front of the villa where the party was being held. It was perched on a cliff, and even from the car Lana could see it was twice as big as Guy's house. The grounds were lit with silver lights, and she heard the sounds of glasses clinking and laughter.

"It's the size of a hotel," Lana breathed. Fir trees lined the driveway and a wraparound terrace overlooked the bay. A row of hedges surrounded a marble fountain, and the stone garage could fit at least six cars.

"Villa Russe is owned by one of the wealthiest couples on the Riviera. Boris and Natalia Petrikoff fled from Russia with a collection of fur coats and a suitcase full of eggs. They had other money, of course. They'd been stashing gold and rubles in a Swiss bank account for years." Guy smoothed his hair in the rearview mirror. He wore a black tuxedo with a yellow silk handkerchief in the pocket.

"A suitcase full of eggs?" Lana repeated.

"Fabergé eggs," Guy clarified. "Boris was Czar Nicholas's cousin, and he commissioned the jeweled eggs for Natalia's birthdays. After the revolution, Fabergé stopped production and the remaining eggs became quite valuable. The suitcase didn't just contain Fabergé eggs; there were gold humidors and diamond necklaces. The story goes that at the Petrikoffs' first dinner party, Natalia was naked under her mink coat because she hadn't brought any clothes. She didn't want to take up room in her suitcase that could be filled with precious items."

Lana had heard of Fabergé. Her mother had told her stories of the most famous jewelry house in Saint Petersburg before the revolution.

"My father wanted to buy my mother a sapphire-and-diamond ring and matching necklace from Fabergé when they got married," Lana recalled. "But she insisted on a small diamond instead. She loves pretty clothes, but she thinks extravagant jewels are cold and glaring."

"It's easy to agree when a woman has natural style. You in that dress, for instance." Guy waved at Lana's white satin gown. Her neck was bare, and she wore silver shoes. "It accentuates your youth but is elegant at the same time."

Lana waited for Guy to finish in his usual biting tone. But he was quiet, and when she looked at him there was something new in his expression.

"Natalia loves to show off her jewelry at parties. Her biggest fear is not being noticed, and the jewels make her feel young and vital. And there's often a Gestapo officer among the guests who offers her a pretty sum for a bracelet or a pair of earrings," Guy went on.

"The Gestapo?" Lana repeated, puzzled.

"They requisition apartments owned by Jews and sell the paintings and rugs on the black market," Guy explained. "Then they turn around and buy jewelry for their wives and girlfriends. You'll see, tonight Natalia will be wearing some exquisite emerald bracelet, and by the end of the night it will belong to an SS officer who'll send it to his wife in Germany."

"I didn't know . . ." Lana stammered. The air had a new chill, and she longed to be sitting in the living room of the villa with a glass of sherry and her copy of *Anna Karenina*.

"We better go inside." Guy took her arm. "Someone at this party must know when the next raid will occur. Our job is to find out who."

Lana followed Guy into a marble foyer. A circular staircase swept up to the second floor, and urns were filled with flowers like birds-of-paradise and camellias.

"I do love my camellias, they remind me of Marguerite in Alexandre Dumas's novel *Lady of the Camellias*. She wore a different-colored camellia on her dress depending on which lover she was waiting for," a woman said as she approached Lana. She was in her late forties with blond hair and a Russian accent. She wore a topaz gown and carried a pearl cigarette holder.

"It was such a tragic story. I cry every time I read it." She smiled at Lana. "When you're my age and married, the only way you experience passion is through books."

"You can't be old," Lana said, admiring the woman's smooth cheeks and small waist. "You have the face and figure of a girl."

"Do you think so?" she wondered. "I wouldn't know. I've removed all the mirrors from the house. It's the only way to remain happy as you get older. Instead, I hold parties and invite beautiful young men and women. If my guests are attractive, I must be too."

"That's great logic." Lana laughed.

"I wish I had done it years ago, it would have saved me the anguish of turning forty." She held out her hand, and Lana noticed the large diamond on her finger. "I'm Natalia."

"It's a pleasure to meet you." Lana took her hand. "I'm Lana Antanova."

"The countess staying with Guy Pascal." Natalia moved closer. "Tell me, what's he like in bed? I know that isn't the kind of thing one discusses at dinner parties, but I can't help but be curious. He's so handsome and virile, he must be a wonderful lover."

Lana gulped. Natalia couldn't expect Lana to answer. She wondered if this was the way all women talked on the French Riviera.

"Did I hear my name?" Guy appeared behind them.

"Only in the best way." Natalia turned to him and smiled. "I've been getting to know the countess. I begged Boris for years to let you be my lover. If that's not possible, I'm happy you found someone as pretty as Lana."

"There's a war on, none of us can have everything we want," Guy said with a smile. "Where's that caviar Boris promised? He said it was shipped from the Caspian Sea and narrowly avoided being torpedoed by a submarine."

Natalia drifted off, and Guy went to get glasses of champagne. Lana took deep breaths.

"You look like a fish twisting on a fishing line." Guy returned and handed her a champagne flute.

"Natalia asked what you were like in bed." Lana blushed. "I didn't know how to answer."

"That sounds like Natalia." Guy chuckled. "She loves to shock people. I can tell she liked you. She doesn't pay that much attention to guests she's not fond of," he said. "The important thing is to gain her friendship so she invites us to more parties."

Lana smoothed her dress. Her job was to fit into the social set. From now on she would try to be more relaxed about sex.

"Don't give it too much thought." Guy squeezed her arm. "I'm going to find that caviar; it's the best thing about the Petrikoffs' parties."

Guy crossed the room, and Lana noticed Captain Von Harmon standing in the doorway. He accepted a glass of champagne from a waiter and walked over to Lana.

"Countess Antanova. I would offer to find you a drink but you already have one." He bowed shortly.

"Captain Von Harmon." Lana greeted him. "It's nice to see you again."

"I'm glad we have mutual friends." Captain

Von Harmon moved closer. He wore some kind of cologne, and his cheeks were freshly shaved.

"The Petrikoffs have a lovely home," Lana commented. "I'm happy to be invited."

"Have you been enjoying yourself in Nice?" he asked.

"I haven't done much besides read at the villa." She took another sip for courage, and her eyes sparkled. "And I blame you."

"You blame me?" he said in surprise.

"You promised to show me around Nice," Lana reminded him. "How would you feel if you asked me to visit the castle of Nice and I'd already been?"

"You compliment me." Captain Von Harmon nodded. "I didn't expect a beautiful woman to sit by the phone and wait for my call."

"Then you underestimate both of us." Lana found she was enjoying herself. It wasn't hard to flirt after a glass of champagne.

"How have I done that?" he inquired.

"By not believing you are handsome enough to wait for, and by not thinking I would keep my word."

"That does make me the villain." He chuckled. "Let me make it up to you. I'm busy on Friday and Saturday. Perhaps I can collect you on Sunday and we'll go for a drive."

"Sundays are when I usually sleep." Lana put her hand to her mouth as if she were stifling a yawn. "What could you be doing that's so important on Friday and Saturday that you don't have time to show a new visitor around?"

Lana needed to get information from Captain Von Harmon. He must know when the next raid was going to happen.

Captain Von Harmon was about to answer when another SS officer approached them. Lana's body stiffened at the sight of Alois Brunner. This time she had no way to escape.

"Good evening, Captain Brunner." He nodded. "May I introduce Countess Lana Antanova? We met at the Casino de Monte-Carlo last week."

"It's a pleasure." Captain Brunner took Lana's hand.

Standing so close to the man who killed Frederic made bile rise to her throat. Her whole body felt chilled and it took all her willpower not to flee. Across the room Guy flashed her a smile, and she clutched her champagne glass and steadied herself.

"Lana is new to the Riviera," Captain Von Harmon said. "She's from Paris."

"Ah, Paris. I enjoyed my time in Paris very much," Captain Brunner replied. His hair was slicked back, and his eyebrows were thick as caterpillars. "The chef at the Ritz learned to make a delicious schnitzel, and I attended a performance of *Die Fledermaus* that rivaled anything I've seen in Berlin. But I completed my assignment in Paris, and it was time to begin my work on the Riviera."

"Your work?" Lana repeated.

"To rid the Riviera of Jews. They are as thick as locusts. And they aren't just French Jews, they're from Austria and Hungary and even Germany." He looked at Lana carefully. "You don't have any Jewish friends, do you, Countess Antanova?"

A chill ran down Lana's spine.

"I led a sheltered life in Paris." She chose her words as if she were walking in a minefield. "My mother escaped the Bolshevik revolution and our friends were mostly Russian. As you must know from being in Paris, there isn't much reason for French citizens to go out. It's impossible to get theater tickets, and the restaurants have strict rationing. I mainly stay inside and read books."

"That sounds terribly dull for someone like you," Brunner replied.

"Someone like me?" Lana looked at Brunner curiously.

Brunner leered at the way her gown hugged her chest, and it took all her strength not to splash champagne in his face.

"A young woman of noble descent. You should have suitors so you can get married and have children," he responded. "Surely there must be men in Paris worthy of your attention."

Lana remembered her cover. She tried to hide her revulsion.

"I'm afraid not, Paris is so depressing. I came to the Riviera for a little fun." Her eyes danced flirtatiously. "The men on the Riviera seem much more interesting."

Guy appeared, and she felt his hand on the small of her back.

"There you are," Guy said to Lana. He held two plates piled with caviar and toast. "I go to find caviar and come back to find you otherwise engaged."

"This is Captain Brunner and Captain Von Harmon." Lana introduced them. "Guy Pascal."

"It's a pleasure, but I'm afraid I have to pull the countess away." Guy bowed. "One of the best things about these parties is finding design ideas for my villa, and there's a piece of furniture I want her to see."

Guy led her upstairs and down a long hallway. He opened the door to a bedroom and pulled Lana inside.

He walked to the minibar and poured two shots. He handed one to Lana and waved at an ottoman. "Sit down and drink this. Brunner was standing so close to you. I thought you might be in trouble."

Lana sunk onto the ottoman and gulped the brandy. "Thank you. I couldn't stand there without wanting to claw Brunner's eyes out. He was bragging about getting rid of the Jews on the Riviera."

"Alois Brunner has one of the most impressive

records in the Third Reich for getting rid of Jews." Guy swirled the liquid in his glass.

Lana listened while Guy told her how Brunner had joined the Nazi Party in 1931 and become Eichmann's right-hand man. He sent 47,000 Austrian Jews to concentration camps in the first year of the war and since then he deported 43,000 Jews from Greece and 25,000 from Paris. In 1942 he was the commander of a train from Vienna to Riga carrying a wealthy Jewish financier named Sigmund Bosel. Brunner took Bosel in his pajamas and chained him to the platform of the car before shooting him. His body remained on the platform until the train arrived in Riga.

Guy finished his story, and Lana gulped her brandy.

"You knew all this and let me near him?" Lana said, and realized her hands were trembling.

"Brunner is in charge, we have to get close to him," Guy urged.

"I don't know if I can . . ." Lana stammered.

"Men like Brunner are predictable. They want to be flattered, then they are as pliable as a child with a new toy."

Alois Brunner had killed Frederic and was responsible for the death of their baby. How could she converse with him when just being near him made her ill?

Guy moved over to her and put his hand on her shoulder.

"We have to stop Brunner at what he's doing. If we don't, we're as bad as everyone else."

"What do you mean?" She looked up at him.

"If we learn when Brunner plans on deporting the next round of Jews we have a chance to save them. That's a few dozen Jewish men and women and children who will live because of us. Can you turn your back on them because Alois Brunner is disagreeable to talk to?" He dropped his hand. "And we're running out of time. Hitler lost some key battles this year. The German army surrendered to the Allies in North Africa in May, and they lost the Battle of Kursk to the Russians in July. Hitler may say he will defeat Stalin, but he's getting worried. It would be a huge achievement for Brunner if he exterminated all the Jews on the Riviera by the spring."

That was less than four months! Sylvie and Odette were Jewish. They had little chance of escaping the raids. Lana couldn't live with herself if she didn't try to help.

"I'm ready to go downstairs." She stood up. Her reflection gazed back at her from the mirror, and she noticed her cheeks were pale.

They stood at the top of the staircase, and Guy put his hand on her arm. Together they floated down the stairs and Lana felt something harden inside her. She saw the Gestapo officers standing in the grand salon and walked toward them.

"I'm sorry for my absence," she said, and

turned to Brunner. "Captain Von Harmon offered to show me around Nice. Perhaps you can give us suggestions, Captain Brunner. You seem so knowledgeable."

"I would be happy to." Brunner nodded. "The botanical gardens are always pleasant; they are one of the first places we're going to clear out."

"Clear out?" Lana repeated.

"Of Jewish families playing tourist." He looked at Lana closely. "You would understand. After all, czarist Russia felt similarly about the Jewish population for centuries." He paused. "The purpose of the pogroms was to rid Russia of Jews. I believe it's getting rid of the children that will make the difference. Some people are content with exterminating Jewish men and women; they think children should be spared. But it's like getting rid of a rat infestation but leaving behind the babies. In a few weeks the problem will arise again. The children must be dealt with too, so that Europe is free of Jews forever."

Lana tried to hide her revulsion. Only the most cold-blooded woman would agree to killing innocent children. She could hardly stand to look at him, but this was a test—to help Odette and Sylvie and everyone else, she had to gain his trust.

She lifted her eyes and returned Brunner's gaze.

"That's a fascinating viewpoint," she answered.

"Shall we get some caviar and you can tell me more?"

Brunner clicked his heels and took her arm. "I'd be delighted."

Chapter Seven

NICE, NOVEMBER 1943

The morning after the Petrikoffs' party, Guy didn't leave the house early for once. Lana heard him rustling around in the kitchen, but she wasn't ready to go downstairs. First, she wanted to wait for a phone call.

She woke up to the sun streaming through the bedroom window and the uneasiness of the previous night faded away. The ocean was as still as a painting, and she wished Frederic were with her. Frederic would have loved the Riviera. He would have taken photographs of the cobblestone alleys in Old Town and held her hand as they strolled along the Promenade des Anglais.

The night before was the first time she had felt the presence of true evil. Brunner's brooding eyebrows reminded her of the angel of death. How could an ordinary man be so consumed with hatred for a whole race of people who had never done any harm?

When she arrived at the villa, she had filled the bath with hot water and scrubbed the scent of Brunner's cologne from her skin. Even when she climbed under the crisp sheets, she still felt defiled.

Her hand drifted over her flat stomach and she thought about the baby. The things Brunner said about getting rid of Jewish children had made her feel ill. For much of the night she couldn't sleep, and this morning she was more determined than ever to do her job.

The phone on her bedside table rang.

"Hello," she said into the receiver.

"Good morning, this is Captain Von Harmon." A male voice came down the line.

"Captain Von Harmon, what a pleasant surprise," Lana answered.

"But you are the one who called me. I received a message from the hotel operator."

"Did I?" Lana let out a little laugh. "It must have slipped my mind. I've been sitting at my window and enjoying the spectacular view. I hope you have a similar view from your room," she said lightly. "I'm glad you called me back."

"I am very fortunate to receive a call from a beautiful woman. What can I do for you, Countess Antanova?"

"You must call me Lana. We've met twice, that must make us friends," Lana prompted. "Then you might do me a favor. I've been invited to a dinner party on Friday night. I wonder if you would accompany me."

"Friday night? I'm afraid that's impossible."

Lana's heart beat a little faster, and she clutched the phone.

"Please," she purred. "It's an important party, and I would feel awkward if I arrived alone."

"What about Monsieur Pascal?" Captain Von Harmon asked.

"Guy and I have a certain arrangement." She made her voice sound seductive. "He understands that I came to Nice to have fun. When I meet a fascinating man like you, Captain Von Harmon, I can't help but want to know him better."

"It's possible I could make time." He wavered. "When does the party start?"

"People dine so late on the Riviera. I doubt they'll sit down before ten p.m.," she answered. "I could meet you so you don't have to drive all the way to Cap Ferrat."

"That would make it easier," he agreed.

"How wonderful!" Lana beamed. "I'll come to you. Where will you be at nine thirty?"

"The lobby of the Hôtel Atlantic," he offered.

"I'll meet you there."

Lana hung up the phone and zipped up her dress. She slipped on a pair of sandals and hurried down the staircase.

"Thank goodness you're still here," she said to Guy when she entered the kitchen. "I was afraid you'd leave."

"Do you mind lowering your voice?" Guy glanced up from his newspaper. "It feels like a woodpecker is attacking my forehead."

Guy wore slacks and a rumpled shirt. Lana

noticed his hair was uncombed and there was stubble on his chin.

"You don't look like yourself." She frowned.

"This is exactly what I look like after I've had too many glasses of champagne and had to stand on a terrace in the freezing cold."

"I drank champagne on the terrace, and I feel fine." Lana walked to the coffeepot and poured a cup of coffee.

"Wait until you enter your thirties. You have the advantage of youth; you're eight years younger than me. And the fur coat Natalia insisted you borrow," Guy grumbled. "Brunner and Von Harmon would have stood out there all night if I hadn't said we had to go home."

"I have wonderful news." Lana sat opposite him. "I know the time and place of the next raid."

Guy put down his paper, eyed her with curiosity. "I was with you all night and we didn't learn anything except the way Brunner likes his omelets. Ham and cheese with shallots."

"I just hung up with Captain Von Harmon. I asked him to accompany me to a dinner party on Friday night. At first he said it was impossible, so I knew it was the night of the raid. But I insisted, and he said he'd meet me at nine thirty p.m." Her eyes sparkled with excitement. "In the lobby of Hôtel Atlantic."

"You think the raid will be on the Atlantic?"

"I'm not sure." She pondered. "But we know it

will be at one of the hotels. Why else would he say he was going to be in the lobby of the Atlantic?"

"It could be." Guy nodded thoughtfully. "Or he could be going there for a drink."

"You said I have to trust my instincts," she reminded him. "I have a feeling about this. If I'm right, all we have to do is alert the guests before Von Harmon and his men arrive."

Guy grabbed his car keys and motioned for Lana to follow him.

"Where are we going?" she asked.

"We don't simply alert the guests. They'll rush onto the Boulevard Victor Hugo and make Von Harmon's job easier." He opened Lana's door and hopped in the car.

"What do we do?" she wondered.

He gunned the engine and smiled. "We help them escape, of course."

Guy kept his foot so hard on the gas pedal, Lana averted her eyes from the cliffs. They drove into Nice and parked on a narrow street in Old Town. Two German officers strolled along the cobblestones, and Lana held her breath. But they were engrossed in conversation and didn't pay any attention to Guy's car.

Guy reached into the back seat and produced a straw hat and a pair of sunglasses.

"Put these on in case someone follows us."

"What a lovely hat." Lana admired the floral bow. "Whose is it?"

Guy glanced up and chuckled. "If you're asking if I go see a woman at night, the answer is no."

"Why would I ask that?" Lana retorted. "I just wondered why you have a woman's hat."

"I'll show you." Guy led her to the trunk of the car. She peered inside and noticed a selection of hats and sunglasses. There were a few coats and scarves.

"In case anyone follows us. There's also a pistol under the back seat if you ever need one." He nodded. "Let's go. We have a lot to do."

Lana put on the hat and walked alongside him. Guy kept glancing behind them, and she was reminded of the danger that lurked everywhere. If any of the German officers they socialized with suspected she was a member of the Resistance, she and Guy would be shot.

They entered a house with a low ceiling. A narrow staircase led up to the second floor.

"Lana, I want you to say hello to the man who's going to drive the boat," Guy said, entering an apartment.

The flat was one large room. A mattress was flung in the corner, and there was a kitchenette with a small fridge.

"What boat?" Lana asked.

"The boat that is going to carry the Jews to Algiers," Guy said as footsteps sounded in the hallway. Lana's eyes widened when the young man entered the room.

"Pierre! What are you doing here?"

"It's a pleasure to see you, Countess Antanova." Pierre greeted her. "Guy told me he was bringing you here today. I couldn't wait to see you again."

She noticed a pair of men's shoes next to the door.

"I don't understand," she said. "What does this have to do with you?"

"Pierre's father, Louis, taught him to drive a fishing boat when he was practically a boy," Guy explained.

"I was ten," Pierre said proudly. "I came home and told my mother one day I'd buy a yacht and sail around the Mediterranean. Just like the wealthy visitors who crowded the promenades in Nice."

"Pierre's father sold his fishing boat a few years ago, but Pierre is still one of the best sea captains in Nice." Guy rubbed his chin. "Which is lucky, because there will be fifty people on a boat that's made to carry ten, and he'll be driving at night without any lights."

"It will be as easy as paddling in the bathtub," Pierre said with the same youthful enthusiasm he had shown when he drove Lana around Nice.

The connection between Guy and Pierre suddenly dawned on her. Perhaps Pierre hadn't simply been waiting for work at the train station.

"Pierre is in the Resistance?" Lana realized. "But you never said anything."

"I didn't want to join the army, then I would have had to fight for Vichy France," Pierre explained. "But I had to do something. It's because of the war that my parents are dead."

"Louis was one of the earliest members of the Resistance on the Riviera. He risked his life smuggling Jews across the Alps to Italy." Guy took a notebook from his pocket. "Let's go over the plan. I'll get the room numbers of the guests from the concierge and knock on all the doors. Then I'll escort everyone to the far end of the harbor where the fishing boats are docked. The Germans don't go there because it smells like fish. Pierre will be waiting in the boat." He scribbled in the pad. "As long as Lana keeps Captain Von Harmon busy from seven p.m. to ten p.m. that will give Pierre enough time to depart."

"What do you mean from seven p.m.?" Lana asked in alarm. "Von Harmon said he'd meet me at nine thirty p.m."

"That's because he expects the raid to be completed by then." Guy kept scribbling. "If we want to prevent the raid, you have to meet him before it starts."

"But how?" Lana asked. The room felt claustrophobic. She noticed there weren't any windows.

Guy paused, and his smile was as bright as the bare light bulb hanging from the ceiling. "You'll think of something."

• • •

Guy left to continue preparations, and Lana stayed at the flat with Pierre.

"I had no idea you were in the Resistance." Lana sipped her water. "Did Guy plant you at the train station to spy on me when I arrived from Paris?"

"No, that was luck." Pierre grinned, sitting on one of the cushions that were scattered on the floor. He was all arms and legs, and Lana was reminded of a wooden puppet she had as a child. "I was waiting for a fare and saw you standing with your suitcases.

"I joined the Resistance to avenge my father's death and because I couldn't watch innocent people being killed," Pierre said. "But it makes me even happier that I work with Guy. I owe him a lot. After my father died, Guy found me in the taxi with the windows closed and the motor running. He thought I was trying to kill myself. I told him I just fell asleep but he didn't believe me. Maybe he was right."

"Oh, Pierre." Tears sprung to Lana's eyes.

"He and his wife let me stay with them and never asked for anything in return."

Lana looked up sharply.

"Did you say Guy's wife?"

Pierre's eyebrows knotted.

"You didn't know he had been married?" he asked, the realization all over his face.

"He told me a few things about his past for our cover, but he never mentioned that he had a wife." Lana felt strangely irritated. She lived in Guy's villa, and yet Pierre knew more about him than she did.

"Please don't tell him I told you," Pierre begged. "Guy would be furious with me."

She shouldn't have been surprised. Guy said it was best if they didn't reveal anything about their pasts that they didn't already know. And yet, Henri had told Guy that she had been married. She wished she could ask Guy why he had hid his marriage without fear of being reprimanded. But Henri and Guy had been in the Resistance longer. There must be a reason for the way information was doled out like the cough syrup she sometimes took as a child.

"Is he still married?" she wondered.

"It's not my place to tell you, you must forget I said anything." Pierre jumped up and started straightening the coffee table.

"How can I trust anything Guy says if none of it is true?"

"It's the same for anyone in the Resistance." Pierre folded the pages of a book. "You don't have to believe what Guy says, you just have to have faith in what he is trying to do."

Guy bounded into the room.

"Everything is all set," he announced. The circles under his eyes had disappeared, and there was a new energy about him. “Lana and I are going to lunch; espionage makes me hungry. Pierre, would you like to join us?”

“I have to work.” Pierre shook his head. “My landlady needs the rent, and the price of petrol keeps going up.”

Guy reached into his pocket and took out a hundred-franc note. “Take this and buy some groceries and a carton of milk. You’ll need your strength when you’re captaining the boat.”

Lana put on her sunglasses back in the car. With so much to think about, she didn’t want Guy to see her eyes.

“Where are we going?” she asked. The road hugged the Mediterranean, and Nice fell away behind them. Cliffs were coated with pink and purple flowers, and yachts glittered on the water like precious jewels.

“It’s a surprise,” Guy said, maneuvering around a sharp bend.

“I’ve had enough surprises for one more morning,” Lana muttered, tying a scarf around her hair.

“What do you mean?” He turned to her.

She couldn’t confide what Pierre had revealed. She had to wait for Guy to tell her himself.

“That Pierre is a member of the Resistance, and that I have to figure out how to distract Von Harmon all night,” she offered instead.

Guy laughed and turned on the radio. "This is a good kind of surprise. Trust me, the drive will be worth it."

The car bumped along the gravel, and Lana was glad she didn't have to talk. Had Guy really been married? There were no half-used lipsticks in a drawer or a woman's robe tucked in a closet. Henri had said that Guy was a wealthy Swiss businessman; he'd never mentioned a wife. Was anything about Guy's past true? And could she risk her life working with someone whose existence was a fabric of lies?

In front of them, the road curved and Lana saw a harbor filled with boats. Villas clung to the hills, and there were forests of fir trees.

"Welcome to Cannes." Guy waved at a sign. "The Boulevard de la Croisette is the most famous promenade on the Riviera. Just wait until you see the Carlton Hôtel. The valets hand-polish your car while you're at lunch, and the concierge keeps a silver water bowl for dogs behind the desk."

The Boulevard de la Croisette was lined with palm trees. Across the way, the Mediterranean seemed even bluer than in Nice. Umbrellas dotted the sand, where waiters delivered drinks to men and women wearing chic sweaters and slacks.

Guy pulled up in front of a building that took up an entire block. It was six stories of creamy stone with red turrets and flags flying over the entrance. Bentleys and Fiats lined the street in front.

"How is this possible?" Lana gazed at men in silk blazers. "There's a war on."

"Which means the black market is booming." Guy put on his jacket. "What better way to spend all that money than at one of the finest hotels in France?"

They entered the lobby, and Lana looked around uncomfortably. It didn't feel right to be standing under crystal chandeliers and surrounded by the scent of Chanel perfume, when in two days, Jewish guests at the Hôtel Atlantic would be pulled from their hotel rooms and forced into the dark night.

"You look like someone died." Guy noticed her expression.

"I was thinking about the raid on Friday night . . ." she stammered.

"That's why we're here." He took her arm. "So we don't think about it for an hour."

Guy told her about the history of the hotel. The Carlton was opened in 1911 by an Englishman named Henry Ruhl. The main investor was a Russian aristocrat, Grand Duke Michael Alexandrovich. No expense was spared on the design. The marble in the lobby was imported from Greece and the twenty-four-carat-gold layering was applied by hand. The dining terrace faced the ocean. Round tables were covered with pink tablecloths and the chairs were upholstered in the same turquoise as the Mediterranean.

They sat at a table by the railing, and Guy ordered dishes that made Lana's mouth water: pigeon with mint and turbot cooked with parsnips and winter squash. "I'm surprised you and your mother never stayed here. The hotel has been the main watering hole for the Russian oligarchy on the Riviera for decades. The grand duke used to take his five-o'clock tea at the hotel bar and there were golf matches and sailing regattas."

Lana never told Guy just how poor they were when she was a child. Her mother took almost any job to support them. They shared a small flat with other families, and her mother used a clothespin to keep her dresses together when they fell apart.

"My mother never had money for holidays until she married." Lana sipped her wine. "And since the war, no one travels that far on vacation. It's too time-consuming to just keep warm and have enough to eat."

"Except you," Guy said meditatively.

"What do you mean?" Lana asked.

"A mysterious young woman arrives on the Riviera to help a bunch of Jews she's never met escape the Nazis."

"Are you questioning why I'm here?" Lana said coolly.

She still felt hurt that Guy hadn't told her he

had been married. But she couldn't ask him without getting Pierre in trouble.

"You're so young to have been married and lost your husband. And you were still a student," Guy answered, eating a forkful of pâté. "I would have thought after your husband died you would want to stay close to your mother in Paris."

"Lots of girls get married when they're young. My mother was nineteen when she married my father," she said evasively. What if Guy was testing her to see how much she would reveal? Everyone had warned her not to give the details of her life to anyone, not even Guy. "Why shouldn't I be here? Many women are in the Resistance."

"Not Russian countesses who are studying chemistry at the university." He took another bite.

"Henri made me believe I could help people," she began. "Especially the children. Children shouldn't have to suffer because adults are at war."

"The children?" Guy looked up from his plate.

Lana bit her lip. She shouldn't have said that. Guy might think she had visited Sylvie and Odette.

"No Jew should die because of his beliefs or the spelling of his last name, but killing the children is even worse. Childhood is about feeling safe and loved, otherwise how will children be able to dream? And without dreams how can the future generation discover planets and cure diseases and create art? The war has to end so the children lead normal lives; otherwise the future of humanity is doomed."

After she finished talking, Guy was quiet. He reached across the table for a bread roll. For a moment their hands touched. Lana was perfectly still. Then he removed his hand and picked up a knife.

"Then we'd better be successful on Friday," he said, buttering his bread.

"Will it be very dangerous?" Lana asked. The courage she felt when she made her speech had passed, and she was more nervous than before.

"What could be dangerous about driving a boat that I bought for a few hundred francs from a fisherman I just met?" His voice turned lighter. "I checked it out from top to bottom, I'm sure it's seaworthy. All Pierre has to worry about are the patrol boats."

"Patrol boats?" Lana said in alarm.

"The Germans aren't stupid. Any of those yachts could be used to carry Jews to safety." He waved at the yachts bobbing in the harbor. "But if the boat is painted black, it will be impossible to see at night. Unless Pierre collides with another boat or hits a rock, he should make it across to Algiers."

"And if he's caught?" Lana asked.

"Then he'll be shot." His voice tightened. "That won't happen. You've seen Pierre drive a taxi, he's as confident as a race car driver. I have the same confidence in him steering a boat," Guy said as the waiter put plates of fish and vegetables with melted butter on the table. He tucked his napkin under his chin and picked up his fork. "This all looks delicious. Why don't we enjoy our lunch?"

After their meal they strolled along the Boulevard de la Croisette. The air smelled of perfume and cigars, and the pavement was as shiny as the handlebars on a bicycle. They turned a corner to spot a group of officers lounging at a café. Their caps rested on the table, and they drank glasses of beer. Guy ignored them, but Lana quickened her step.

Guy took her arm and led her through the old town.

"I want to show you something," he said. They climbed brick stairs until Lana's calves burned and she thought she couldn't take another step.

"Where are we?" she asked when they reached the top. In front of them was a church with a clock tower. Windows were placed high in the walls and there was a courtyard with a sundial.

"This is the Eglise Notre-Dame d'Espérance." Guy rested on a bench. "It's one of my favorite churches. Construction began in the sixteenth century. For the next three hundred years architects and craftsmen worked to create a place where people could go to find peace and hope.

"Hitler not only wants to exterminate half the European population but also he has no respect for the past. Churches are being bombed all over Europe, and the contents of museums are under wraps in secret locations, possibly never to resurface again. What will the world look like in a hundred years if everything that is important is gone?"

Lana saw a couple strolling along the path. The woman wore a navy coat and had a wedding ring on her finger. Lana's heart ached for Frederic so much that for a moment she couldn't speak.

"That's why we're here," Lana said softly. "So that Hitler doesn't win."

Guy looked at her, and his eyes were as green as the grass.

"We should go." He stood up. "I have to buy Pierre a pair of waterproof boots. I don't want our captain to get cold feet."

Guy dropped Lana off at the villa and went into Nice to run errands. She entered the kitchen and heard a knock.

"Giselle," she said, opening the door. "What a lovely surprise."

Giselle wore her usual uniform of slacks and a blouse smudged with paint. Even attired as she was, she looked sophisticated.

"I saw Guy drive off and thought you wouldn't mind if I stopped by."

"Please come in." Lana ushered her inside. "I was making some tea."

Lana brought out a tray with tea and lemon and honey and they sat in the living room.

"I wanted to ask you a favor," Giselle said, stirring honey into her tea.

"What kind of favor?" Lana asked. Despite their time as friends, she still hadn't learned anything more about Giselle. Giselle seemed so eager to do things together: asking her into her villa for a drink, inviting her to visit the perfumeries in Grasse. And yet she hardly revealed anything about herself. Lana recalled the engraved humidor in Giselle's living room. The way Giselle became so agitated when Lana examined it. For all Giselle's welcoming manner, there was something about her that was guarded and closed off.

"I have to go away; I hoped you might take care of my chickens," Giselle explained. "I used to ask my neighbor Madame Bouchard, but she's getting old. The last time I went away, she forgot to collect the eggs and the chickens sat on them for days."

"Of course I will." Lana smiled. "Where are you going?"

"To take care of some business," Giselle said evasively. She waved around the room. "I love what you've done here: it's so pretty and inviting."

The villa did look better. Every day she filled the vases with flowers and polished and dusted the furniture.

"Guy said he used to feel like he was living in a museum and now it feels like a home," Giselle commented. "He's very appreciative."

"When did he say that?" Lana asked.

"A couple of days ago when he came to get some eggs. I think he likes being domesticated." Giselle grinned at Lana. "I couldn't live with a man telling me what to do. I need my independence."

Lana stirred honey into her tea and took a sip. She had to pretend that talking about being Guy's mistress was the most natural thing in the world.

"Guy doesn't tell me what to do," she rejoined. "We lead separate lives."

"You might think that, but he'll start wanting to know where you've been or checking your receipts," Giselle countered.

She smiled meaningfully and picked up her teacup. "Men can't be happy having women as lovers, they have to own them."

Lana tried to seem sophisticated and worldly. She ran her fingers over the rim of her cup and smiled.

"It's not like that with me and Guy," Lana

assured her. "He knows I'm not ready to settle down. I'm on the Riviera to have fun."

"How many women have said that and suddenly they're spending all their time fixing the man's favorite cocktail?" Giselle chuckled.

She uncrossed her legs and pointed to the bottles of Scotch on the sideboard. "Just be careful. One day you'll come home to a diamond engagement ring and you won't know how to say no."

Lana opened her mouth and then closed it. She couldn't ask Giselle if she knew that Guy had been married.

"I should go, I have to let the chickens out of their coop." Giselle stood up and smiled her dazzling smile. "I came to the Riviera to be an artist, and I spend half my time raising chickens. I'm tempted to get a rooster; the hens seem lonely without any males around. But roosters are only good for their meat, they don't provide eggs. And I could never kill anything."

Giselle left, and Lana took her teacup upstairs to her bedroom.

The phone rang and she picked it up.

"Lana, darling. It's your mother," Tatiana said when she answered.

"Oh, hello!" Lana started.

For a moment she forgot that she had given her mother her phone number. She'd never wished to speak to her mother more. But talking to Tatiana on the villa's phone was difficult. She couldn't tell her about Alois Brunner, or how every time she passed a group of German soldiers she felt nervous and vulnerable.

"I hope it's all right that I called. I hadn't heard from you. I wanted to see how you are."

"I'm fine." Lana sunk onto the bed and tried to keep her voice light. "Guy took me to Cannes. We ate lunch at the Carlton Hôtel."

"Jacques and I have always wanted to go to the Carlton!" Tatiana exclaimed.

"It was wonderful," Lana agreed. "We ate steamed turbot with parsnips and winter squash. I can't wait to tell Sister Therese. We used to laugh that the only vegetable left in France was rutabaga."

"That's one of the things I wanted to tell you." Her mother's voice dropped. "I went to the convent to deliver some books, and Sister Therese was gone."

"What do you mean gone?"

"She didn't come back from the market one day. No one knows where she went."

"I'm sure she'll turn up." Lana tried to squelch the uneasy feeling in her stomach. "Perhaps she went to visit the sister convent in Lyon."

"I'm sure you're right," Tatiana agreed. "I'm glad you're having fun. Guy sounds like he knows all the best places."

"He does." Lana nodded. "He's showing me a lovely time."

• • •

Lana hung up and paced around the room. She wished there was someone she could ask about Sister Therese. But she hadn't had any contact with Henri since their first meeting. And it would be too dangerous to phone the convent.

Thinking about Sister Therese reminded her of the little Jewish girls at the convent: Esther Cohen and Ida and Sophie Rosenberg. She wondered if they were still alive. Her heart ached, and her resolve to help the children grew even stronger.

The raid was in two days, and she would spend the next day brushing up on current events so she could engage Captain Von Harmon in conversation. But on Saturday she was going to the market. Then she would visit Odette and they'd have a picnic at the kitchen table. Odette might not be able to behave like a normal little girl, but Lana could still try to make her happy.

Chapter Eight

NICE, DECEMBER 1943

Lana stood in Giselle's kitchen and filled a bowl with birdseed for the chickens. Giselle had asked Lana to drive her to the train station and said she could borrow her car while she was away. Lana was grateful: she could get to Nice that evening to see Captain Von Harmon without Guy having to drive her. They both agreed it would be best if they weren't seen together on the night of the hotel raid.

The afternoon sun warmed her back as she walked out of the chicken coop. It was hard to imagine that at this moment Captain Brunner and Captain Von Harmon were plotting to throw dozens of Jews out of their hotel rooms and march them down Promenade des Anglais to the train station.

She scattered birdseed on the ground and entered the garden shed. Behind the shed was a space that Giselle used as her studio. Lana had never been inside, but suddenly she had the urge to look around. Perhaps she could ask Natalia Petrikoff for help in getting Giselle a gallery show.

Canvases were stacked against the wall, and

there was a table strewn with paints. Lana poked her head inside a little fridge and laughed. Giselle loved her little luxuries. She would keep a chilled bottle of gin and a carton of goose pâté close by for when she took a break.

She turned and noticed a painting resting on the easel. It was of a man in his thirties with a strong jaw and long eyelashes. His blond hair flopped over his forehead, and he held a bunch of flowers.

Could it be the man whose initials were on the humidor?

Lana flipped through the canvases to see if there were other portraits, but they were only still lifes of fruit bowls.

A church bell chimed. Lana strode through the garden to the kitchen. There wasn't time to wonder if Giselle was hiding something. In four hours Captain Von Harmon would leave his hotel to meet Captain Brunner at the Hôtel Atlantic, and she had to do everything she could to stop him.

When she returned to Guy's villa, his car was already gone. She opened the front door and ran up the staircase to her bathroom.

She ran water for a bath and wished that she were in Paris with Frederic practicing Chopin in the living room. After her baths, she used to wrap herself in a towel and sit beside him. Frederic would laugh that he was too distracted to play, and they'd end up making love on the sofa.

Hot water filled the bath and she stepped into the tub. There was no point in dreaming about the past. The only thing she could do was make herself so alluring that Captain Peter Von Harmon couldn't resist her.

Lana turned onto the Avenue Durante and parked Giselle's car. The Hôtel Excelsior wasn't as grand as the Carlton Hôtel in Cannes, and it didn't sit on the main promenade like the Hôtel Negresco. Instead, it was set back on a leafy street and seemed more like a nineteenth-century château with a peaked roof and ivy creeping up the walls.

The lobby resembled the living room of a private home. There was a fireplace with a roaring fire and bookshelves filled with leather-bound books. A man in a dark suit stood behind the concierge desk. An elevator bore grille doors.

"Good evening." Lana approached the desk. "I was looking for one of your guests: Captain Von Harmon."

"Captain Von Harmon is staying with us," the man acknowledged. "But I'm not able to give details about our guests."

"I wouldn't dream of asking for private information," Lana replied. "After all, the Hôtel Excelsior is a well-respected hotel."

"Then what can I do for you, Madame . . . ?"

"Countess Lana Antanova." She reached into

her purse and took out an envelope. “I wonder if you can deliver a letter.”

“A letter?” He looked at the envelope suspiciously.

“To Captain Von Harmon,” she said, and slipped a fifty-franc note into his palm.

His cheeks colored, but he tucked the money into his pocket.

“I would be happy to help.” He bowed.

She smiled her most flirtatious smile. “I was hoping you’d say that. If you don’t mind, I’ll sit in your lobby and wait for a reply.”

Captain Von Harmon appeared ten minutes later. Lana almost didn’t recognize him without his Gestapo uniform. He wore slacks and a shirt, and his hair was damp as if he had stepped out of the bath.

“Countess Antanova, what are you doing at the Hôtel Excelsior?” He approached her. “We were supposed to meet at the Hôtel Atlantic at nine thirty.”

Lana purposefully shifted on the chair so Captain Von Harmon would be distracted by her legs. She had chosen a knee-length gold evening gown from her mother’s collection and paired it with silver heels.

“I’m sorry if I’m disturbing you,” she began. Her voice rose, and she bit her lip. “Guy and I got into a terrible argument, and I had nowhere else to go.”

"If the argument was about me taking you to the dinner party . . ."

"No, of course not. I told you I can see whomever I like." She twisted her hands. She leaned forward so he could see more of her décolletage. "It was about the war."

"The war?" he repeated.

"It was awful, you should have heard him," Lana said, shivering. Her eyes widened and she pointed at the guests crossing the lobby. "Is there somewhere we could go that's quiet? Perhaps where I could get a cup of tea. It's made me so anxious; I feel ill."

Captain Von Harmon paused, and she could almost see him calculate in his head whether he had time before the raid.

"A cup of tea is a good idea. Why don't we go into the bar and sort this out?"

When the waiter appeared, Lana announced she'd changed her mind and asked for a Scotch. She had to get Captain Von Harmon drunk for her plan to work.

"What do you mean that you and Monsieur Pascal got into an argument about the war?" Captain Von Harmon asked when the waiter delivered two Scotches.

"Guy is a good man, but he's Swiss. And the Swiss have always had plenty to eat and drink," she said, sipping her Scotch. "I tried to see it from Guy's point of view. His country has never gone through a war or suffered in any way. He doesn't understand what it's like to love your country so much and not be able to help." Her words choked, and she blinked back a tear. She had to sound devastated or Captain Von Harmon might send her away. "I tried to explain, but he got so angry and I . . ." She gulped. "Forgive me; it's hard to talk about. I had to come see you. You were the only person who would understand."

"I would understand?" Captain Von Harmon repeated, frowning.

"Hitler is trying to return Germany to its former glory, and I want the same for Russia," she tried again. "I want to be able to visit my home country and know the places my mother used to talk about: the architectural beauty of Saint Petersburg instead of Leningrad and summers at our old dacha in the country. How wonderful it would be to attend balls at the Winter Palace.

"Don't get me wrong, Guy doesn't outright support the Allies. But he remains completely detached." She placed her glass on the table. "Don't you see? How can I remain neutral when Russia is desperate for Hitler and the German army and men like you to rescue it from the communists?"

"I can't save Russia personally." He chuckled uncomfortably.

"But you understand why Russia needs Hitler. He took Germany out of the gutter and gave its people back their dignity. And look at what he's accomplishing now. He's deporting all the Jews from Poland and Austria and Germany, just like Russia needs to get rid of the communists." Her voice became urgent. "I couldn't help myself. Guy told me to leave."

"To leave?" he repeated.

"I thought he was going to hit me. He picked up a bottle and held it over his head as if he was going to throw it." Her eyes widened. "I was so frightened, I grabbed my shoes and ran. He'll calm down when he's sober, but in the meantime I had nowhere to go. I came here, I hope you don't mind."

"I see, but I'm afraid I have an important engagement." He rubbed his brow. "I can meet you at the Hôtel Atlantic as we planned."

"What will I do until then?" Lana asked in alarm. "Captain Brunner said that Nice isn't safe at night." She waved at her gown. "And a woman in an evening gown can't sit in a hotel lobby. People will think . . ."

"I sympathize, but my plans can't be changed. If you want to wait in my room . . ."

"Captain Von Harmon!" Lana exclaimed. "Just because I'm distressed doesn't mean I would put either of us in a questionable position."

"My apologies." Captain Von Harmon flushed. He was obviously struggling with what to do, and Lana reached up and patted his shirt collar.

"If we could just sit here and talk until the dinner party," she coaxed. "Then Guy's rage will blow over and everything will be all right."

Captain Von Harmon slumped against his chair, and for a moment Lana felt sorry for him. He was so simple; he believed a gentleman couldn't disappoint a woman.

"If I went to my room and made a phone call, perhaps I could stay longer." He wavered.

"Would you? I'd be so pleased." She leaned forward so he could smell her perfume. "Why don't we ask the waiter for a menu, and I'll order something while you're gone. I always get hungry when I'm emotional, and I haven't eaten since lunch."

Lana took as long as she could deciding what to order without rousing his suspicions. The waiter delivered another round of drinks, and Lana asked questions to distract Von Harmon from going to his room.

She learned that he grew up near Hitler's castle in Berchtesgaden and came to Hitler's attention when he delivered cheese from his parents' dairy. Hitler took a personal interest in the teenager who carried a copy of *Mein Kampf* in his bicycle basket and whose blond hair was the color of butter.

Captain Von Harmon joined the Youth Party at the age of fourteen. He rose quickly in the ranks until Eichmann himself asked him to become a member of the Gestapo. He served beside Eichmann in Poland when he had 600,000 Jews deported. And he was at the Wannsee Conference in 1942 and assisted Eichmann in the deportation of thousands of Jews to Belzec and Treblinka.

Whenever Von Harmon was about to leave she asked another question, despite her revulsion. Finally the clock struck nine and she excused herself to the powder room.

"I'm afraid I have news," she said when she returned. "I rang the hostess of tonight's dinner party, and it's been called off. Her husband got food poisoning."

"Called off!" Captain Von Harmon exclaimed. His eyes were glazed from the Scotch and he pulled at his shirt collar.

"Marta promised she'd reschedule," Lana said. "I hope you'll be available again."

"Of course, but what will you do tonight?"

"I'd love to stay longer, but I've already taken up too much of your time." She put her hand over her mouth as if she were yawning. "I suppose I'll go home. I'm terribly tired. It's been a lovely evening," she said with a little smile. "You're a wonderful storyteller, I should employ you to read to me before bed."

Captain Von Harmon's cheeks colored, and he jumped to his feet.

"You can't go home. What about Guy?"

"He'll have gone to his event by now, and when he returns I'll be snug in bed." She waved offhandedly. "He was quite drunk, tomorrow he won't remember our argument."

"Then at least allow me to call a taxi."

Lana didn't want to leave the hotel with him. She had parked Giselle's car outside. "You're not even wearing a coat. I don't want to be responsible for one of the most important Gestapo officers in Nice catching a cold."

"I'm not that important." He shrugged. "I'm only fourth in charge on the Riviera."

"You're important to me." She kissed his cheek and rubbed the lipstick with her palm. "Good night, Peter. I hope I can call you Peter. I feel that tonight, we have become firm friends."

It wasn't until she had driven away that she let herself relax. The whole time she sat opposite Captain Von Harmon at the bar, she was afraid he would cut the evening short. And she worried about his calling a taxi; she couldn't have anyone follow her.

Now she pulled up in front of the dock. Her purse lay on the passenger's seat next to her shoes. Her feet ached from wearing heels, so she drove barefoot.

She rolled down the window to breathe in the salty air, relieved that her role this evening was over. A few carefully chosen words of flattery and several rounds of drinks and Captain Von

Harmon had become as pliable as a child. She couldn't wait to tell Guy about her success.

A German jeep was parked in the middle of the road. A soldier waved at her to stop.

"Can I help you?" He poked his head inside.

"Guten Abend," she said in German. "I wanted to park and go for an evening stroll."

"I'm afraid that's not possible tonight," he replied. "There's been a disturbance. A man has been shot."

"Been shot?" Lana repeated.

"He was trying to steal a boat," the soldier said. "But not anymore. Now he's on his way to the morgue."

Her eyes scanned the harbor for Pierre's boat, but there were only a few fishing boats rocking at the shore. She spotted Guy's car parked at the end of the dock, but he was nowhere in sight. She wondered whether the soldier was talking about Guy.

"Are you feeling all right, fräulein? You're quite pale," the soldier asked.

"I need to walk in the fresh air." She opened the car door. She had to get to Guy's car and see if he was all right.

The soldier put his hand on the door. Lana could see his gun gleaming in the dark.

"I can't allow that," he said. "The area is being searched in case of an accomplice."

Lana gulped and peered onto the dock. Guy

could be hiding somewhere. He might be trying to avoid the German soldiers. She couldn't leave without trying to find him.

She briefly put her hand on top of the soldier's. "Please, I ate something bad at dinner," she explained. "If I don't get some air, I might faint."

The soldier wavered, and Lana thought he would let her get out. But then he closed the door firmly.

"I'm sorry, fräulein, I have to follow orders," he barked. "You are welcome to sit in the car until the sickness passes."

Lana tried to hide her disappointment. There was a lump in her throat, and she tried not to panic. She remembered standing outside the window at the convent and seeing Frederic face Alois Brunner. How helpless she had felt, the crack of the gun and Frederic falling to the floor. Her voice faltered, and she took a deep breath.

"Of course, I understand," she said with a little smile. "I'll just take a moment and I'll be on my way."

There was no point in staying at the dock. The soldier wouldn't let her out of the car. If he suspected she was looking for someone he might get suspicious. She had to drive to the villa and wait for Guy there.

The villa was dark when she arrived, and she fumbled with her house key. She stumbled into the living room and turned on the light.

"There you are," Guy said. "I was wondering when you'd be back."

Guy stood up from where he had been sitting on the sofa, and Lana couldn't help herself. She dropped her purse and burst into tears.

"Well, that's not much of a greeting after the night we've had," he murmured.

Lana barely heard him. She buried her head in her hands and kept sobbing.

"I went down to the dock. A soldier said a man had been shot. Then I saw your car, and I thought . . ."

"The damn car." Guy sighed. "Some German soldiers were sniffing around it so I had to leave it there and drive the van."

The plan had been that Guy would transport the Jews to Pierre's boat in a florist's van. Guy's car would be waiting at the dock. Guy would drive his car to the villa, and Pierre would return the florist's van when he got back from Algiers.

"It's parked in the garage in case an inquisitive neighbor wonders why Guy Pascal traded his convertible for a florist's van," Guy continued.

"So you weren't shot?" She gasped.

"Do you see any holes in my chest?" He waved at his dress shirt. "That thief almost deserved to be shot; who cheats a fisherman out of making a living?"

Guy took a handkerchief out of his shirt pocket and handed it to her. "Tell me what happened.

How did you get Captain Von Harmon to miss the raid?"

Lana gulped and sunk onto the sofa.

"I went to the Hôtel Excelsior and told Captain Von Harmon we got into a terrible fight," she began. "Then I asked if we could discuss it in private."

"In private?" Guy said sharply. "It's all very well to flirt with him at a party, but if you went to his hotel room I'll . . ."

Lana looked up and noticed the change in Guy's expression. His fist was knotted in a ball, and his eyes flashed.

"I wouldn't dream of doing that," she corrected. "We sat in the bar."

"That's better." Guy nodded. "I hope you didn't drink too much. I don't want to be responsible for turning you into an alcoholic."

"I hardly drank anything," she said, and the tears started again. "I was so frightened. What would have happened if I had failed?"

"But you succeeded." Guy sat beside her. He took the handkerchief from her and dabbed her eyes.

"I had to say the most terrible things." She thought about the way she talked about Hitler and the Jews. "I was afraid he wouldn't believe me."

"Soldiers have guns as weapons, but we only have our intelligence," Guy mused. "Whatever you said allowed dozens of people to be on their way to safety."

Lana thought again of her fear when she saw Guy's car parked at the dock. She hadn't been so frightened since she stood outside the convent window in Paris.

"I wanted to look for you . . ." she stammered. "But the soldier had a gun, and he wouldn't let me out of the car."

"It's a good thing you listened to him." He soothed her. "We're overwrought. The best thing to do is get some sleep. Tomorrow morning I'll fix us both eggs with horseradish. It's the best cure for hangovers."

"I don't have a hangover, I hardly drank," she reminded him.

"There are different kinds of hangovers. You've had a lot of shocks this evening." He stood up and took her hand. "Go to bed, everything will seem brighter in the morning."

His hand was warm on hers, and she rose from the sofa.

"Lana," he said when she was halfway to the staircase. She turned, and his eyes were luminous under the light of the chandelier. "I'm proud of you, you did great work."

Lana stood on her balcony, and the breeze touched her cheeks. The moon had come out and the sky was full of stars.

Of course she was too nervous to sleep. The success or failure of the raid had rested on her shoulders.

But there were other things that had been different about the night. She remembered driving so fast to the villa, with only the thought that Guy was dead. And then finding him sitting in the living room and not being able to control her sobs. It all felt too familiar. She had been reminded of hurrying to the convent to tell Frederic about the baby and seeing him talking to the Gestapo officers.

"Oh, Frederic," she breathed. "If only I could have done something to save you."

She lay on the bed and stared at the ceiling. Guy was right; she was wound up by the events of the night. The next day everything would go back to normal.

Chapter Nine

NICE, DECEMBER 1943

The third morning after the thwarted raid, Lana stirred a pot of oatmeal in the kitchen. Guy had left the villa early, and she didn't know when he would return. But when she tried to take a bite of oatmeal, she couldn't swallow.

For the last two days, she had been too nervous to eat anything except soup and toast. What if something had happened to the boat? It could have been stopped when they reached Algiers. Or Pierre could have run into trouble on his return. Guy tried to reassure her. The trip would take Pierre at least twenty hours each way. All they could do was wait.

The front door opened, and she heard footsteps in the hall. Guy appeared, holding two shopping bags.

"You left the house so early," she said when he entered the kitchen. "I made oatmeal but didn't know when you'd be back."

"I was up with the roosters." He set the bags on the counter. "I thought I'd go into town and get some things for breakfast." He took her hand and did a little waltz around the kitchen.

"What are you doing?" She laughed.

"I feel ten years younger." He let her go. "The mission was a success. The Jews were safely transported to Algiers, and Pierre is back at his flat. He's hungry and exhausted, but nothing that a few good meals and some rest won't fix."

"I can't tell you how relieved I am!" Lana exclaimed. "I was so worried, I couldn't sleep."

"I told you Pierre was an experienced sailor." He grinned. "You and I are going to have a feast to celebrate."

Guy prepared fried eggs and toast. There were grilled tomatoes and sautéed mushrooms.

"You said you don't know how to cook." Lana set down her fork. Her appetite had returned, and she had eaten almost everything on her plate.

"I feel like I can do anything after a successful mission." He wiped his mouth. "I'll let you in on a secret."

"What kind of secret?"

"Before every mission, I write a note and bury it in the garden."

"A note?" She raised her eyebrows.

"Saying how grateful I am for the good things in my life and what I'd miss," he said ruminatively. "If anyone finds them, they'll know I had a heart."

"I hadn't thought of doing that," Lana said.

"That's because this was your first time." He sipped his coffee. "A lot of things come to mind when you can't sleep and you don't know whether tomorrow night you'll be in the same bed or five feet underground."

Lana's heart beat faster, and she looked up. "But you weren't in danger that night. Everything went perfectly."

"Thanks to you. I'm sure Captain Brunner was quite dismayed that Von Harmon ruined his plans." Guy smiled.

Guy learned that when Von Harmon hadn't made his phone call, the two other officers involved in the raid thought something went wrong. The raid had been canceled.

Guy reached into his pocket. "I bought something for you when I was in town."

She snapped open the velvet box, and inside was a silver pen.

"It's a Caran d'Ache fountain pen. It's a Swiss brand; they're my favorite pens." He took it out of the case. "You can use it to write to your mother."

"It's beautiful, but you didn't have to buy me anything."

"Good work should be rewarded," Guy answered. "I ran into Natalia in Nice. The Petrikoffs are having a dinner party in two weeks, and I said we'd go."

"Of course." Lana nodded, sipping her coffee.

"I better hurry." Guy ate the last bite of grilled tomato. "I promised Pierre I'd help him fix the boat. Then I have an appointment with the tailor.

I got a small tear in my dress shirt, and I'm going to order a new one." He chuckled. "The Resistance work is taking a toll on my wardrobe."

Guy left, and Lana filled the sink with dish soap and hot water. The clock in the living room struck eleven, and she turned off the faucet. The sun streamed through the window, and puffs of clouds floated over the horizon. It was a beautiful day, and she was going shopping at the market. Then she was going to the narrow house on Rue Droit for an indoor picnic with Odette.

Lana remembered how lonely Odette had been the last time she visited her. Sylvie was so frightened for Odette's safety. Guy wasn't the only one who felt better now that the mission was over. Lana somehow felt lighter, and she wanted to help the two people who needed it most.

Lana strolled along the cobblestones of the Cours Saleya. The street was covered with canopies and tables overflowing with fruits and vegetables. Vendors sold jars of spices and buckets of flowers.

For once, the German soldiers were absent and the air hummed with the sound of people chattering in French. Neighbors greeted one another, reminding Lana of the markets in Le Marais that she and Frederic frequented early in their marriage.

Her shopping bag was filled with pears and

oranges. She had a tin of ham and a bunch of carnations for Sylvie. She'd bought a vanilla crème and milk and sugar for coffee for Odette.

Boom.

Lana dropped the bag on the ground. Her heart hammered; she looked around for a shooting. As she bent down to retrieve her bag, she noticed a man beside her.

Lana looked up and recognized Charles Langford. He wore a navy sweater over gray slacks.

"Lana!" He bent down and handed her the bag. "This is a wonderful treat. What could be better than running into a friend?"

"Charles," Lana said, feeling glad to see him. "I'm not usually that clumsy. I heard a bang and thought someone fired a rifle."

"That's the noon cannon shot, haven't you heard it before?" he asked.

"I don't think so." Lana shook her head.

"It's fired from the town hall every day to announce the lunch hour." Charles's face broke into a grin. "It's one of the most civilized traditions on the Côte d'Azur."

"I'll remember that," Lana said, feeling calmer. "We seem to run into each other everywhere."

"The Riviera isn't a big place." He shrugged. "We have our own market in Menton, but it's so close to the mountains, the fish isn't fresh. Here the fishermen unload the catch and bring it straight to Cours Saleya."

"It feels like Paris before the war," Lana commented, glancing around. "Everyone is in a good mood, and no one is looking over his shoulder."

"The Germans don't like the outdoor market, they'd rather have their meals served on a plate," Charles said. "You must be thirsty. Why don't we sit at a café and I'll buy you a lemonade."

"You don't need to do that." Lana wavered.

She didn't have time to sit with Charles. She needed to take her purchases to Odette.

Charles took her arm and steered her toward a café. "I told you that Menton is boring. I'm not going to lose my chance to sit in the sun with a pretty young Parisian."

They sat at an outdoor table, and Charles ordered two lemonades.

"Tell me everything you've been doing in Nice," Charles said when the waiter brought their drinks.

She reached into her bag and brought out a book. "I stopped at the bookstore in the Palais de Justice. I bought *The Stranger* by Camus and Proust's *Remembrance of Things Past*. I've never read it. My mother is a huge reader and says it's not to be missed."

"I thought you were going to switch to lighter reading," Charles teased her. "Proust is one thousand pages, and his writing can be quite melancholy. But I understand your mother's love of reading. My parents are the same way.

They used to host literary salons at the house in Menton. That American writer F. Scott Fitzgerald would come, and the Duke and Duchess of Windsor attended whenever they were on the Riviera."

The Duke and Duchess of Windsor were supporters of Hitler. Was Guy right and were Charles's parents Nazi sympathizers? And what about Charles?

"Your parents know the Duke and Duchess of Windsor?" Lana asked in awe.

"The Riviera used to be the place to be seen. That's where the jet set was born," Charles reflected. "But everyone is gone. The Hôtel du Cap is closed, and the Germans have requisitioned every hotel in Nice." He sipped his drink and looked at Lana. "You must know that. You were talking to Von Harmon at the casino."

"I told you we weren't together." Her cheeks flushed. "Von Harmon was just seated next to me at the blackjack table."

Lana slipped the book into the bag and another book spilled out.

"What a coincidence, *The Jungle Book.* I always loved Rudyard Kipling. It was one of my favorite books as a child!" Charles picked it up. "I even named our dog Mowgli."

Lana froze. She had bought the book for Odette because she thought it might lift Odette's spirits. Lana had read it years ago and fallen in love with the tales of Mowgli and his animal friends in the jungles of India.

"It's a gift," she said hastily. "For the daughter of the concierge in my mother's building."

"You're sending a book to Paris?" Charles inquired.

"You can't shop in Paris these days; it's so cold, and there aren't any taxis. The bookstores hardly have any stock, and everything is overpriced."

Charles nodded and handed her the book.

"We are lucky on the Riviera, at least we have sunshine," he agreed. "Actually, I'm having a party next Friday night, and I'd like you and Guy to come."

Lana shook her head.

"I don't think so. Guy is very busy."

Guy was suspicious of Charles. Guy would never agree to attend his dinner party.

"Lana, no one is that busy on the Riviera." Charles gave a small smile. "Please. It would make me happy, and I think you'd enjoy it."

Lana couldn't think of another excuse.

"All right, we'd love to," she accepted. "Thank you, this has been very pleasant." She stood, eager to get to Rue Droit. "Guy is expecting me home."

"I'll walk you to your car," Charles offered.

Lana had been planning to walk to Sylvie's, but now she would have to pretend to drive away.

Charles whistled when they arrived at Giselle's car.

"This is a beauty," he said. "You must be quite the race car driver."

"Hardly." Lana laughed. "It belongs to a neighbor. I only have it for a few days."

Lana stepped into the driver's seat, and Charles closed her door.

"I'll call with the address for the party," he said, resting his hand on the window. After Charles left, Lana reparked the car on the Promenade des Anglais and walked to Rue Droit. She glanced around to make sure no one had followed her and knocked on the door.

This time it was Sylvie who answered the door after Lana whispered her name. She seemed even thinner than Lana remembered. Her face was pale, and the circles under her eyes were more pronounced.

"Lana, what are you doing here?" Sylvie ushered her inside.

"I brought some things for Odette. And flowers for you." Lana showed her the bag. "I had to come. I can't stop thinking about how hard it must be for you and Odette."

"These are lovely, and you have been so kind. If you hadn't brought Odette home that day, she might have been stopped by German soldiers." Sylvie accepted the carnations. "But you shouldn't be here. If anyone sees you entering the home of Jews, we may all be shot."

"Don't worry, I've been careful," Lana assured

her. "If Odette can't go outside, I thought we'd have an indoor picnic."

The look of desperation in Sylvie's eyes softened, and she nodded toward the kitchen.

"Odette is upstairs. I was just making tea. Would you like to join me?"

Lana followed Sylvie into the kitchen and sat at the table.

"I'm afraid we have to share a tea bag," Sylvie apologized. She poured tea into a cup and handed it to Lana. "I've used all my rationing coupons."

"I'll bring tea bags from the villa." Lana accepted the cup. "And coffee. We have a whole basement stocked with coffee."

Lana noticed Sylvie's look of surprise and couldn't help feeling guilty. Guy's wealth afforded them little luxuries. Life was so different for Sylvie and Odette. Jacob was dead, and Sylvie struggled to find work that hired Jews. They had to exist with the barest necessities.

"A whole basement full of coffee!" Sylvie's eyes widened.

"I know I'm lucky and . . ." She stumbled, but Sylvie seemed to sense her distress and smiled warmly.

"We're very grateful." Sylvie poured her own cup of tea and sat opposite Lana. "Why are you being so kind?" she wondered out loud. "You don't even know us."

Lana remembered seeing Odette cowering

between the buildings when the woman's dog was shot. The fear in her eyes had reminded Lana of her terror when Frederic was murdered. And Odette had seen her father gunned down in front of her. How could Lana not feel close to her when they both experienced the worst thing imaginable?

Lana studied the way Sylvie's shoulders were almost concave and the sharp planes of her cheeks.

"This war isn't fair to anyone, but it's worst for the children. I can't bring back Odette's father or allow her back in school. I have to find some way to help. So that one day Odette will look back on this time and instead of just remembering the terrors of war, she'll also recall little kindnesses," Lana tried to explain.

Sylvie made a choking sound, and her body shook with tears. Lana handed her a handkerchief, and Sylvie wiped them away.

"I'm sorry, I know I should be stronger. But it's so hard without Jacob. I've never been alone." She hiccupped. "Sometimes I hear Odette's footsteps outside my room at night, and I put a pillow over my head so she doesn't hear me cry."

"Where are your parents?" Lana asked.

"They're dead," Sylvie replied. "I was born in Alsace, near the German border. In 1940, the Germans annexed Alsace, and my parents decided to join me and move to Paris. I was already living there and married to Jacob." Sylvie twisted her wedding band. "They were killed in a German bombing raid walking in front of their apartment. Now Jacob is dead too." She gulped. "Who knows what will happen to me and Odette."

"I'm sorry." Lana touched Sylvie's hand. "But you mustn't talk like that. You and Odette will be all right."

Sylvie blinked and kept talking.

"We moved to Nice in 1941. Jacob got a job at the Hôtel Negresco in Nice, and it seemed like the perfect opportunity. On the Riviera, Jews were still allowed to work, and Odette could attend school." Sylvie's eyes darkened. "But then the Germans took control. Jacob wanted to escape to Italy, but I was afraid. If only I had listened to him, Jacob would be alive."

"You can't blame yourself," Lana said. "Escapees going over the Alps are captured all the time. You and Jacob could both have been killed and Odette would be an orphan."

"Jacob and Odette shared a special bond," Sylvie continued. "They did everything together. Odette misses him so much."

"Odette has you. She'll be all right," Lana comforted her. "You can read to her and teach her how to sing."

Sylvie seemed to wilt like a flower parched with thirst.

"I barely get any afternoons off. And what

if something happens to me? The Germans have turned a blind eye on Jews singing in the cabaret because they don't want to miss their entertainment."

"I can visit Odette in the afternoons," Lana volunteered. "I'll watch out for her."

"Why risk your life to help us?" Sylvie asked.

Lana wanted to say so many things: That she knew what it was like to lose the person she loved most in the world. That she considered having a family the greatest gift, and that if she couldn't have one with Frederic, she could help another one. But revealing anything about her past could put them all at risk.

"Because I'm here and I can." Lana stood up and gathered her bag. She held out the book she'd purchased at the market. "I brought Odette a book. Is it all right if I go upstairs?"

Sylvie jumped up and hugged Lana.

"Sometimes I think God has forgotten us. But maybe I'm wrong. He's too busy trying to fix things that it takes time for him to reach us."

Odette was sitting at her desk when Lana opened the door. She seemed to be staring off into space, but she turned at the sound.

"What are you doing here?" Odette asked suspiciously.

"I thought we could have an indoor picnic," Lana said, and handed Odette the book. "I bought this for you. It's one of my favorite books."

Odette put it on the desk. "Thank you. I used to read every night before I went to bed, but my mother doesn't let me turn on the light. Even with the curtains closed, she thinks the Germans can see that someone is home. We creep around in the dark. It's as if we're already ghosts."

"Don't talk like that," Lana said.

"Why not?" Odette challenged. "This house is a coffin if I can't go outside."

"Odette, you have to listen to me," Lana said sharply. "When you're young, everything seems like it will last forever. But one day the war will end and life will return to normal."

Lana noticed a large map on the wall where Odette had been looking when she entered.

"What's that?" she asked.

"It's a map of England." Odette rubbed her eyes. "I had an English pen pal named Bernadette. My father wanted to show me where she lived. I can't write to her anymore because my teacher, Madame Blanche, mailed the letters, and I don't go to school."

"I could try to mail your letters," Lana offered.

"How would you do that? The Germans control everything, even the post office. I heard my parents talking about it. Germans read every letter."

Lana shouldn't have said anything. There would be another raid soon, and Pierre would take the boat to Algiers. He could mail the letter from there. Odette was so miserable; she had to do something to make her feel better.

"Why don't you give them to me," Lana suggested.

Odette jumped up and went to her bedside table. She removed a stack of envelopes and handed them to Lana.

"We used to have so much fun writing. Bernadette has a pony named Puddles. She was going to send me a photo, but I don't know if she ever did," Odette commented. "You can read them if you like. Madame Blanche always read them to correct the spelling."

"We'll find out." Lana slipped the envelopes into her bag.

"Do you really think she'll get my letters?" Odette asked eagerly. "If I had someone to write to, I wouldn't be so lonely."

Odette's eyes sparkled, and Lana thought she looked so pretty. Her cheeks glowed, and her hair framed her face.

Lana stood up and took Odette's hand. "Now why don't we go downstairs and eat that vanilla crème."

After they ate all the food, Lana walked quickly to Giselle's car. As she prepared to drive away, she saw a man in a long coat and a hat hurrying toward her. He opened the passenger door and stepped into the car.

"Don't say a word, just start driving," Guy barked. Fear turned to anger as she recognized him.

"What are you doing here?" she demanded.

"I said don't talk." He looked behind them. "Just drive."

They drove through Old Town in silence. Guy used his hands to give her directions. Lana turned onto the main road. He glanced in the rearview mirror, and his features relaxed.

"There aren't any cars behind us, we're safe now." He took off his hat. "You can slow down, I wouldn't want to plunge to our deaths because I made you take the turns too fast."

"You didn't answer my question," Lana said, easing up on the gas pedal. "Why were you following me?"

"I wasn't." Guy unbuttoned his coat. "I was standing in the tailor's with sewing pins digging into my neck and saw you leaving a house." He looked at Lana. "Who were you visiting?"

Guy had seen her leaving Sylvie and Odette's.

"It doesn't matter to you," Lana said stiffly. "You don't know them."

"Everything you do affects me and Pierre and the mission," Guy reminded her. "I'm guessing there aren't any members of the Russian aristocracy living in narrow houses on Rue Droit. They own villas in the hills with manicured lawns and views of the Mediterranean."

Lana's heart beat so fast, she thought it must burst.

"All right. It's a Jewish family. Sylvie, and her daughter is Odette," she admitted. "Odette's not allowed to go outside, so I brought her some things."

"You must see why it's dangerous for you to visit Jews," Guy said calmly. "What if Captain Von Harmon had you followed to make sure he could trust you? If he saw you coming out of a home occupied by a Jewish family, he'd have you shot."

All of a sudden she didn't care about anything except telling Guy about Frederic and the reason she was in Nice. She pulled to the side of the road and turned off the engine. The Mediterranean was a turquoise bracelet far below and the sun melted into the horizon.

"What are you doing?" Guy said as a car whizzed by. "You almost drove off the cliff."

"You think I'm going to get us killed no matter what I do, so I may as well tell you everything," Lana retorted. "My husband, Frederic, was a music student in Paris. He taught piano at the convent because he believed children's talents shouldn't go to waste. That included Jewish children." She took a breath and plunged on. "One day, Alois Brunner appeared at the convent and accused Frederic of hiding Jewish children at the school, which was true. Brunner suspected he had one hidden in the piano and made him open the lid, and when Frederic wouldn't hand over Esther Cohen, Brunner shot him." She gasped for air. "If I can fill one day of Odette's life during wartime with something other than loneliness and death, I'm not going to miss that chance."

"You're overwrought," Guy said calmly. "Why don't you get out and let me drive?"

"You might only be able to help people who are faceless names on a hotel guest list, but I'm not like that." She didn't move. "Odette needs me, and I'm not going to turn my back on her. If you want to send me back to Paris, that's fine. Tell me and I'll book the next train."

Guy was silent, and Lana's whole body quivered. She shifted her skirt and waited for him to say something.

"I should drive straight to the villa and throw your clothes in a suitcase. And then I should make you call a taxi because being seen driving you to the train station could be dangerous," he began. "But I'm not going to. We all have our Odettes and our Sylvies, and you'll learn to put them behind you. In the meantime, I can't afford to lose you. You're not afraid to get close to the enemy and pulled off the last mission superbly."

"What do you mean I'll put them behind me?" Lana demanded, the line having lodged in her head.

"You think that if you save other people, you

will bring back the ones you lost," he said evenly. "I'm sure Frederic was a fine man, and Esther Cohen was just a child. But getting yourself killed by taking presents to a mother and daughter you just met isn't going to bring Frederic and Esther back to life. We've got a whole city of Jewish men and women and children to save. I heard a rumor that Brunner is planning a raid on the streets above Old Town. Jews have lived there since the sixteenth century; there are more Jewish bones in the cemetery than anywhere else in the South of France."

Lana was too stunned to argue. How dare Guy talk about Frederic and Esther as if he knew them? Frederic was the bravest man she ever knew. He did everything to help others without thinking about himself. Esther was an innocent child. Esther had already lost her own father, shouldn't she be allowed a little happiness?

She still felt guilty that she couldn't stop Frederic's death and that she lost the baby too. But she also understood that, in a way, Guy was right. He had been the one to see her emerge from Sylvie's house. But he could have just as easily been Von Harmon or Brunner.

"I knew it was dangerous," she said grudgingly. "I'll be more careful in the future."

"That's better. Who would eat my omelets if anything happened to you?" Guy said, and his smile—that easy smile that had been replaced just a few minutes ago by an expression as dark as a thundercloud—returned.

When they arrived back at the villa, Lana went straight to her room.

She picked up the hairbrush on her dressing table. Frederic had bought it for her at an antiques store last Christmas. She argued the money should be spent on an extra blanket, but Frederic said she deserved pretty things.

For Frederic everything had been simple. He helped everyone he could: Elaine and Vivienne, Esther Cohen, and the other children at the convent.

"I want to do good, Frederic," she said aloud, pulling the brush through her hair. "If only you were here to guide me. It seemed so simple when I joined the Resistance, but now I see it's not." She sighed. "I wanted to help others survive the war. But I never thought I'd end up at war with myself."

One of Odette's letters poked out of Lana's purse. The envelope hadn't been sealed, and she took it out. The letter was written in French and in Odette's flowery cursive.

> Dear Bernadette,
> I don't know if this letter will reach you, but I thought I'd write anyway. Our teacher said your teacher would translate it for you. I wanted to learn English so I

can write you a whole letter, but now I don't know if I ever will. Everything is different since the Germans arrived in Nice. I'm supposed to wear a yellow star, and German soldiers are everywhere.

It's all because Hitler thinks the Jews should be exterminated. It doesn't make sense, we're all the same. My hair might be a different color than my friend Annalise, but we both like books and hate brussels sprouts.

Our teacher, Madame Blanche, said that God watches over the children, but I'm not at school anymore. We have to keep the curtains drawn so the Germans don't find us and I'm not allowed to play outside. How can God watch over me if he can't see me?

I thought of writing a letter to Hitler, but it wouldn't help. If all the important leaders can't change his mind, what good would a twelve-year-old Jewish girl do? I'll keep writing to you instead. Please send photos of your pony.

Your friend, Odette

Lana closed the letter and sighed. Is that why Odette didn't want to stay inside? Because she was afraid God couldn't see her?

She went into the bathroom and washed her

face. A black dress hung in her closet, and she slipped it on and walked downstairs.

Guy was hunched on a sofa in the living room. A bottle of brandy sat on the coffee table, and he held a shot glass.

"Are you going somewhere?" Guy looked up.

"I want to talk to you," she said shakily.

"In that case you might like one of these." He reached for another glass.

"No, thank you." She shook her head. "It's too early for a drink."

"It's never too early to drink during war," he said, and there was a half smile on his face. "In the car, I forgot to tell you how sorry I am you lost your husband. You're so young; it must have been a terrible shock."

"It was. The afternoon Frederic died, I was going to the convent to tell him I was pregnant," she replied. "It seemed silly to be happy about a baby when Paris was occupied by the Germans, but I knew he would be thrilled. Frederic loved children as much as I do."

"I didn't know." He glanced at her stomach.

"There's nothing to know." She shrugged. "I lost the baby the day Frederic was shot."

"I'm sorry," Guy said gruffly.

"That's why I'm here. There was no point in staying in Paris and feeling sorry for myself; at least here I can do some good."

Guy poured himself another brandy. His eyes

were bloodshot, and he passed the glass under his nose.

"I ran into an old friend this morning. He told me about a Resistance worker I knew in Paris named Maurice. Maurice was an interior designer. There were rumors that he had been a frequent guest at Berghof, Hitler's chalet in Bavaria before the war. There was even a photo of Hitler and Maurice in a 1938 issue of the British magazine *Homes and Gardens*." Guy chuckled. "The magazine did a three-page spread with photos: a paneled library and a grand hall filled with Teutonic furniture and a theater where Hitler held screenings of Hollywood movies.

"In fact, Maurice was only at the chalet to sell Hitler a globe. But when the war started Maurice could drop references to smoking cigars on Hitler's terrace and eating the cook's potato soup." Guy paused and sipped his brandy. "That familiarity served Maurice well when he joined the Resistance. He hired a design assistant named Eloise, and together they were hired by SS officers, who were eager to put their own touches on their Paris apartments. You wouldn't believe how many German bombing raids were thwarted because of the information Eloise passed on to Maurice.

"An SS officer named Hedrick became infatuated with Eloise and started buying her gifts and taking her to dinner. Eloise and Maurice were thrilled; Eloise would learn all his secrets. But one night he suggested she take home a casserole. Eloise lived in the same building as a Jewish family named the Morgensterns. They never had enough to eat, so she gave them the casserole. A few days later the Gestapo came to the Morgensterns' door. It was just a routine check to see if they had papers, but Hedrick recognized his casserole dish on the dining table. Apparently the dish was Meissen china; it was a gift from his mother. He asked Mrs. Morgenstern where she got it, and she wouldn't say. After the SS officers rounded up the Morgensterns, Hedrick went to Maurice's design studio, showed Eloise the casserole dish, and then he shot them both. You think it's important to help Odette and Sylvie, but you're putting them in danger too. The only way to succeed in this game is to cut out your own heart."

The living room was quiet, and Lana heard a frog outside the window.

"You said you wanted to talk about something," Guy finished.

"I wanted to know the names of the guests who will be at the Petrikoffs' party that we'll be attending in two weeks," she said quickly. "I like to be prepared."

Guy smiled at Lana over his glass. "That's what makes you a good Resistance worker. You're always thinking ahead."

Chapter Ten

NICE, DECEMBER 1943

Lana was sitting at the dining table and sipping a cup of coffee when the phone rang the next morning.

"Lana, it's Charles Langford."

"Charles, how nice to hear from you," Lana said.

Charles had always been so kind to her, saving her from having to talk to Brunner at the casino and buying her a lemonade when she ran into him at the market. But these meetings were starting to feel like more than coincidences. Lana chided herself; she was behaving like Guy. She was lucky to have Charles as a friend.

"I called to give you details for the party. It's Villa Gold in Menton. Cocktails are at seven but come earlier if you like. I can show you and Guy the grounds."

Lana had forgotten about Charles's invitation.

"Yes, of course," she said, wondering how she was going to tell Guy.

"I'm looking forward to it," Charles said easily. "Ever since we ran into each other at the casino I've been trying to remember where I met Guy before. I'll figure it out by then."

Lana was about to thank Charles for the

invitation when the front door opened. She said goodbye and hung up the phone.

"Who was that?" Guy asked, entering the dining room. He wore a jacket and carried a pile of envelopes.

"It was Charles Langford, actually," Lana replied.

"How did he get this number?" Guy asked.

"I suppose from the telephone book." She shrugged. "He invited us to dinner on Friday night."

"I hope you said we were busy," Guy said shortly.

"I tried. But he said no one is that busy on the Riviera."

"Langford will say anything to get what he wants," Guy muttered, sitting opposite Lana.

"I don't know what you have against Charles." Lana defended him. "He's only been kind."

"Why would he call out of the blue?" Guy asked, sifting through the mail.

Lana couldn't tell him that she bumped into him on the way to see Odette. Guy would be furious.

"It wasn't quite out of the blue," she admitted. "I ran into him the other day."

"You didn't tell me."

"I didn't know I had to report every encounter," Lana retorted. "Would you like me to keep a list with dates and times?"

"I'd like you not to accept invitations to dinners from Nazi sympathizers."

"You have Charles completely wrong. But so what if he's friendly with the Germans?" She crossed her arms. "We go to the Petrikoffs' parties, and they have German officers as guests."

"That's different. The Petrikoffs and other White Russians want Germany to help save Russia from the communists. They're not actively handing Jews over to the Gestapo like Langford."

Lana added a spoonful of sugar to her coffee and stirred it angrily.

"You have no proof," she insisted. "Charles could have been trying to help the Jews escape across the Alps and failed."

"Men like Langford don't fail." Guy grunted. "They sit in their fancy villas and sail their yachts as if the war were merely a set of obscure references on the radio. All they have to do is turn it off and the whole problem of Jewish shops being looted goes away."

"You live in an expensive villa, and you know plenty of people with yachts," Lana pointed out, her blood boiling. She didn't know why she was so upset; she hadn't been that keen to go to Charles's party.

"I'm on the Riviera for one reason: to save as many Jews from the gas chambers as possible." Guy rested his elbows on the table.

"You don't know anything about Charles," she responded.

Guy was about to say something but stopped. He stood up and buttoned his jacket.

"Tell Charles we'll come."

Lana put down her coffee cup in surprise.

"I don't know why I didn't think of it before," Guy continued. "What better way to find out if Langford is delivering information to the Gestapo than by catching him in the act?" He turned to the door. "Plus, I've heard Langford's chef cooked at the Hôtel München Palace before the war. His German meat loaf is supposed to be delicious."

Guy left, and Lana finished her coffee. She was about to take the cup into the kitchen when the phone rang. Perhaps Charles forgot to tell her something about the dinner party.

"Hello," she said into the receiver.

"Countess Antanova." A male voice came down the line. "This is Alois Brunner."

Lana stared at the phone. She jumped, and the coffee cup dropped on the floor.

"Is everything all right?" Brunner asked. "It sounds like there was a crash."

She crouched down and picked up the pieces.

"This is a pleasant surprise," she replied. "How did you get my number?"

"Captain Von Harmon gave it to me," Brunner answered. "You had cocktails with him the other night."

Her skin turned cold, and she took a moment to answer.

"We had a pleasant evening," she said with a little laugh. "I needed a little distraction. After all, at the party I told you Captain Von Harmon offered to show me around Nice. You were going to give me suggestions."

"You have an excellent memory," Brunner agreed. There was a silence before he continued. "The thing is, Captain Von Harmon had to go to Berlin." He paused. "His wife is having a baby."

Lana gulped and took a deep breath.

"He didn't say anything about it," she commented. "Captain Von Harmon is excellent company. He has quite a war record; I was impressed."

"Captain Von Harmon is a skilled officer," Brunner said.

Lana regained her composure. She straightened her shoulders and clutched the receiver.

"You haven't told me why you're calling," she said coolly. "I imagine it's not often that a high-ranking member of the Gestapo makes a phone call to a woman in the middle of the day."

"You're right, Countess Antanova," he said. "I thought I'd offer my services to show you around the Riviera since Von Harmon is indisposed."

"That's very kind, but it won't be necessary," she replied. "Guy and I attend plenty of parties.

We've been invited to a party at the Petrikoffs' in two weeks. Perhaps you'll be there."

Lana hoped that he would say he was busy.

"I'll check my calendar. It would be a pleasure to see you."

"And you," she said, and then stopped. She had to know if Von Harmon had been sent away permanently. "Maybe Von Harmon can come. Will he be back from Berlin?"

"That depends on the baby." Brunner chuckled. "I'm sure he hopes so. I heard Berlin is covered in snow. Goodbye, Countess Antanova, it was a delight to speak with you."

Lana said goodbye and hung up the phone. It had been a mistake to give the operator at Von Harmon's hotel her phone number. She never expected Brunner to call her.

She swept up the remaining pieces of the broken cup and took them into the kitchen. There was a knock at the front door, and Lana wondered who it could be. She hurried to the entry and opened it.

"Giselle!" she exclaimed. "I thought you weren't coming home until tomorrow."

"I finished my business a day early," Giselle said, kissing Lana on both cheeks.

"Please come in. It's lovely to see you." Lana ushered her into the living room.

Giselle followed her and sat on the sofa. She glanced around the room. "I hope I'm not interrupting. Where is Guy? He's never here when I'm around."

"Guy is just busy." Lana waved offhandedly. "Can I offer you something to drink?"

"Yes, please." Giselle took off her coat while Lana fetched her a glass of water.

"I hate traveling," Giselle said, sitting in a chair in the living room. "I can't sleep in a strange bed, and I never pack properly. I'm always too hot or too cold."

Lana noticed a heart-shaped bracelet around Giselle's wrist as she sat on the sofa.

"What a pretty bracelet," she said.

Giselle glanced down at it.

"I bought it for myself. That's why I went away. My great-aunt died and left me some money." Giselle twirled the bracelet. "I should be practical and set the money aside, but I couldn't resist. After all, the black market won't last forever."

Lana poured a glass of water for herself. So many things had happened since Giselle left, but she couldn't talk about any of them.

"You never told me where you were going." Lana tried to think of something safe to say.

"Didn't I?" Giselle frowned. "I was in Paris, settling my aunt's estate."

"Paris!" Lana was grateful to have something to talk about. "My mother says the black market is flourishing in Paris. No one shops at the stores anymore."

"I've always admired Parisian women. Even if Hitler took away all the perfumes and lipsticks in Paris, they would still be so sophisticated." Giselle gave a small laugh. "It must be something in the soufflé."

"I miss Paris, but it's so dreary in winter. Was the weather very bad?"

"The weather?" Giselle repeated absently.

"The weather in Paris on your trip," Lana prompted. "Last winter it snowed every day in December. I didn't know one could be so cold."

"The streets were covered in snow." Giselle nodded. "I'm glad to be back in the Riviera. Even the chickens seemed happy to see me when I got home. I bought them presents."

"For the chickens?"

"You didn't think I spent all the money on myself." Giselle's eyes danced. "I got them blankets to keep them warm at night."

Giselle left, and Lana put the dishes in the sink. The phone rang, and she walked into the living room.

"Lana." Her mother's voice came down the line. "I'm glad you answered. I haven't talked to you all week."

"Is everything all right?" Lana asked.

"As good as it can be under the occupation. I started my Christmas shopping," Tatiana said. "I know there's a war, but that doesn't mean we can't give gifts. I found a beautiful pair of boots for you, but I wonder if it gets cold enough on the Riviera."

Lana imagined her mother meeting some Russian on a street corner and exchanging a set of wineglasses for winter boots.

"You don't need to get me anything. Keep them for yourself. My neighbor Giselle just returned from Paris and said the streets are covered in snow."

"You mean rain," Tatiana corrected. "I wish it would snow. There are never any taxis, and when I arrive home, I look like Mrs. Lippman's dog after a bath."

Lana and Tatiana chatted about Christmas, and then Lana hung up the phone. Her head throbbed, and she went into the bathroom for an aspirin.

She was certain Giselle had said it had snowed in Paris. She went back over their conversation, and something stirred in the back of her mind. Someone had said it was snowing. Captain Brunner, Berlin buried in snow.

Chapter Eleven

NICE, DECEMBER 1943

It was Friday morning and that night was Charles's dinner party. Lana was eating breakfast. It had been three days since Alois Brunner called, and Lana had barely slept. It was only the view from her balcony, the orange sun and the satiny Mediterranean, that gave her the energy to get out of bed and go downstairs to the kitchen.

She missed her mornings with Frederic in Paris before they went to the university. Even when there wasn't butter for the toast or later bread at all, just sitting together in the small kitchen kept her happy all day.

Now she poked at the congealed oatmeal Guy had left on the stove as her thoughts whirled through her head. Brunner's tone had been inscrutable over the phone. It was impossible to know if Captain Von Harmon had really gone to Berlin because his wife was having a baby or if he was being punished for missing the raid.

And she couldn't stop thinking about Giselle. Giselle had lied and said she had been in Paris when her real destination could have been Berlin. Lana remembered the heart-shaped bracelet Giselle brought back from her trip. Women never bought heart-shaped jewelry for themselves. Perhaps it was from a secret lover.

Then there were Sylvie and Odette. She had gotten herself involved when Guy had warned her to stay away. She had to ask Pierre to mail Odette's letter when he returned to Algiers after the next escape. It was too risky to mail it from France; the Germans controlled the post office, and the mail could be censored. What if it was intercepted and the Gestapo discovered a Jewish family was living in the house on Rue Droit?

The only good thing was Guy had hardly been at the villa for the last few days. Pierre had come down with a terrible cold, forcing Guy to fix the boat himself. And with Guy gone and Pierre sick, Lana resolved to visit him at home. She took a bicycle from the garage and started down the hill toward Nice.

Lana climbed the narrow staircase to Pierre's flat and knocked on the door.

"Countess Antanova!" Pierre exclaimed, ushering her inside. "What are you doing here?"

"I brought some things to help your cold." She held up a bag.

"Lozenges and tissues from the pharmacy, and chicken broth from the butcher." She arranged the contents on the table.

"I can't accept all this." Pierre shook his head.

"Of course you can." Lana walked to the

stovetop and emptied the broth into a pot. "You risked your life driving the boat."

"Guy told me you came down to the dock the night of the raid." Pierre followed her.

"I wanted to make sure the boat left safely." Lana nodded. "Then a soldier told me that a man had been shot. I was so worried about you and Guy."

"You can't imagine what it was like," Pierre recalled. "The passengers tried to smuggle things on board, and I had to tell them the extra weight would sink the boat. One woman had a bump under her coat, and I thought she was pregnant. It turned out she was hiding a photo album."

Pierre started coughing, and Lana handed him a tissue.

"I was so relieved when we reached Algiers," he continued. "Then on the way back, the boat started leaking, and I got this cold. I feel terrible that Guy has to fix the boat."

"Don't worry about Guy," Lana told him. "He just wants you to get better."

"Guy is a quick learner. He's learned more about boats in the last month than I've known my whole life," Pierre said with a smile. "He said after the war he's going to buy a sailboat and name it *Aimee*."

Lana looked up sharply. Her skin turned cold, and she felt oddly jealous.

"Was that the name of Guy's wife?" she asked, handing him the cup.

"No." Pierre sipped the chicken broth. "It was the name of his daughter."

Lana's eyes widened and she gasped.

"Guy had a daughter?"

"You mustn't tell Guy that I told you," Pierre urged. "I saw a photo of her after Guy's wife died, and Guy told me about her. She was about three years old with dark hair and blue eyes."

"What happened to her?" Lana breathed.

"Guy didn't say. He was so upset about his wife at the time, I didn't press him," Pierre replied. "I shouldn't have said anything, it's just . . ."

"Just what?" Lana prompted.

"When we were loading the boat, a little girl was afraid of the water and refused to get in." He fiddled with his cup. "The girl's mother was terrified they would be left behind. Guy picked her up and whispered in her ear, and her face broke into the biggest smile," Pierre remembered. "I've never seen anyone so good with a child."

Lana couldn't have been more stunned if Pierre said that Guy performed *Rigoletto* at the opera house. She knew Guy was in his thirties and had been married. But he never talked about children. She couldn't picture him with a daughter.

Pierre doubled over in a fit of coughing. She unwrapped a lozenge and handed it to him.

"That cough sounds terrible. You should see a doctor," Lana urged.

"I can't afford a doctor." Pierre wiped his brow with a cloth.

Lana thought quickly. She could help Pierre, if he could do the same for her.

"I'll find a doctor and pay for it," she responded. "If you'll do me a favor."

"What kind of favor?" he asked.

Lana took the envelopes out of her purse.

"The next time there is an escape, I need you to give them to someone in Algiers who can mail them to England." She handed them to him. "And in the future there might be more."

Pierre turned it over. If he noticed the childish writing, he didn't comment on it.

"I would do that for you without your finding a doctor." He slipped it into his pocket. "After all, isn't the point of being in the Resistance that we all work together?"

Lana left Pierre's flat and stumbled into the sunshine. She remembered the pain and grief of her miscarriage and wondered what had happened to Guy's daughter. But Pierre had made her promise not to mention it to Guy, and she couldn't break her word. After all, if Guy didn't open up to her, there was no way to help him.

It was better to concentrate on the reasons Henri had sent her to the Riviera. That evening was Charles's dinner party, and in less than two weeks they were attending the party at the

Petrikoffs'. There were plenty of things to keep her busy without worrying about Guy.

It was early evening and Guy drove through the center of Menton. Lana peered out the window at the painted houses that were stuck together. Old men played boules in the town square. A stone basilica sat on a hill.

"It's so pretty," Lana said. "As if nothing has changed in a hundred years."

"Don't let the simple cottages fool you," Guy grumbled, steering the car toward the mountain road. "The homes above Menton are some of the most glamorous on the Riviera. I haven't been in Charles's house but I've seen it from the outside. It's the size of a Scottish castle."

"When have you been invited to a Scottish castle? I'm sure you're exaggerating," Lana returned, patting her hair.

The car kept climbing, and Guy was right. The houses were huge, with marble columns and swimming pools overlooking the bay.

Guy turned off the road, and the car bumped along a gravel drive that ended in front of a stone manor with trellises of jasmine climbing the walls.

"Lana, Guy." Charles stood on the steps. He was dressed in a blazer and slacks. "I'm so glad you came."

Charles led them inside. The house resembled

the pictures of an English estate in one of her mother's design magazines. There was a paneled library and a breakfast room with pretty floral wallpaper. The living room contained floral rugs and sofas covered in chintz.

"My mother decorated the house. She loved the Riviera, but she missed her roses." Charles chuckled, waving at the wallpaper covered with roses. Lana admired a painting of an English village on the wall.

"What a beautiful painting," Lana commented.

"That's a Turner." Charles followed her gaze. "I'm quite fond of it myself. It reminds me of growing up in the English countryside."

Charles went to fix them drinks, and Lana turned to Guy.

"Charles is so polite and welcoming," she said under her breath. "And the decor of the house is lovely."

"Just because his parents have good taste doesn't mean they're good people," Guy snapped. "Coco Chanel has the best taste in Paris, and now she's in bed with a German diplomat."

Lana had heard the rumors about Chanel, but she didn't want to believe them.

"You don't know that," she whispered.

"If Coco Chanel feared the Gestapo, she would have fled to New York like Schiaparelli," he said. "Instead, she's taken up an entire floor at the Ritz, right next to the German military."

Lana opened her mouth to reply, but Charles entered the room, carrying two glasses.

"I remember where we met," Charles said to Guy, handing him a glass. "It was at a house-warming party in Villefranche-sur-Mer. You knew the names of all the cheeses at the dessert table."

"I am Swiss," Guy said, accepting the cocktail. "We're taught to know the difference between an Emmentaler and a Gruyère."

Charles led them around the grounds while the other guests arrived. Lana had expected dozens of people like at the Petrikoffs' party, but dinner included only two other couples and a man of about sixty.

"This is Thierry and his wife, Lucille." Charles introduced a dark-haired man and a pretty brunette. "Thierry is my bank manager. He accepts my dinner invitations because he wants to make sure I'm not spending my savings on expensive caviar."

"Nonsense, Charles is the most frugal client I have. He doesn't even gamble," Thierry said lightly. "The only money he spends is on books."

"And this is Hank and Sally Eastwood. The Eastwoods are American," Charles continued. "I was so happy to have friends on the Riviera who speak English. But Americans talk too fast, and Hank's accent is almost impossible to understand."

"I'm from the South; even my wife can't understand me." Hank chuckled, shaking their hands.

The last man had thinning hair and a goatee.

"And this is Raoul Gunsbourg. Raoul is from Bucharest. He's the director of the Opéra de Monte-Carlo, one of the best in the arts." Charles beamed. "We're fortunate to have him."

Lana looked at Raoul with interest. She had no idea that Charles was involved in the opera.

"I'm the lucky one," Raoul offered. "Not only do I get to lead the opera, I'm invited to wonderful dinners."

"Raoul's only fault is his modesty." Charles turned to Lana. "Did you know that it's because of your Czar Alexander III that Raoul is here? It was on the czar's recommendation that Albert, Prince of Monaco, ask Raoul to become the director of the Opéra de Monte-Carlo."

"All this history of the Riviera is fascinating," Guy said to Charles. "They should employ you at the tourist center in Nice."

Lana shot Guy a look, but he only continued to sip his drink.

Charles went to check on the dinner, and the other guests spread out on the lawn. "Why were you so rude?" she demanded as she joined Guy.

"Didn't you see Gunsbourg's expression? He's a mouse trying to avoid a cat," Guy replied.

"What are you talking about?" Lana was puzzled.

"Have you heard of René Blum? Blum founded the Ballet Russe de Monte Carlo in 1932. Two years ago Blum went back to Paris to visit his family and never returned. He was put on a train from Drancy to one of the camps in the east."

"By Brunner?" Lana gasped.

"Exactly." Guy applauded her. "Gunsbourg is next on Brunner's list. You know how serious Brunner is about the arts. The Germans have shut down the opera house, but when it reopens he plans on replacing Gunsbourg with someone who'll perform his beloved Wagner," Guy said. "Charles is pretending to be Gunsbourg's friend until he can turn him over to the Gestapo."

"You're making this all up," Lana spluttered.

"Weren't you listening to Charles's banker? Charles doesn't gamble, and yet we saw him at the casino, full of German officers."

"You've had it out for Charles from the beginning. He's only been polite," Lana countered. "He invited us to this dinner party."

"I just don't want Brunner getting his hands on more Jews." Guy grunted. "Let's go inside. We're here now, and I'm starving."

Lana's cheeks burned, but she followed Guy into the house. The meal was excellent. Lana couldn't remember the last time she had eaten tender beef or sweet squash. For dessert there was a pavlova and passion fruit.

After dinner, the men smoked cigars in the

library, and Lana wandered down the hall. She heard music and peered through the door. Raoul sat at a grand piano. He turned at the sound of her entrance.

"Excuse me," Lana said. "I didn't mean to interrupt."

"Countess Antanova, please come in." Raoul stood up. "I couldn't resist. It's a Bösendorfer piano. I haven't seen one since before the war."

"You play beautifully." Lana entered the room.

"I aspired to be a pianist, but my parents insisted I become a doctor. I was a medic during the Russo-Turkish War. After that, I promised myself I'd devote the rest of my life to music."

Lana remembered Frederic's parents making him take chemistry at the university in Paris.

"Charles told me that your mother escaped Russia and you were raised in Paris." Raoul interrupted her thoughts.

"Charles told you that?" she said in surprise.

"Charles knows I'm eager to meet fellow émigrés." He nodded.

"I've never been to Russia. My mother fled before I was born," Lana responded. "But she misses Russia very much."

"We all miss our homes," Raoul commented. "All my family in Bucharest are dead. I have been lucky to live on the Riviera, but it's not safe here anymore. Things have become dangerous since the Germans arrived."

"Could you immigrate to Switzerland?" Lana asked before she could stop herself.

"The Swiss took in Jewish artists and musicians at the beginning of the war, but not anymore." He shook his head.

"There must be a way to cross the border," Lana urged.

"Even having the correct papers wouldn't be enough." He shrugged and sat down at the piano. "I'm not a young man, and I've led a good life. After all, who gets to hear Tchaikovsky performed every night and earn a living at the same time?"

Lana was about to answer when she heard footsteps.

"There you are." Charles stood at the door, addressing Raoul. "I've been sent to convince you to give an after-dinner performance."

"It would be my pleasure." Raoul nodded and turned to Lana. "Countess Antanova, would you choose a piece?"

Lana gulped and remembered the hours she spent listening to Frederic on the piano.

"Chopin's sonatas have always been a favorite," she said softly.

Raoul's eyes flickered with happiness. "An excellent decision."

Raoul played piano in the drawing room, and then it was time for the guests to leave.

Lana and Guy waited in the entry while Charles retrieved her cape.

"Thank you for coming." Charles gave the cape to Lana and shook Guy's hand. "I hope you enjoyed yourselves."

"We had a wonderful time," Lana gushed. "The food was delicious, and your home is lovely."

Charles leaned forward and kissed Lana on the cheek.

"Then you'll have to come back." He beamed. "Next time we'll have pears from my garden."

Guy took Lana's arm and led her to the door. Suddenly he kissed her. His hand rested briefly on the small of her back. The kiss was sweet and warm and she inhaled the scent of his aftershave.

Guy turned to Charles and there was a twinkle in his eye.

"Now I know what you're hiding up here in Menton."

"Hiding up here?" Charles repeated, puzzled.

"You don't want anyone to steal your chef. Those were the best beef tips I've had."

Lana was quiet on the drive back to Cap Ferrat. The moon was full, and the air was thick with floral perfumes. She couldn't believe that Guy had kissed her. But he didn't mention it, and she wasn't going to be the one who brought it up.

Guy pulled into the driveway and turned to Lana.

"You haven't said a word since we left."

"I've been thinking about something. I talked

with Raoul Gunsbourg at the party. He's terribly worried about being captured by the Gestapo." She smoothed her cape. "I had an idea. Perhaps you could escort him over the border to Switzerland?"

"Take Gunsbourg to Switzerland?" Guy spluttered. "Why would I do that? There are thousands of Jews on the Riviera. I can't simply escort them all."

Lana looked at Guy, and her eyes were filled with anguish.

"You heard him play the piano. And think of everything he's accomplished at the Monte Carlo opera house. You're a Swiss citizen, you can save him."

"If that were possible, we wouldn't have to use a boat," Guy argued. "The security at the Swiss border has tightened. They're checking everyone's papers."

"Maybe you can't take dozens of Jews across the border," Lana persisted. "But surely you can make up some story. Gunsbourg is your uncle and you're taking him to a spa for his health."

Guy drummed his fingers on the steering wheel.

"Charles planned this very well," he said.

"I don't know what you mean."

"He accomplishes two goals." Guy turned to Lana. "He hands Gunsbourg over to Brunner's friends at the border and gets me arrested at the same time."

"That's ridiculous," Lana scoffed.

"Charles is in love with you, he probably has been since you met on the train." Guy waved at the villa. "He'll appear at the door the minute I'm dead with a starched handkerchief and a Pimm's cup."

Lana was about to protest and changed her mind.

"So what if he is in love with me? It doesn't change anything. You and I have a relationship that is just for show," she retorted.

"We don't need Charles mooning around," Guy said stubbornly. "All his attention might turn your head, and you'll forget why you're here."

Guy couldn't possibly think that. He said that she was doing a good job. A thought occurred to her.

"You're jealous!" she said, turning to Guy. Guy didn't like Charles because he had feelings for her himself. "Is that why you kissed me? Because he was paying me too much attention?"

Guy ran his hands over the steering wheel.

"Of course I'm not jealous. I kissed you because I want to keep Charles on his toes." He waved offhandedly. "Charles is like a bloodhound. You can't get distracted."

Chapter Twelve

NICE, DECEMBER 1943

Two days later, Lana jumped on the bicycle and rode into Nice.

She left the bike in town and walked the few blocks to Sylvie's house on Rue Droit. Guy had said Brunner was planning a raid of the streets above Old Town soon. Many of the narrow houses with their shutters and planter boxes filled with pansies belonged to Jews. She wondered what would happen to them if she and Guy couldn't stop the raid.

Footsteps sounded on the pavement, and she darted into the alley. She peered into the street and saw two Gestapo officers smoking cigarettes. There was a clattering sound, and a cat jumped over a garbage can. One officer took out his gun and motioned the other officer to follow him.

Lana's heart raced, and she pressed herself against a building. She remembered Guy's warning that Captain Von Harmon might have her followed. She didn't want to be seen walking near Sylvie and Odette's house. But then the officer said something in German, and they continued down the street. The smell of their cigarettes dissolved into the still air, and she let herself breathe.

"Odette," Lana said with relief when she knocked and Odette opened the door.

"You look like you saw a ghost." Odette led her into the parlor.

"A cat jumped in my path and frightened me," Lana said quickly. She didn't want to scare Odette by telling her about the German officers.

The room was dark, but something about it felt different. Lana's carnations were in a vase and candles stood on the mantel.

"It looks nice in here," Lana commented.

"I convinced my mother to let me light candles last night." Odette followed her gaze. "They looked so pretty, I could almost imagine I was lying in a field and gazing up at the stars."

"And you're wearing a different dress." Lana noticed Odette's blue dress with a white collar.

"It was a birthday present. I didn't think there was any point in wearing it if I can't go outside, but I decided to describe it in my letter to Bernadette." She looked at Lana eagerly. "Come upstairs to my room. I wrote four more letters."

Lana and Odette climbed the stairs, and Odette sat at her desk.

"Did you mail the letters?" She turned to Lana.

"They will be on their way to England soon," Lana said cautiously.

Odette flung her arms around Lana.

"I knew you would! My mother didn't believe me, but I was certain you could do it."

Lana turned to the window and noticed a different map spread out on the desk.

"What's this?" she asked Odette.

"It's a map of Old Town. My father made it. Before the occupation we used to go on walks. My father wrote down the names of all my friends with their addresses." She pointed to the houses with dots under them. Underneath the dots were scrawled names in an unfamiliar handwriting. "I'm going to copy it and send it to Bernadette. Maybe after the war, she can come and stay with me."

"Are your friends Jewish?" Lana inquired.

"Some of them." Odette shrugged. "Some are school friends, and some friends belong to the temple. "

"Could I borrow this for a while?" Lana asked, trying to hide her excitement. If she had this map, she would have the addresses of many of the Jews who lived in Old Town. She and Guy could knock on their doors and warn them before the raid.

"Why do you want it?" Odette asked.

"I haven't explored Nice," Lana said evasively. "And Old Town is so pretty."

Odette rolled it up and handed it to Lana. "My father made lots of maps. Just promise you'll bring this one back."

"I promise."

Lana leaned the bicycle against the garage and let herself into the villa. Guy's car wasn't in the driveway, and she wondered when he would return. She ran up to her bedroom and placed the map on the bedside table.

She had to come up with a way to explain the map to Guy without telling him about Odette. The envelopes peeked out of her purse. There was so much to think about. Odette was counting on her to get the letters to Bernadette. Then she had to think of a plan for Bernadette's letters to reach Odette.

If only she could ask Frederic's advice. He had given Vivienne piano lessons because it wasn't safe for Vivienne to leave her house. And he taught the Jewish children at the convent.

"You must have run into obstacles, Frederic. You would know what to do," she murmured. "You would never let the children down."

The top envelope was open and she took it out of her purse. Odette said she didn't mind if Lana read her letters. She couldn't help but be curious. What was it like to be Odette, to have lost a parent and to wonder what each new day would bring?

> Dear Bernadette,
> I didn't tell you in my last letter the most important thing that has happened. I was too sad to talk about it. But since I plan to keep writing to you, I think you should know. German soldiers shot and killed my

father. At first, I wished I had died too. All I wanted was to be with him again. But the Jewish faith isn't like Christianity. There isn't a heaven and hell, there's only one place where all the Jews go. What if it's so big that I couldn't find him? I'm not afraid of dying—I see people die every day. But I am afraid of being alone. I've been alone so often since the Germans arrived, and it's the most terrible feeling in the world.

Things are better now. My mother is happier since I promised to stay inside. I forgot how pretty she is when she smiles! And I have a new friend named Lana. She's going to make sure you get these letters. She's a grown-up, but she seems to understand what it's like to be a child.

I thought I wouldn't have much to write about because I can't go out, but I've already filled a page. I'm going to draw you a picture of a dress I got for my last birthday. I bet you have a whole wardrobe of pretty dresses. Perhaps you can take a picture and send it to me.

Your friend, Odette

Lana closed the letter and slipped it back in the envelope. *Oh, Odette! How can a child be so innocent and wise at the same time?*

A door opened downstairs, and Lana crammed the envelope in the drawer. She ran to the staircase as Guy entered the living room. His overcoat was draped over his arm, and he wore slacks and a black turtleneck.

“Where have you been?” she asked, walking quickly down the staircase to join him. “You’ve been gone all day.”

“Switzerland.” Guy dropped his coat on the end table. “Raoul Gunsbourg is safely on his way to Geneva.”

“Switzerland!” Lana exclaimed.

“I was wrong the night of Charles’s party.” He walked to the bar and filled a glass with Scotch. “I still believe every life is worth saving. When the war is over, the survivors need music and literature to help make sense of everything that happened. If men like Gunsbourg don’t make it, they won’t have anyone to guide them.” He sipped his drink. “We’ll be living in the Dark Ages.”

“But what about Charles . . . ?” Her voice drifted off.

Guy leaned against the cushions and for a moment he looked tired. But then his eyes met hers, and he smiled cheekily.

“Charles will never suspect I had anything to do with it,” he assured her. “I called him yesterday to thank him for the party. I said you and I were staying at Hôtel de Paris in Monte Carlo and invited him to join us.”

"You did what?" Lana exclaimed. "What if he had accepted?"

"Then I would have piled you into the car and driven to Monte Carlo," he said mischievously. "But I knew he would say no. Charles Langford would rather spend all day ironing his expensive shirts than sit and watch you and me play footsie under the table."

"But what if Charles called Hôtel de Paris and asked if we were there?"

"I took care of that too. I have a concierge friend there." Guy finished his drink. "Raoul was very grateful. He said if we're ever in Geneva after the war, he'd like to take us to the opera."

Lana's eyes welled up. Suddenly it was all too much. Raoul escaping to Switzerland, and Odette's letters to Bernadette. She wanted a time when the most excitement in her week was Giselle's chicken laying eggs.

"I thought you'd be happy," Guy said, noticing her expression. "I was going to open a bottle of champagne to celebrate."

"I am happy." She pulled herself together. "But there's something I have to tell you."

"I hope you haven't found any other artists who need saving." Guy groaned. "Because I haven't slept in twenty-four hours, and I'd do anything for a hot bath and bed."

"It's nothing you have to do tonight." She walked to the staircase.

She grabbed the map and ran back down to the living room.

"Do you remember when you said Brunner is planning a raid on the streets above Old Town?" she asked.

Guy stood at the bar, refilling his Scotch glass. "We don't know what day and even if we did, it's going to be difficult. It's easy to knock on the door of every hotel room and tell the occupants they have to leave. But there are dozens of streets in Old Town. It will take us ages to approach every house, and we have no idea which ones are occupied by Jews."

Lana spread the map on the coffee table.

"The houses with the dots under them are occupied by Jews."

Guy studied the map for a long minute and looked up at Lana.

"Where did you get this?" he demanded.

"It doesn't matter where I got it," she returned, nervous at his tone.

"Of course it matters!" Guy snapped. "I need to know where it came from. How else will I know that it's accurate?"

Lana straightened her shoulders. She faced Guy, and her eyes were bright.

"You didn't tell me how you got Raoul over the border, and I didn't ask," she said. "You're the one who said I need to trust my instincts; it's time you trusted me too."

Guy's brow knotted together, and a scowl flashed across his face. He downed his Scotch. His eyes were dark and brooding. She thought he would tell her to leave.

But he put the shot glass on the bar and crossed the room. Suddenly his mouth was on hers, and his arms were around her. Her pulse raced, and she could taste the Scotch on his breath. This wasn't like the moment in Charles's foyer when he had kissed her to make Charles jealous. This kiss was real. She could feel it in the pressure of his mouth and the way he pressed her against him.

He released her.

"I'm sorry, I shouldn't have done that."

"Why did you?" She gulped.

He sighed and ran a hand through his hair. They stood more than a foot apart now.

"Because this war is about saving people who are walking around with a death sentence because they happen to be Jewish. And then I enter the villa, and here you are with your blond hair and those blue eyes, looking as if you spent the day deciding what to serve at dinner," he said. "Some days I want to indulge in that fantasy: that I'm coming home to my beautiful wife and the most important thing we have to discuss is who we should invite to our next party."

Outside, the sun set over the garden. The swimming pool glimmered in the golden light, and the sound of distant cars drifted through the window.

She touched her lips and tipped her head at Guy.

"Sometimes I'd like to indulge in that fantasy too."

Chapter Thirteen

NICE, DECEMBER 1943

Lana woke early the next morning and drew back the curtains. It had rained during the night, and the hills were as bright and green as emeralds. A bank of fog settled over the Mediterranean, and she longed to curl up with a cup of hot tea and read Proust's *Remembrance of Things Past*.

The phone on her bedside table rang, and she picked it up.

"Countess Antanova," a male voice said. "It's Captain Von Harmon. I hope I didn't wake you. I've always been an early riser; it's the most inspiring time of day."

Lana sat on the bed and pressed the phone to her ear.

"Captain Brunner said you were in Berlin."

"I just returned," Captain Von Harmon replied. "My wife had a baby boy."

"Congratulations, you must be pleased."

Lana felt an overwhelming sense of relief. Alois Brunner had been telling the truth. Captain Von Harmon was in Berlin for the birth of his child. Her role in the raid hadn't caused him consequences. She wasn't sure why she was glad. Von Harmon was a member of the Gestapo, after all. But being personally responsible for his punishment made her feel terrible.

"His name is Wolfgang Adolf Von Harmon," Captain Von Harmon answered proudly. "The führer sent a note of congratulations."

"Of course he did." Lana made her voice flirtatious. "If Wolfgang is anything like his father, he will be a fine man."

"I don't deserve your compliments, Countess Antanova. I left Nice without saying goodbye." He paused. "I would like to make it up to you by having dinner tonight."

Von Harmon was inviting her to dinner, even though he was married. The invitation made her uncomfortable. It was one thing to flirt with him, but it was another to accept a date. She wondered what kind of a woman he thought she was. And yet it was her job to get close to him. She couldn't let guilty feelings about his wife interfere with her work.

Lana counted to ten before she spoke.

"Really, Captain Von Harmon," she said playfully. "Do you think I'm that boring that I'm free every night?"

"My apologies, quite the opposite," he admitted. "I found myself thinking about you often when I was away. If tonight doesn't work, it will have to wait until next week. I'm afraid Brunner has me tied up."

Lana sat up straighter. Did that mean the raid

on the streets above Old Town would be this week?

"I can't turn down a man who is so good at flattery," she purred. "I'll try to change my plans. Where would you like to meet?"

This time it was Captain Von Harmon who waited before he answered.

"Why don't we meet in the lobby of my hotel, the Excelsior," he suggested. "I've been traveling so much, it would be nice to stay close to home."

Lana hung up the phone and slipped on a dress. She ran downstairs and found Guy in the dining room. A book was open in front of him, and there was a pot of coffee and two cups.

"You're awake early." He glanced up. "I was reading an Agatha Christie book. Sometimes you need something to take you away from this war. A detective story with an ornery French detective named Hercule Poirot is just the thing."

"You won't have time to read this week," Lana said excitedly. "Captain Von Harmon is back in Nice and invited me to dinner tonight. I'll be able to find out the date of the raid on Old Town."

"We thought Von Harmon was banished to Berlin for missing the raid."

"Apparently not. His wife had a boy, and Hitler sent a note of congratulations himself," Lana said. "We're dining at the Hôtel Excelsior."

Guy closed the book and stirred sugar into his coffee.

"Or Von Harmon is in disgrace and is being used as bait to bring you in."

"What do you mean?" Lana asked.

"If Brunner is growing suspicious, he could have arranged the dinner," Guy said thoughtfully. "It's a trap, and you'll be arrested."

"That's ridiculous. When Brunner called the other day he was completely cordial," Lana said.

"It doesn't matter. It's too dangerous. You can't go."

"Of course I'm going!" Lana returned. "It's the only night Von Harmon is free this week."

"I'm not going to have you captured on my watch," Guy snapped. "It's all getting too close. You don't know what they do to female spies. They'll torture you until that blond hair falls out and those long legs are covered with more wounds than a matador at a bullfight." He looked at Lana. "By the time they're finished, you'll be begging them to shoot you."

Lana gulped, and a chill ran down on her spine.

"We have the map; I'm not going to miss this chance." She lifted her chin. "Von Harmon is quite taken with me. All I have to do is keep flattering him until I get the information."

Guy drummed his fingers on the dining room table.

"You can go on one condition; I'll be there too. I'll hide in the kitchen or behind a palm tree if

I have to," he decided. "But I won't let you be alone with him."

Lana poured herself a cup of coffee, but the pungent aroma made her stomach turn.

"If you want to spend the evening hunched behind a potted palm, I'm not going to stop you." She sniffed the cup and placed it back on the saucer. "This coffee is too strong, it's bad for your nerves."

Lana sat across from Captain Von Harmon at the Hôtel Excelsior's restaurant and listened to him describe his family's apartment in Berlin. From the outside she was the picture of grace and calm: she had spent an hour in her dressing room fixing her hair and adjusting the neckline of her dress to show just a hint of cleavage. But ever since Guy had dropped her off near the hotel, she had been so nervous she could barely breathe.

"Joseph Goebbels invited my family to stay at his villa on the lake next summer," Von Harmon was saying. "It's only twenty-five kilometers from Berlin, but it's like another world. There's a private cinema and a park."

"I'm sure you'll have a wonderful time," Lana said, admiring the photo of a pretty blond woman and two small children he had handed to her. "Your wife is lovely, and such handsome children, you must be so proud."

"The new baby, Wolfgang, isn't in the photo

but he has the same blond hair. Tomas and Clara and Wolfgang are everything I could ask for. But three children under the age of five isn't easy for Helga." He looked at Lana. "She doesn't have much energy left for me."

"She gave birth a short time ago. It was just last week," Lana reminded him.

"I can't fault my wife. She is doing exactly what the führer wishes." He picked up his fork. "But I'm getting lonely."

"Lonely?" Lana repeated.

"Everyone needs companionship. I thought that's where you and I might form an arrangement."

Lana glanced around for Guy. But she found only waiters carrying large trays. She rubbed her lips together and smiled provocatively.

"Captain Von Harmon," she purred. "That's a very tempting invitation. I can't tell you how flattered I am. And after we were just talking about you being invited to stay at Joseph Goebbels's villa. Obviously, you're one of the most important men in Germany."

"You flatter me," Von Harmon cut in, but he was pleased.

"I'm only saying the truth." She tilted her head and made a small pout. "But I can't possibly accept. I'm living with Guy."

"Countess Antanova, life on the Riviera is going to become harder in the next few months.

We are building barricades on the boulevards to allow only certain cars through. Rationing will be strict; anything not grown locally will disappear from the shelves. Even wealthy men like Guy Pascal will find it difficult to buy the most ordinary things like bread. I can still give you this." He waved at the plates of scallops. "And so much more."

Lana imagined the boulevards with their palm trees and white benches scarred by barbed wire fences. She pictured German officers stuffing their faces with steak while Odette and all the other children starved. But she couldn't leave. She pasted a smile on her face and played along.

"What kind of things?" she asked.

"I'm owed favors," he said delicately. "I can give you jewelry and perfume and all the dresses you want."

"You don't think very highly of me if you think I could be convinced with perfume or diamonds." Lana touched the neckline of her dress provocatively. "I am a woman with a heart, after all."

Captain Von Harmon gazed at the outline of her breasts and his eyes were lit with desire.

"I don't understand," he stammered.

"Love, Captain Von Harmon," she said in a cold tone. "Love is the only reason a lady would accompany a man to his bed."

"I didn't mean to offend you, Countess

Antanova." He bowed his head. "I will be the most ardent suitor you could know."

Lana waited, and then she lifted her eyes to meet his.

"It's a tempting offer." She leaned forward. "Can I take a few days to think it over?"

"The offer is only good tonight," he said shortly. "I thought we were of like minds. Unless you have been leading me on."

Von Harmon's eyebrows arched as if he was tired of playing the game.

"Then how can I refuse?" She touched his hand. "After all, the führer himself writes you letters. You're an important man."

"Since I returned from Berlin, I occupy a suite." His voice was thick as if he had drunk straight cream. "We can have our dessert there."

Lana's heart hammered, and she tried to think. Where was Guy? He would never forgive her for going up to Von Harmon's suite. But she hadn't found out the day and time of the raid. If she didn't accompany Von Harmon, she might lose her chance.

"You've convinced me," she said, and gathered her purse. "Do you mind if I freshen up?"

"Why don't I go up and get things ready?" he suggested. He stood. "The hotel staff can be a little stuffy; I wouldn't want them to get the wrong idea."

"That's an excellent plan." She nodded.

"It's suite two thirty-eight." He grasped her hand and brought it up to his lips. "Don't keep me waiting, Countess Antanova. We still have so much to discuss."

Lana leaned against the sink in the powder room. She had been standing there for fifteen minutes, but she was still too shaken to move.

She hadn't thought of what she would do if Von Harmon propositioned her. She pictured his thin lips roaming over her body and felt sick. And she and Guy were getting closer. She couldn't sit across from Guy at breakfast and eat his soft-boiled egg when she had been intimate with a member of the Gestapo. But if she didn't go to bed with Von Harmon, she was sending more Jews to their deaths.

Frederic had thought nothing of using his body to shield Esther Cohen. Shouldn't she use hers if that was the only way to achieve their goal? She studied her face in the mirror and made her decision. She had to go through with it. It was better not to think too much. Sometimes, the only thing to do was act.

The door to the powder room opened and she heard the strains of the piano. She marched through the marble lobby and waited in front of the elevator.

As the elevator doors opened, Guy stepped out. He grabbed her arm suddenly and jostled her through the lobby. He didn't stop until they were outside the hotel and had turned onto Boulevard Victor Hugo.

"What are you doing?' she demanded.

"Hurry, please get in the car." He opened her door and jumped into the driver's seat. He waited for her to slide into the passenger seat and turned the key in the ignition.

"I can't leave," she said over the roar of the engine. The top was down, and the wind blew her hair. "Von Harmon is waiting for me in his suite."

"I'll explain when we get back to the villa." He glanced at her. "Just keep your head down in case we're followed."

Finally they reached the villa, and Guy jumped out. He took her hand and ran up the steps.

"You were supposed to watch us, not interfere," she said, anger rising inside her. "What will happen when I don't show up in the suite? And I don't have the date of the raid, you ruined everything."

Guy closed the curtains and took the phone off the hook. It was only when the room was in total darkness that he faced her.

"Von Harmon isn't waiting for you; he's dead."

Lana gasped.

"What did you say?"

"I thought it would be a good opportunity to search his room for information while you were at dinner." Guy took off the overcoat he had been wearing. "I was about to leave when Von Harmon entered, so I hid in the closet. Von Harmon took off his clothes and put on a robe. Then he took his pistol and placed it under his pillow."

Lana put her hand on the side table. The room blurred and she felt dizzy.

"He put a gun under the pillow," she whispered.

"I've placed rose petals on a pillow to welcome a woman to bed but never a pistol," Guy said darkly. "I don't think he planned for you to get up in the morning."

"How is he dead?" she stammered.

"I shot him." Guy's voice was blank. "Don't worry, no one saw me. I stole his wallet and his watch. They'll think it was a robbery."

"I was having dinner with him," she said, frightened. "I'll be a suspect."

"I took care of all of that. I left the gun with fingerprints."

"You left your fingerprints on the gun!" Lana's eyes widened. "You'll be arrested."

"Not my fingerprints. The gun belongs to a well-known thief named Yves," Guy corrected. "Yves lives in Casablanca now, but it will take the authorities ages to figure it out," he said, sounding pleased with himself. "I told you I keep a pistol under the back seat of the car."

"Why were you carrying the gun, and how did you know Von Harmon invited me to his suite?" she asked.

"I had to have a gun. You were meeting with Von Harmon," he explained. "What if something went wrong?"

Lana glanced up at Guy. He wanted to protect her.

"I didn't know he invited you to his suite," he continued. "But when I saw the champagne bucket and matching robes, I had a good idea. I was going to go downstairs and warn you. That's when he arrived. Thank God I got there first. . . ."

Tears sprung to Lana's eyes.

Guy took her in his arms, and this time she kissed him first. His lips were firm and powerful, and his hand pressed against the small of her back. When they parted she gasped for breath.

"I didn't mean to do that." She gulped. "I was afraid and I'm overwrought."

"Can we just not talk for a minute?" he whispered.

Lana took in his dark hair and those emerald-green eyes, and her body trembled with desire.

He touched her mouth, and she shivered. Then he kissed her again, and she fell into his embrace. He took her hand and together they walked upstairs.

Guy's bedroom was dark, and he turned on the light. Lana barely noticed the padded headboard and the bedside table piled with books. All she was aware of was Guy unbuttoning her dress and the warmth of his fingers against her skin.

He nuzzled her neck, and she reached up and pulled off his turtleneck. His shoulders were wide and smooth, and she ran her hands over his chest.

"You're all I think about," he whispered, pulling her onto the bed.

She lay against the pillows and watched Guy strip off his slacks. He perched above her, and she waited while his eyes took in every part of her body.

He dropped to his side and turned her face to his.

"I don't have any right to do this." His voice was choked with emotion. "But I've never wanted a woman more."

She pressed her finger against his mouth.

"I want you too," she whispered.

Guy gently pushed her on her back. He climbed on top of her, and she arched to meet him. Then it was all a tangle of lightness and heat and sensations she never wanted to end.

Afterward they lay on the bed, and she watched Guy's chest rise and fall.

He turned on his stomach and kissed her nose. "You make me very happy."

The moon was a white ball outside the window, and she felt something new she couldn't name. She wasn't a young newlywed who believed being in love could keep away the war. She was a woman who had seen the worst kind of evil happen right before her eyes and realized she couldn't stop living. When Frederic was shot and she lost the baby, all she wanted was to sleep. For a while she couldn't see the point of getting up to face a new day. But then she came to the Riviera and met Sylvie and Odette. She realized there was so much good she could accomplish. Now it was impossible to ignore the attraction between her and Guy. And why should she? If she made the decision to live, how could she stop from feeling?

Perhaps it was time to stop asking Frederic for advice. She was alive, and so was Guy.

She reached up and kissed him.

"You make me happy too."

Chapter Fourteen

NICE, DECEMBER 1943

Lana woke in Guy's bed the next morning and was afraid he would regret what had happened between them. But he pulled her close and repeated the intimacy of the night before. Afterward, she lay and listened to him showering in the bathroom. She expected to feel embarrassed surrounded by his things. But instead, she buried herself in the sheets and was completely at home.

He appeared in the bedroom with a towel wrapped around his waist.

"Dress in something warm," he said, pulling on slacks and a sweater. "We're going somewhere special."

Lana sat against the headboard and gazed at the heavy clouds hanging over the horizon. "But it looks like it's going to rain."

Guy peered outside. "It's just a thick fog. It will burn off and be a beautiful day."

"Can't we stay here?" Lana waved at the bedspread.

"That's a tempting offer." He kissed her. "But who knows how long we'll be on the Riviera, and there's somewhere I want to show you." His eyes danced, and she had never seen his smile so bright. "Don't worry about your hair and makeup. You couldn't be more beautiful than you already are."

Guy went downstairs, and Lana slipped on a robe and padded back to her bedroom. Guy's mention of time on the Riviera caught her off guard. The Gestapo were still deporting Jews; they had work to do here. She wondered if he knew something he wasn't telling her. Perhaps Henri had communicated to him that he had other plans for them. She searched her closet for a sweater and put the thought out of her mind. For now she would pretend they were new lovers instead of Resistance workers in the middle of the war.

The convertible maneuvered along the sharp cliffs, and Lana turned to admire the view. They were so high up; the Mediterranean was like a child's drawing. Clouds as fat as marshmallows slid across the sky. The air was fresh and moist and smelled of piney shrubs.

Driving with Guy today was different than it had been before. Instead of careening around the turns, he drove so slowly that cars honked to let them pass. Guy muttered that some people couldn't appreciate the beauty of the Riviera and waved them on.

Lana wanted to ask how they planned to thwart the raid on Old Town given what little information they had, but she was afraid to break the spell. They talked about everything except the war, and sometimes they didn't talk at all. Guy hummed a Maurice Chevalier song, and Lana leaned against the headrest, and her heart brimmed with happiness.

The car stopped beside a field of lavender, and Guy unloaded a picnic basket. He pulled a blanket out of the trunk and spread it on the ground.

"Your car is equipped for everything, even picnics." Lana laughed as he opened a bottle of wine.

Guy stopped what he was doing and sat beside her.

"If you're asking if I've done this before, the answer is no." His eyes were serious. "I already told you. When I joined the Resistance I swore to myself that I wouldn't get involved with a woman."

"What changed your mind?" Lana gulped and wondered if he was going to say it had been a mistake—the night before had been magical but couldn't happen again.

Guy leaned forward and kissed her. His whole body seemed to be part of the kiss, and when they parted she could still feel his lips on her mouth.

"For a long time I wondered what I was doing in the Resistance. I wanted to stop those German bastards from blowing up railway stations, but that didn't stop the emptiness of being alone. The war splinters people: either they can't be trusted, or they're so wrapped up in their own misery they retreat into themselves. It's difficult to really know someone. Some care so little for their own lives, they become careless with the lives of others. And for some it's the opposite. They've lost so much already, they're afraid to care for someone new and lose them too. Life changes in a blink of an eye. If you're on the wrong side of a rifle, you find yourself dead." He wrestled with the bottle of wine. "But then you appeared, and I remembered what it was like to embrace living. At first I told myself it was just the pleasure of having someone to talk to after so much time by myself. But I know now that it's something more. It's wanting to get up in the morning and having the energy to get through the day. It's not thinking about the future because you want each hour to last forever. I could sit all day at the breakfast table because looking at you is like being bathed in sunshine. You're fearless and bright and everything is easier when we're together." He looked at her and his voice was hoarse. "I don't know exactly where this will go, but I'm not ready for it to end."

They kissed again, and Guy poured glasses of wine and pointed at the village far below.

"That's Villefranche-sur-Mer. It was a simple fishing village until about forty years ago, when a group of artists arrived. Now artists and poets mingle with fishermen, but it still retains its charm. Everyone knows one another, and you won't find anyone wearing expensive jewelry."

Lana peered at the narrow houses clustered around a horseshoe-shaped bay. Instead of elegant villas dotting the hills, there were farms with lopsided barns.

"It was the first place I saw that made me feel I understood art." Guy kept talking.

"What do you mean?" Lana wondered.

"I grew up visiting museums and galleries, but I'd never been moved by a painting." He pondered. "I stood in this spot and saw the sun stretching over the horizon and fields choked with color, and I understood. There's beauty in this world that even Hitler can't take away."

Lana recalled that was the way Frederic felt about music. It was wonderful that Guy felt the same about art.

The first raindrops fell as they started on the food. Guy scrambled to load the car, but by the time he closed the hood they were both wet.

"Could we stop and get something hot to drink or maybe a bowl of soup?" Lana asked as the car approached the center of Villefranche-sur-Mer. The wind had picked up and rain splashed the windshield.

"I don't know if anything is open." Guy grunted, keeping his eyes on the road.

“Please,” Lana urged. “My clothes are wet, and I’m freezing.”

Guy turned to look at her as she shivered. His expression softened. “All right, I can’t have you catching cold like Pierre.”

He parked and grabbed a jacket from the back seat. He held it over Lana’s head, and they ran into the nearest café.

The waiter brought them menus, and Guy placed them on the table.

“Two potato soups.” He ran his hands through his hair and grimaced. “And a couple of whiskies if you have them.”

Guy’s mood had darkened, and Lana felt slightly irritated. It wasn’t her fault that it had started to rain. And she couldn’t drive back to Cap Ferrat soaking wet. She opened her mouth to say something when an older woman entered the café.

“Monsieur Pascal, is that you?” The woman approached their table.

“Madame Broussard.” Guy looked up. “It’s nice to see you.”

“Nice to see me as if we saw each other yesterday! Stand up, let me see if you’re still so skinny.”

Guy rose reluctantly, and the woman kissed him on both cheeks.

“Too thin but as handsome as ever.” She turned and looked at Lana. “You forgot your manners. Aren’t you going to introduce me?”

"Countess Antanova, this is Françoise Broussard. She owns the best restaurant in Villefranche."

"The only restaurant," Françoise corrected. "The rest are merely cafés that serve food my own mother could make. Françoise's has a chef. It's been too long, you must come for dinner."

"We'll do that." Guy nodded. The waiter brought their soups, and he sat down. "Right now we're having bowls of soup to keep warm."

"Monsieur Pascal used to be one of my best customers," she said fondly. "Always with that pretty wife and gorgeous little girl."

Guy's soupspoon clattered to the table. Françoise glanced from Guy to Lana and put her hand over her mouth.

"Monsieur Pascal . . ." she stammered. "I'm sure this is perfectly innocent. I didn't mean . . ."

"It's all right. I'm not indiscreet," Guy said quietly. He placed his napkin on the table and sat back in his chair. "My wife died."

Françoise's chest heaved, and she twisted her hands.

"*Merde!* I didn't know."

"I didn't tell you," Guy said, trying to smile. "If you don't mind, we'll finish our soups. I promised the countess I wouldn't let her catch cold."

Françoise left, and Guy picked up his spoon. His face was blank, and even his eyes seemed drained of color.

"My wife's name was Marie. We had a daughter named Aimee."

"I'm sorry," Lana whispered.

Guy signaled the waiter for another whiskey.

"Let me have one more of these, and I'll tell you the whole story."

Lana waited while Guy gulped the whiskey.

"I'm Swiss. I was born and raised in Geneva," Guy began. "My father is a successful businessman, and my mother is American. My mother came to Switzerland on holiday, and my father swept her off her feet." He smiled fondly. "I had a charmed childhood: skiing in the Swiss Alps and vacationing on the French Riviera. Then I met Marie. I spent a summer in Montreux, and she was working at an auberge where I was staying." He chuckled. "I had the impression that all French girls were stuck-up and only interested in fashion like the ones I'd met in Paris, but Marie was different."

Lana started to protest, and Guy squeezed her hand.

"Present company excluded." He grinned. "Marie was raised on a farm near Reims. She was fresh and young and lovely. We had a wonderful summer, and then she got pregnant. We were married in a stone church in Montreux. I was madly in love; I would have married her anyway."

Guy signaled the waiter for another whiskey.

“I wanted to stay in Switzerland, but she longed to be near her parents when we had the baby. I understood. My parents had moved to America several years before because my mother wanted to be closer to her parents. Her parents wouldn’t travel to Europe because they were afraid there was going to be a war.

“Marie’s father was Jewish, so when the war started her parents sold the farm and moved to the Riviera. Everyone thought the Riviera was safe for Jews. They bought a little farm above Villefranche-sur-Mer, just a few cows and goats, but enough to get by. I urged them to come to Switzerland, but Marie has a sister, Celine. Celine and her children lived with them in Villefranche, and her parents wouldn’t move to another country.

“Her parents only had a small house, and there wasn’t enough room for all of us. And I didn’t want to intrude; after all, I could afford a place of our own. We rented a place in Nice, and Aimee was born.” Guy nursed his glass. “All the cheesy things people say about becoming a father were true. The minute Aimee set her blue eyes on me through the hospital window, I was head over heels in love.

“Even with the Italian occupation, life was better than I could imagine. In July of ’42 there was an Allied bombing raid on the railway station in Nice. Aimee was only three, and Marie thought it would be safer if they stayed with her parents and sister for a few weeks. The house would be crowded, but it would be better than staying in Nice. I had some business here, but I was going to join them soon. They had been there only a few days when there was a farm accident." Guy stopped and Lana noticed his hands were shaking.

"Aimee was run over by a tractor. It had nothing to do with the war, but Marie blamed herself. She returned to Nice with her parents. They were going to stay with us in Nice for a while and help her recover.

"A week later the French police conducted a raid on our neighborhood. Hitler was getting impatient that Mussolini was too lenient with the Jews. So at the Germans' request, the French police stepped up their attempts to get rid of the Jewish population.

"I wasn't home when the police knocked on the door. Marie's father pretended he couldn't find his papers, and they started to drag him away."

"How do you know?" Lana cut in.

"Our landlady saw the whole thing," Guy answered. "Marie screamed at the policemen that they would have to take her too. Marie and her parents were escorted to the train station." He gulped. "I traced them to Drancy, where a Gestapo officer named Alois Brunner put them on the train to a camp."

"Brunner!" Lana gasped. The familiar scene flashed before her eyes: Frederic opening the piano and Brunner insisting he hand over Esther Cohen. Then hearing the gunshot that seemed to pierce her own heart.

"Marie must have been very brave." She faltered, wondering how to comfort him.

Guy stared at the rain on the windowpane.

"The smart thing would have been to go back to Switzerland or join my parents in America," he said absently. "But I didn't tell my parents what happened. My mother still thinks I'm eating Marie's soufflés and hiking in the French Alps."

"Why did you keep it a secret?" Lana was shocked.

"I wasn't ready to leave France. I don't know why. Perhaps I was still hoping that Marie was alive." He shrugged. "Or maybe I was punishing myself, or I worried that I would leave behind my memories of Marie and Aimee." His voice was gruff. "I decided I would help Celine and her children escape to Switzerland. I got them across the border, and then I returned to Villefranche. I was going to sell the farm and go back to Geneva. That's how I met Henri. He heard I helped Celine escape and asked me to do the same for other Jews on the Riviera. Then he told me about Alois Brunner." His eyes were hard as marbles. "I decided I couldn't live in a world with men like Brunner, so I made myself a promise. I'm not leaving France until one of us is dead."

"Is the villa yours?" Lana asked.

For the first time since he started the story, Guy's expression turned lighter.

"Henri and I agreed to keep my cover as close to my past as possible," he answered. "It makes it more difficult to get caught in a lie. I come from a wealthy family, so I was able to buy the villa. And if anyone in Switzerland asks about Guy Pascal, they'll find I was a well-respected member of the community."

They finished their soup and dashed back to the car. The rain turned into a soft drizzle, and Guy pulled up in front of the villa.

"I'm glad you told me." Lana watched the wipers crisscross the windshield. "When Frederic was murdered and I miscarried our baby it was the worst day of my life. I can't imagine what it's like to lose a child."

"For weeks I asked my doctor for something: a prescription of pills or a vial of poison that I could add to my nightly brandy," Guy said meditatively. "But that's the funny thing about doctors. They say they want to help you, but they only want to stitch you back together. They won't do the one thing that will stop the pain.

"Then I saw the relief in Celine's eyes when she and her children arrived safely in Switzerland. If I could do something to help others and avenge

Marie's and Aimee's deaths at the same time, it was worth living with my own pain."

Lana's eyes filled with tears, and she turned to kiss him.

"How did you come to own the villa and be part of society on the Riviera?" she asked after they parted.

"Buying the villa was easy. Many houses were for sale; all the Americans were scurrying home. I met Natalia and she introduced me to people," he recalled. "She is very well connected. She told everyone that a wealthy Swiss industrialist just bought a villa in Cap Ferrat and they must include me at their parties."

Lana felt oddly jealous. She sat back and smoothed her hair.

"You must have been a hit from the beginning. A single and handsome foreigner."

Guy noticed her pained expression. He put his hand on her chin and drew her close.

"I didn't notice any of the women; I still missed Marie." He kissed her deeply. "Until now. Now all I can think about is you."

She kissed him back. There was a small rip in the convertible top and a raindrop splashed her nose.

"I bought this convertible for our honeymoon," Guy grumbled, wiping the rain from his cheek and offering her his handkerchief. "It looked good in the showroom, but it's been nothing but trouble. Give me a British Rover any day."

"Nonsense." She laughed, accepting the handkerchief. "You're much too handsome to drive a boring car."

Guy went to run errands, and Lana sat in the living room. It was the first time Guy had opened up about his past, and she felt close to him. She understood now why Guy hadn't wanted to stop in Villefranche for a bowl of soup. He'd been afraid of running into someone he knew and having to explain what happened to his wife and daughter. But why had he taken her to the picnic spot in the first place? Was it for the view or to share his past? She rubbed the finger where she used to wear her wedding ring. The people they had loved and lost were impossible to leave behind.

Chapter Fifteen

NICE, DECEMBER 1943

The Petrikoffs' party was in full swing when Guy and Lana arrived. A band played in the ballroom, and men wearing dinner jackets and smoking cigars wandered in and out of the library. Guy went to join them, and Lana stood at the bar.

"Countess Antanova, it's wonderful to see you again." Natalia Petrikoff approached her. A diamond-studded cap covered Natalia's hair and she wore a white evening gown with flowing sleeves.

"It's lovely to be here," Lana replied, glancing around the room. She was glad she had borrowed Giselle's gown.

"I was hoping you and Guy would come," Natalia confided. "So I could see if the rumors were true."

"Rumors?" Lana repeated, her heart beating faster.

Had someone seen her with Captain Von Harmon the night of his death?

"There's a rumor that you and Guy are the most romantic couple on the Riviera." Natalia waved her cigarette holder. "He's been singing your praises to anyone who will listen. He's positively devoted."

Lana took a sip of her champagne and smiled.

"Guy enjoys giving compliments; it's part of his nature."

"I'm glad that Guy found love," Natalia said merrily. "When he first attended our parties, I wondered if he knew how to smile," she mused. "I even took it on myself to help him. I went to the pharmacist and asked him to blend the most seductive perfume. I thought Guy might enjoy a small dalliance. But then I was afraid my husband would smell it. It would be so inconvenient if my husband was in love with me." She smiled. "It's wonderful to see romance blossom in our corner of the war. Especially when one hears terrible stories." She leaned closer to Lana. "Like what happened to Giselle Saint Claire. A friend happened to be in Berlin last week and heard the most fascinating story."

Lana put her hand on the sideboard to steady herself. She hadn't seen Giselle in a few days. Lana had been so busy with the Jews' escape from Old Town and Guy. Now she felt slightly guilty. Giselle was her friend; she should have checked in on her.

"Giselle?"

"Your neighbor," Natalia replied. "It's all very hush-hush. My friend is well connected, but you must promise to keep it a secret. It's not the kind of thing one would like to get out. After all, Giselle is part of our circle. It could hurt all of us."

"You have my word," Lana said, trying to keep her expression calm.

"I should have suspected something about Giselle from the beginning," Natalia reflected. "She used to attend our parties, and she was always alone. I thought she was too beautiful to be without a man. She never even flirted; for a while I thought she liked women." Natalia shuddered. "But apparently she had a German lover."

Lana felt like she had been punched in the stomach. She waited until she caught her breath.

"There's nothing wrong with having a German lover," Lana answered smoothly, in character.

"Nothing at all," Natalia agreed. "I've considered taking a German lover myself. They're so virile; they're supposed to be wonderful in bed. My friend said that Giselle's lover was part of a plot to kill Hitler last March—the brandy bomb. A German officer named Henning von Tresckow gave Hitler two bottles of Cointreau brandy to take on his plane to Berlin. The brandy held a bomb, but the fuse didn't go off. If it had, the führer's plane would have been blown to bits over the Bavarian Alps."

"Is that so?" Lana asked, and wondered if her

voice was too bright. Could Natalia tell that her whole body was trembling?

"Apparently the case went unsolved for months. Come to think of it, we rarely saw Giselle during that time. But many members of our set have their little quirks. You might see them at three parties in the same week and then they hibernate like bears in the winter. My friend confided that Hitler was adamant the Gestapo keep searching until they uncovered who planted the bombs. Two weeks ago, Giselle's lover, Hans Markel, was implicated. After his capture, he was tortured and hanged." Natalia clucked her tongue. "One can only hope Hans didn't mention Giselle's name. The one thing the Bolsheviks and Germans have in common is they're not kind to prisoners."

"That's terrible." Lana gasped.

Her mind went immediately to the engraved humidor box in Giselle's living room. That's why Giselle grew so flustered when Lana asked where she got it. *HM—Hans Markel*. It was a gift to her lover.

"You promise you won't breathe a word of this, not even to Guy," Natalia insisted. "I shouldn't have mentioned it. But some things are so awful to think about. It somehow relieves the burden of knowing when you share it with someone else." She smiled. "And for some reason I feel close to you. At first I thought it was because I could see myself in you when I was young. But it's more than that. You're different than most of our friends. You listen when someone talks." She glanced around the room. "Just be careful. These days we should be wearing protective armor like the knights in the Middle Ages instead of these frivolous evening gowns. We have to protect ourselves. If Giselle had a secret lover who was a traitor, who knows what other people are hiding."

Natalia wandered off, and Lana gulped her champagne. Suddenly she had the sensation of being watched. She looked up to find Alois Brunner approaching.

"Countess Antanova." He nodded. "It's lovely to see you. You are a vision of beauty, a welcome distraction as I've had a disturbing week."

"Did something happen?" Lana asked, trying to keep her voice steady.

"Captain Von Harmon was murdered in his hotel room recently," Brunner said shortly.

Her stomach dropped. Of course, she knew Von Harmon's death would come up soon, but Brunner's mention of it made her doubly nervous.

"How horrible!" Lana put her hand to her mouth.

"Apparently it was the night that you joined him for dinner." He looked at her closely. "I thought perhaps you might be able to help me."

"Help you?" she repeated.

"The police said it was a robbery. You were at the hotel; perhaps you saw something suspicious." Brunner waved his glass. "Someone lurking around the elevator or a disturbance on his floor."

Lana took a deep breath. She turned to Brunner, and her eyes were as bright and clear as the chandelier floating above them.

"I did have dinner with Captain Von Harmon, but it ended abruptly," she began. She couldn't tell Brunner that Captain Von Harmon propositioned her. He might construe it as a motivation for her to shoot him. "I wasn't feeling well and needed to go home." She looked at him levelly.

Brunner's black eyes roamed over her beaded bodice, and Lana tried to hide her revulsion.

"My apologies if I've caused any offense, Countess Antanova," he said, bowing. "I didn't mean to imply that you visited Von Harmon in his room."

It took all Lana's willpower to keep her expression blank.

"Please send my condolences to Von Harmon's wife. No woman should experience the grief of losing a husband."

The rest of the dinner party passed in a blur. Lana was desperate to leave, but Natalia would be hurt if they didn't stay for the dancing. Lana noticed a Gestapo officer with short blond hair and was reminded of the portrait in Giselle's studio. Perhaps it had been of Hans. Maybe that was why Giselle never seemed to paint when Lana was around.

Finally, Guy collected their coats, and they walked down the steps to the convertible.

"Natalia outdid herself this time," Guy said, backing down the driveway. "God knows where she got the steak. It must have cost a mint."

"Brunner questioned me about Von Harmon, but I think I satisfied him," Lana said distractedly.

Guy's head turned abruptly.

"What did you say to Brunner?" Guy maneuvered around a bend.

"I told him that I wasn't feeling well at dinner and had to go home," she answered. "He believed me."

"Then tonight was a success on all fronts," Guy said, and smiled. "I learned the date and time of the raid on Old Town."

"How?" Lana asked.

"By hanging around the kitchen; it's the best place to be at Natalia's parties," he said. "I sample the entrées before anyone else and hear the gossip. One of the waiters warned the chef that there's going to be a raid on the streets above Old Town on Friday."

Would she have time to warn Sylvie? Could she get Sylvie and Odette to Algiers, then to England?

"That's in five days!" Lana's pulse quickened. "How will we stop it?"

"Don't worry, we have the map. Pierre and I will warn everyone, and the boat will leave on Thursday night. When Brunner and his men show up, all they'll find is empty houses."

"What if they're monitoring the homes? They'll be suspicious if everyone is gone."

"I thought of that." Guy nodded. "We'll ask residents to leave the lights on in case any German soldiers are patrolling the streets at night. And there'll still be enough foot traffic during the day so no one will grow suspicious."

"I'm going with you, it will be faster if we all work together."

"That's too dangerous." Guy shook his head. "With Von Harmon dead, you can't be seen anywhere that might be suspicious."

"What will I do?" she asked. "I feel useless staying at the villa."

"You can go to Giselle's for company," Guy suggested.

For a moment, Lana had forgotten about Giselle. She looked up at the night sky and wondered where Giselle was now. Perhaps the Germans had captured her too. Perhaps she was being interrogated as they spoke.

"Giselle is gone. I don't know if she's coming back."

"What do you mean, she's gone?"

Lana told Guy about her conversation with Natalia, despite Natalia's warning.

"That's what you were talking about with Natalia," Guy said when she finished.

"I feel terrible, I knew something was different about Giselle. The first time I visited she said she hadn't been with a man in years, but there was a humidor with an inscription in the living room. And she said she only painted still lifes, but I found a portrait of a man in her studio. And there were other things."

Guy pulled into the driveway of the villa and turned off the engine.

"What other things?" he inquired.

Lana told him that she thought Giselle had lied about going to Paris. There was the great-aunt who had died and the heart-shaped bracelet Giselle brought back from her trip.

Guy turned to Lana, and even in the dark she could see that he was concerned.

"An engraved humidor isn't so unusual. She could have picked it up anywhere. And why shouldn't Giselle buy herself a bracelet? We're at war, and there are hardly any men. She can't wait for a new lover to buy her jewelry."

"I suppose you're right." Lana felt a little better. "What do we do now?"

"We wait and hope she returns," Guy said. "The Gestapo are very hard on traitors. Some eager officer would take particular pleasure in torturing Hans's mistress. She wouldn't know of our activities, I think."

Lana pictured Giselle with her high cheekbones and delicate mouth locked in a cell, tortured for any scrap of information, and her breath constricted.

"I never mentioned the Resistance," Lana assured him. "She doesn't know what we are doing."

Guy looked at Lana. He drummed his fingers on the steering wheel.

"I hope you're right," he said. "A lot of Jews are counting on us to help them escape."

The next raid! She remembered her terror after the last raid; the German soldier stopping her at the dock, the fear that Guy might have been shot.

"What if the Gestapo come around and ask questions about Giselle? It could be dangerous for us and Pierre."

"We don't have a choice." Guy opened the car door. "If we don't stop the raid, dozens of Jews will be marched down the Promenade des Anglais to the train station and then to Drancy."

She followed him up the steps and prayed the mission would be successful. In a few days she and Guy would be eating a celebratory omelet in the villa's kitchen. Because right that minute, the future seemed as dark as the night sky.

Half an hour later, Lana was in the living room when the phone rang.

"Lana," a male voice said. "It's Charles Langford."

"Charles!" Lana exclaimed. "This is a surprise."

"I wanted to thank you and Guy for coming to the party in Menton. I hope you had a good time."

"It was lovely, thank you." Lana sat on the sofa.

"I'm calling because I'm having a Christmas party and wondered if you and Guy would come. It's going to be very festive."

They had just been to Charles's house. Would Guy agree to go to Menton again? He had helped Raoul across the border without incident; perhaps his view of Charles was softening.

"I'll have to ask Guy." She hesitated.

"Please say you'll come," Charles said. "It's very festive. I bring out all my parents' decorations. What's the point of Christmas if one doesn't celebrate it with friends?"

Lana couldn't think of an excuse to say no.

"I'd love to come." Lana twisted the phone. "And Guy will be there if he's available."

"Excellent. I'll call soon with the details." He was quiet for a moment. "I was going to ask Raoul Gunsbourg to perform a small concert, but he disappeared."

Lana's tongue felt as if it were glued to the roof of her mouth.

"Disappeared?"

"After the dinner party. No one knows where he went."

Lana swallowed and tried to sound uninterested. "That's odd," she said offhandedly. "I suppose you'll have to get someone else to perform."

"I don't know anyone who plays so beautifully. Hopefully he'll turn up." Charles's voice was cheerful. "It would be lovely to hear Brahms's lullabies at Christmas."

She hoped that Charles hadn't noticed the tremor in her voice.

Lana said goodbye and walked up the staircase. Her legs were stiff, and there was a pain in her neck.

She stripped off her evening gown and turned on the faucet in the bathroom. She wouldn't let herself think about it now. All she wanted was to submerge herself in bath salts and forget about the Riviera and the war.

Chapter Sixteen

NICE, DECEMBER 1943

Lana finished making her bed and walked to the balcony. The overnight rain had cleared, and the sun was bright. Guy had left that morning before she was awake. There were last-minute details to take care of before the raid, and she didn't know when he would return.

Lana tossed and turned all night thinking about Giselle. It must have been so lonely for Giselle to keep her relationship with Hans secret. She prayed that Giselle was safe.

She gathered her jacket and walked to the door. Right now she had to warn Sylvie about the raid on the streets above Old Town. Then she would worry about Giselle.

Lana parked her bicycle in the alley. A man with dark hair opened the door and peered outside.

"I was looking for Sylvie," Lana said, flustered.

"Sylvie isn't here." The man opened the door wider. "Please come in."

"Who are you? Lana asked, suddenly becoming frightened.

The house seemed even quieter than before.

The curtains were drawn, and there was a small box on the coffee table.

"My name is Gerard." He held out his hand. He was short and wore a brown sweater and slacks. "Please sit down."

"I'm Lana." Lana shook his hand.

Was this a trap?

"Where are Sylvie and Odette?" she asked.

"Odette is fine, she's upstairs." Gerard nodded.

Lana let out a sigh of relief. But he still hadn't told her what he was doing there.

"Will Sylvie be home soon?" she inquired.

"Would you like a cup of tea?" he asked. "There's a pot in the kitchen."

"No, thank you." She shook her head. Gerard's even tone and evasiveness made her nervous.

He sat opposite her and rubbed his hands.

"I'm the manager of the cabaret where Sylvie works," he said. "There was a raid last night."

"A raid!" Lana jumped up. "Where is Sylvie? Is she safe?"

Gerard bowed his head. When he looked up, there was a tear in his eye.

"I'm afraid not," he said quietly. "Sylvie is dead."

Lana sunk back onto the couch. She was afraid she was going to faint.

"But Sylvie can't be dead!" She steadied herself. "The Gestapo don't disturb the cabarets; they don't want to lose their entertainment."

"They hadn't until last night." Gerard sat next to her. "An hour before the show started, two Gestapo officers entered the nightclub and asked for the girls' papers. Someone may have told them that we had Jewish girls working there. I pretended to go to my office for the papers and ran to warn them. The other girls escaped through the back door, but Sylvie insisted on going to her dressing room." He handed her the box. "I found this in the drawer of her dressing table after the Gestapo officers left. Perhaps she had gone to retrieve it."

Lana opened it, and inside was Sylvie's wedding ring on top of a photo of Sylvie and Jacob with Odette.

"Sylvie never wore her wedding ring onstage." Gerard hung his head as if it were his fault. "I'm very sorry. Sylvie had a beautiful voice; she was the best girl I had."

"Oh, Sylvie!" Lana cried, and her heart beat wildly.

Odette had no family. There was no one to take care of her.

"Odette can stay with me for a few days," Gerard said, as if he could read her thoughts. "There's an orphanage in Lyon; someone in the cabaret will take her there."

Lana thought of the Jewish children at the convent in Paris. Sister Catherine had tried to hide them so that Brunner and his men wouldn't find them.

"That's very kind, but it won't be necessary." Lana regained her composure. "Odette can stay with me."

"Sylvie told me about you bringing Odette home after that woman's dog was shot. She was very grateful," Gerard said. "But this is different. You can't take care of Odette. You only knew Sylvie and Odette for a short time."

"It's true we hadn't known each other long," Lana acknowledged. "But Odette needs a family. She can't go to an orphanage. I live in a villa in Cap Ferrat. She'll be safe there."

Gerard was silent, thinking it over.

"I only want the best for Odette." He hesitated. "Taking in a Jewish child would be risky for both of you."

Lana stood up and smiled.

"What about if I go upstairs and ask her?"

Gerard nodded.

Odette was sitting on her bed when Lana opened the door. She threw herself against Lana, and her small body convulsed in sobs.

"Why did they shoot my mother? She didn't do anything wrong." Odette's voice was fierce.

"It had nothing to do with your mother," Lana offered. "Sometimes during a war, innocent people are killed. I told Gerard you could come with me. That is, if you want to."

"Go with you where?" Odette wondered.

"To the villa in Cap Ferrat," Lana answered.

"I can't leave," Odette said stubbornly. "All my mother's things are here."

"You can't stay here alone. I'll come back for her things. The important thing is to take you somewhere safe."

Odette was quiet as if she was thinking.

"My mother trusted you. She believed you cared about us."

Lana walked to the closet so Odette wouldn't see the tears in her eyes.

"Do you have a suitcase? We'll take your dresses and books."

"I don't need any of those things. I just want the box," Odette said.

"The box?" Lana turned around.

Odette stood up. "The box from my mother's dressing room."

For a moment Lana could see the young woman Odette would become: strong and brave and forever changed by the war.

"Of course, we'll take the box. I'll pack a few things, and we'll go downstairs."

Gerard offered to lend her his car so she could take Odette to the villa. She would return it later and come back for her bicycle. She felt a surge of relief when she drove through Old Town. But the minute they left Nice, Lana's courage wavered. She drove along the cliffs faster than ever before.

She pulled into the driveway of the villa and

Odette hopped out of the car. She gazed up at the stone facade and green lawn, and her mouth dropped open.

"It's like the movie star homes in magazines," she breathed.

"Not quite, but it's pretty." Lana smiled. "I'm afraid you won't be able to see the rooms. You must go straight to the attic. It will be safe up there, and we'll figure out what to do when Guy gets home."

"Who's Guy?" Odette scrunched her nose.

Lana gulped, and for the first time since Gerard had told her about Sylvie, she thought about Guy. What would he say when he discovered what she had done?

"Guy is the man who owns the villa. He's a good friend. But we must hurry, we don't want anyone to see us." Lana took Odette's hand and led her quickly inside.

A light bulb hung from the attic ceiling, and the walls were covered with faded wallpaper. Boxes stood in the corner and there was an armchair with frayed stuffing.

"I'll bring up some books," Lana said, trying to remain upbeat. "And a blanket and pillows from my bedroom."

"How long will I be here?" Odette asked uncertainly.

"I don't know," Lana said honestly. "Guy will have a plan."

She hoped that was true. Odette ran her small hand over the wallpaper.

"It's nice, but I want to be at home." Odette's voice was plaintive. "At least I could go downstairs and make my own meals. What will I do if I get hungry?"

"I'll fix a tray," Lana suggested. "There's bread and cheese and tomatoes. I'll make sandwiches for both of us, and we'll have a picnic."

"I'm tired of having indoor picnics." Odette started crying again. "I want to be a normal child who goes to school and plays with friends and comes home to dinner with her mother and father."

"I want that for you too," Lana breathed into her hair. "More than anything in the world."

Lana left Odette in the attic and went to the kitchen to make her something to eat. She heard footsteps and saw Guy standing in the doorway. His jacket was draped over his shoulder, and he carried a package.

Seeing his face, the bright eyes and angular cheeks, she realized how much she had missed him.

"You're home," she said happily.

"I brought you something. I went shopping and realized I don't know what kind of perfume you like. The saleswoman asked me to describe you. I said you are a modern woman who can take care of herself but there are parts of you that you don't reveal. And when you're wearing an evening gown with a cape draped around your shoulders, you're the most mesmerizing woman in the room." He placed three perfume bottles on the table. "She suggested Je Reviens by Worth if you want something romantic, Joy by Jean Patou if you appreciate a floral scent, or Shalimar if you prefer something exotic."

Lana examined the bottles and felt a catch in her throat.

"I couldn't decide, so I bought all three. I also got this in case you don't like any of them." He reached into the bag and brought out a box of chocolates. "It's impossible not to like pralines."

"I love all of it," Lana said hoarsely. "But why?"

Guy took her in his arms. He kissed her tentatively, and she kissed him back.

"I know you were worried about Giselle," he began. "Resistance work can be overwhelming. There's so much responsibility with no room for error." He stroked her cheek. "I didn't want you to forget that you're a desirable woman. And a woman who deserves pretty things."

"I am worried about Giselle. I hope she isn't in trouble," Lana said, opening the bottle of Shalimar. The scent reminded her of her mother. Her mother's perfume always preceded her when she entered a room. "Thank you, I'll wear all of them. It was very thoughtful."

Guy pulled out a chair and sat down.

"You made two sandwiches." He waved at the counter.

Lana turned, and her heart beat a little faster. "The sandwich isn't for you, it's for Odette."

"Who is Odette?" Guy asked.

"I told you about Odette, Sylvie's daughter," Lana said nervously. "They're the Jewish family who live on Rue Droit. Odette's father was killed by German soldiers more than a month ago."

Guy's eyes darkened, and he stepped back.

"What is Odette doing here?"

"Her mother was shot and killed last night. Odette's in the attic."

Lana told him about her visits to Odette and the Gestapo showing up at the nightclub. When she was finished, Guy started toward the staircase. His jaw was clenched and lines formed on his forehead.

"Where are you going?" Lana demanded.

"To take Odette to the orphanage."

"You can't do that! Her mother was murdered."

"That's what orphanages are for." Guy's voice was clipped.

Lana's mind went to Brunner when he discovered Esther Cohen hiding in the piano at the convent. Frederic gave his own life to protect her. An orphanage wouldn't be safe for Odette.

"You can't take her to an orphanage," Lana

pleaded. "Odette is Jewish, she'll be sent to a camp."

"She can't stay here," Guy insisted. "The last thing we need is a Jewish child in the attic."

"Why not?" Lana said boldly. "You check the house for bugs, and no one saw us coming inside."

"You don't know for sure." Guy shook his head. "German soldiers are everywhere. Someone could have seen you and Odette leaving Old Town."

Lana had been in such a hurry, she hadn't checked if anyone followed them.

"It doesn't matter," she said stubbornly. "Odette is too upset, she can't go to the orphanage."

Guy thought for a long time.

"The escape of the Jews in Old Town takes place in three days. Pierre will take Odette on the boat to Algiers, and from there she'll go to England. You must see that's the only choice. If she stays here, we're all in danger."

Lana debated what to do. She could go with Odette, but then she would be letting down Henri and Guy and Pierre.

"Odette doesn't know anyone in England," Lana said. She thought about Bernadette. But Bernadette was a child, and Lana knew nothing about her family. And a letter could take weeks to reach her. "She's twelve years old. What will she do?"

"I have a contact there," Guy replied. "He can arrange for her to stay with a family. Many families are accepting Jewish orphans."

Odette would be safer in England. After the war, if they survived, Lana could collect her.

Lana heard a car outside and froze. The car kept going, and she let out her breath. Guy was right. Sending Odette to England was the best option.

"All right," she agreed. "But she's staying here until then."

Lana finished making the sandwiches and took Guy to the attic to meet Odette.

Odette sat in the chair, her arms circling her knees.

"You must be Guy." Odette rose and held out her hand. "Thank you for letting me stay in your house. I know it's dangerous with me being Jewish."

Lana expected Guy to say it was only for three nights, but he simply returned Odette's handshake.

"I'm sorry that you're in the attic, but we don't want anyone to see you."

"I'm used to it." Odette shrugged. "When the war ends, I'll have to do a lot of living." She lifted her shoulders. "To make up for everything my parents will miss."

They ate the sandwiches, and Odette curled up to take a nap. Guy left to run errands, and Lana sat in the living room.

The tray sat on the coffee table. Lana remembered how she used to bring a tray to the living room while Frederic practiced piano. She'd curl up on the sofa with a cup of tea, and he'd take bites of a sandwich between concertos. Now she cared for Guy and Odette in the same way. It was hard to imagine that Frederic would never meet Odette, that he knew nothing about her work in the Resistance.

The phone rang, and she picked it up.

"Lana, sweetheart." Her mother's voice came down the line. "I've missed talking to you. I wanted to see if you're all right."

"It has been too long; I've been busy," Lana answered. "You sound upset, is anything wrong?"

"Jacques was arrested and taken to the police station."

"Arrested!" Lana's pulse quickened.

"It was frightening. Jacques was at the store, and a Jewish man was accused of stealing a box of cigars. Jacques defended him, and German soldiers took him to the police station. I had to go down with his Cartier watch and convince them to let him go."

"You bribed an official!" Lana exclaimed. "You could have been thrown in prison too."

"I could tell by his silk handkerchief that he wasn't opposed to bribes. I'm just relieved Jacques is home." Tatiana paused. "How is the Riviera?"

"Every day there is something new." Lana pondered. Odette's comment about living stuck in her head. "It feels so odd that Frederic is gone. So many things happen that he'll never experience. I worry that I'll forget him."

"I know how you feel," her mother agreed. "When I first arrived in Paris, I found a Russian tearoom that sold your father's favorite cakes. Once a week I'd go and sit by myself. I couldn't even afford a coffee, but just sitting at the table and seeing the glass case filled with the *moloko* cakes and poppy seed *sushki* he loved brought him closer."

Lana pictured her mother sitting serenely in a noisy tearoom.

"Don't tell Jacques, but I still go there sometimes." Her mother's voice tinkled. "Now I don't eat the blintzes because they're bad for my waistline."

They wrapped up their conversation and said their goodbyes.

Lana noticed Odette's suitcase standing in the entry. She had brought it in from Gerard's car and left it there when they went to explore the attic. On top of it was a packet of Odette's letters to Bernadette. Lana opened one and went to stand by the window.

Dear Bernadette,

I don't have much to report, but I wanted

to write to you anyway. Every night my mother performs at the cabaret, and I am home alone. I don't mind too much. I have The Jungle Book Lana gave me for company. My mother has a voice like Edith Piaf. When I was younger I wanted to be a singer, but now I'm not so sure. She hates working at night because she can't sit with me before bed.

I don't think I'll be a chef like my father either. For a while I wanted to be a doctor. But what if a patient was sick and I couldn't save him? I'm tired of people dying. I want to do something that brings people together. Maybe I'll work as a translator so people from different countries can read one another's books. You must have someone who will translate my letters. Our teacher was going to translate the letters from our pen pals, but I can't go to school anymore. I'll figure out a way to read them. And I'll learn so much about life in England. Isn't that the important thing? That people of all nationalities learn to communicate with one another. If that happens, maybe there won't be another war.

What do you want to be when you grow up?

Your friend, Odette

Lana folded the paper and slipped it in the envelope. Odette must have written it before Sylvie died. What would it feel like to be Odette? To have no one left and worry about the future every day?

She rustled through Guy's albums and found a record of Chopin's sonatas. She placed it on the phonograph and sat on the sofa. The room filled with the lilting melody, and she pictured Odette huddled in the attic. She thought about Frederic giving Vivienne piano lessons, and the baby who would have grown up to appreciate music like Frederic. Then she put her head in her hands and cried.

Chapter Seventeen

NICE, DECEMBER 1943

Lana spent the next morning making the attic more comfortable for Odette. She took up a lamp and small table. They ate porridge for breakfast, and Lana found notepaper and a pen so Odette could write to Bernadette.

After they finished breakfast and Odette was content with her books, Lana went to Giselle's to feed the chickens. She didn't know when Giselle would return. At least she could make sure her chickens were fed.

The smell of smoke greeted her when she entered Giselle's gate, and Lana was afraid something had caught fire. The door was slightly ajar, and she walked toward the living room. Giselle, shoulders hunched, sat on the sofa. A cigarette case rested on the coffee table.

"You're here!" Lana exclaimed in surprise. "I didn't mean to barge in, I thought you were away. I came to feed the chickens. I didn't know you were home."

Giselle glanced up. There were dark circles under her eyes; her normally glossy skin looked translucent.

"Thank you, that's very kind. I've never seen

the chickens look so content.” Giselle smiled thinly. “I’ll have enough eggs until New Year’s.”

Lana was silent. There were so many things she wanted to ask Giselle. She didn’t know where to begin.

“Would you like a cigarette?” Giselle waved at the cigarette case.

“No, thank you.” Lana shook her head. “I only smoke at parties.”

“I gave it up for years. My fingers turned yellow, and I developed a cough. But I started again about a month ago.” She inhaled deeply. “The war will do that to you. What does it matter if you have a bad habit when the world has gone mad?”

Lana looked at Giselle. She wasn’t sure how she felt. She was relieved that Giselle was safe, and angry that Giselle kept so many secrets at the same time.

“I was at a party at the Petrikoffs’ and Natalia told me about your German lover. You lied about not having a man in your life, and you lied about being in Paris.”

“Natalia! She always has the best gossip.” Giselle let out a little laugh. She looked at Lana, and her eyes were wide. “I didn’t mean to lie to you, but it was so nice to have a friend. You can’t imagine what it’s been like the last few months.”

Lana remembered that Odette was waiting at the villa.

"You shouldn't have lied," she said abruptly. "And I was worried about you. I thought you had been captured."

"Natalia has great gossip, but it's not always true. Hans wasn't my lover. I am not a traitor."

"Then what was he?" Lana asked. "Why do you have a humidor box engraved with his initials? And why didn't you tell me you were in Berlin?"

"I should have told you," Giselle acknowledged. "But you have to believe me: I've done nothing wrong. Hans and I were childhood sweethearts. We grew up together in Strasbourg, near the German border," Giselle began. "When Hans was twelve he gave me a promise ring and said we'd be together forever. A few years later he joined the Hitler Youth. All the local boys were doing it; it made him feel useful.

"In 1938, Hans was invited to become a member of the Gestapo. He thought it would be safer than fighting in the German army if there was a war." She paused. "Strasbourg was in France but controlled by the Germans. He was afraid there would be a draft and he'd be sent to fight the Russians.

"Hans moved to Berlin, and I stayed behind. At first we visited each other, but I started hearing what the Gestapo was doing—burning shops and herding Jews into ghettos. I told Hans he had to choose between me and the Gestapo."

Giselle took out another cigarette. She fumbled

with the lighter, and Lana noticed her hands were shaking.

"Hans chose the Gestapo, and I moved to Paris. I didn't have any training, so I became an artist's model." She smiled weakly. "I always loved anything to do with painting. The pay was minimal, so I took a lover. Armand was an officer in the Free French army." She flicked ashes into the ashtray. "He was killed in North Africa and left me a safe-deposit box with enough gold and jewelry to start a new life.

"So I came to the Riviera. I didn't lie to you about not wanting a man in my life. All I wanted was to paint and enjoy the sunshine. But then Hans showed up a few months ago. I almost didn't recognize him. His hair was long, and he was so thin; I could see his rib cage.

"I had no idea Hans would do anything like plant a bomb until after it happened. He told me about the failed assassination attempt and asked me to hide him. He believed Hitler was going to destroy Europe and had to be stopped. What was I to do?" Giselle asked plaintively. "I couldn't send him away; he'd be killed. I let him stay in the studio and tried to figure out a way to get him over the Alps. Then the Germans arrived, and the escape routes were cut off. You don't know how desperate I became. I was afraid to leave the house. Even going to the market in Nice was agonizing.

"A month ago Hans received a letter from a

childhood friend in Strasbourg. It was addressed to me. Hans had given him the address; he was certain his friend would help him. He offered to get him papers. It was just before you arrived on the Riviera. I warned him it could be a trap, but he swore his friend could be trusted," she said slowly. "I don't know, maybe he really believed that. He was going stir-crazy; he always had to be doing something."

"Natalia's friend heard a story that you were in Berlin," Lana cut in. "What were you doing there? Why did you say you were in Paris?"

"I was afraid you'd ask questions. It was easier if I said I was in Paris," Giselle answered. "I heard on the radio that an accomplice in the assassination attempt had been caught. I knew it was Hans. I was afraid there might be things in his apartment." She waved her hand. "Photos of us and old love letters."

Lana pictured Giselle going through memorabilia and winced. Once Giselle and Hans hadn't been a man and a woman on opposite sides of a war. They were teenagers planning a life together. Giselle seemed older than Lana because she was sophisticated and worldly, but they were only a few years apart.

"And where did you go now?" she asked. "You didn't tell me you were leaving again."

"I went to his mother's house in Strasbourg." Giselle swallowed.

"To Strasbourg!" Lana said in alarm. "What if his parents alerted the authorities? The Gestapo could have followed you here."

"No one knew I was there. Hans's father is dead, and his mother was at work. Even if I didn't approve of Hans's activities, he was a good son. I had to give his mother his belongings; it was all she had left of him."

Giselle stubbed the cigarette into the ashtray. She took out another cigarette and looked at Lana.

"You've been a wonderful friend, and I felt terrible for lying to you," Giselle finished. "If there is any way I can repay you, just ask."

Lana thought for a moment. She had to return Gerard's car, and she had promised Odette she would collect Sylvie's things. But she couldn't do that on her bicycle.

"There is something. I need to run a few errands later today. Is it all right if I use your car?"

"Keep it for as long as you like," Giselle said with a little smile. "But think of something important I can do. You can't understand how I feel. I'm tired of this war, and I'm tired of hiding."

Later in the afternoon, Lana picked up a box of Sylvie's belongings from the house on Rue Droit. She stopped at a creamery on Rue Saint-François de Paule to get cheeses for Guy and Odette. As she left the creamery, a male voice called her name. Alois Brunner stood across the street.

"Countess Antanova." He joined her. "This is a pleasant surprise."

Lana arranged the shopping bag so that it hid Sylvie's box.

"Captain Brunner, what a pleasure." She greeted him. "What are you doing here?"

Captain Brunner pointed at the creamery.

"The same thing you are. This creamery sells the best Camembert in Nice," he said. "When I was in Paris I grew quite fond of French cheeses."

Lana glanced down at her packages.

"I don't know for how much longer," she said with a smile. "With all the new rationing, soon one won't be able to find small luxuries like fresh cheese anywhere on the Riviera."

Brunner's eyes danced. He stepped closer, and Lana had to stop herself from moving away.

"You can always come to me," he offered. "I'd never let Countess Antanova go hungry."

"That's very kind of you." She nodded. "If you'll excuse me, I have to go. Guy is waiting for me."

"It's nice to see two people care about each other," Brunner reflected. "I'm happy to have run into you. I'm having a New Year's party. I'd like you and Guy to come."

Lana swallowed. First Charles invited them to his Christmas party, and now they were receiving an invitation from Brunner. The whole point of Lana's mission on the Riviera was to be invited to parties. Yet, she couldn't help but feel that Brunner's invitation was a summons.

"A New Year's party," she repeated.

"I'll be in Berlin over Christmas, but I'll return in January. It will be at the Hôtel Excelsior." He eyed her carefully. "Your calendar can't be full so far out. You must come."

The box with Sylvie's things seemed so heavy; all she wanted was to get away.

"Of course, we'd be delighted." She nodded.

"Excellent." Brunner beamed. "I look forward to our next encounter, Countess Antanova." He clicked his heels. "It's always a delight."

Lana waited until Brunner entered the creamery. Then she hurried down the street to Giselle's car.

The drive to Cap Ferrat seemed to take forever. Lana could barely control her thoughts. Had Brunner seen her at Sylvie's house and followed her to the creamery? Was he surveying the neighborhood in preparation for the raid on Friday?

By the time she arrived at the villa, she had convinced herself that the Gestapo had taken Odette. She raced up the front steps and flung open the door. She heard voices and ran to the attic.

Guy and Odette sat across from each other on a

blanket. A backgammon board lay between them, and there were two empty plates.

"Lana!" Odette's eyes sparkled and her brow was creased in concentration. "Guy taught me how to play backgammon. If I win, I get a macaron."

"The macaron was delicious, but I can't eat anymore." Guy rubbed his stomach. "I'll get fat."

Lana opened her mouth to say something, but the words didn't come. Tears filled her eyes and she sunk onto the ground.

"Why don't we get one now?" Guy noticed her expression and turned to Odette. "We'll be right back."

Lana followed Guy downstairs to the kitchen.

"Did something happen?" he asked.

Lana told him about Giselle and her run-in with Alois Brunner.

"I was afraid the Gestapo might have come to the villa," she finished. "Then I saw you together and I . . ."

Guy poured a shot of brandy and handed it to her.

"Here, drink this. You had a shock."

"I know it was wrong to collect Sylvie's things," she said. The brandy steadied her nerves, and she felt better. "But I promised Odette. It's all she has left of her mother."

"It was risky," Guy said thoughtfully. "But it's done, and you're safe."

"That's the thing: no one is safe!" Her voice was frantic. "When Frederic died, Henri asked me to join the Resistance and I thought it was the perfect chance to help others. But what if my mother is being watched because of me? And if Brunner finds out I was friends with a Jewish woman, we could all be in danger." She took another sip. "I'm like a tightrope walker at the circus. But if I fall, it's not just me who gets hurt. I'll take everyone down with me."

Lana clutched the glass and paced to the window.

"That's what war is." Guy crossed the kitchen and touched her arm. "We could be buying fish at the market and get blown up by a bomb," he reflected. "Think of all the good you've done. Because of you, the raid on the Hôtel Atlantic didn't happen. And now you've gained the respect of the officer in charge of the Riviera. Who knows how that will help the Resistance? Not to mention what you've done for Odette. You gave her love and attention and shelter when she would have been alone."

Lana sipped the brandy and let Guy's words soothe her. He had never spoken so warmly.

"I already told you what you've done for me." He took her hands.

"For you?" She looked into his eyes.

"You and I share similar stories. There's not a day that I don't miss Aimee: The way she danced to the phonograph. How her hand felt in mine. But what you experienced was just as bad: you watched your husband being murdered and then you lost your unborn child.

"You could have moved into your mother's flat and let her take care of you. Instead, you accepted Henri's offer and came to the Riviera. You haven't been afraid to do anything. From the moment I saw you slicing tomatoes in my kitchen, you've made me want to be a better man."

Lana remembered the first time she saw Guy, with his tan skin and white shirt, like some kind of bronze god.

"I was so angry at you." She laughed. "I thought you stood me up for no reason."

Guy wrapped his arms around her and kissed her.

"You're not angry anymore," he whispered.

"No, I'm not," she conceded. He pulled her close, and suddenly she needed him to make love to her.

"I want you," Guy echoed her thoughts.

"I want you too." Lana leaned into him. "But we can't. Odette is waiting for a macaron."

"She can wait a little longer," Guy whispered.

Guy took her hand, and they climbed the staircase to his bedroom. Lana wondered whether Odette would worry if Lana didn't return to the attic. But then she felt the heat of Guy's body next to hers and her thoughts slipped away. They wouldn't be gone long, and they had to enjoy each other while they could. Who knew what the next day would bring.

Chapter Eighteen

NICE, DECEMBER 1943

Lana was a bundle of nerves the day before the planned escape from Old Town. Guy had gone to Marseille to get supplies for the boat, and she spent her time with Odette and drinking endless cups of tea.

Somehow it felt different from the last time they helped Jews escape. Then she didn't know what to expect. Now she knew how many things could go wrong: there could be another disturbance at the dock, or the boat could spring a leak.

Lana tried to contain her anxiety, but Odette could sense something was off. She read the same story in *The Jungle Book* twice, and she forgot to cut the orange she brought to the attic for Odette's breakfast.

Her biggest worry was how to tell Odette that she was being sent to England to live with strangers. Odette was beginning to trust her. How would she feel when Lana put her on the boat and said they wouldn't stay together for the war after all?

There was a knock at the front door, and Lana opened it.

Pierre stood on the porch. His scarf was wrapped around his neck, and he wore a fisherman's sweater.

"Pierre, come in." She ushered him inside.

"I'm sorry if I'm disturbing you." Pierre followed her into the living room.

"I'm happy to see you." She waved at the tea set on the coffee table. "Would you like some tea? My mother always drank tea to calm her nerves, but it's not doing any good."

"My father was a coffee drinker. He drank it from the moment he woke up until his last fare of the day." Pierre sat on an armchair. "It was the only way to keep alert while he was driving the taxi."

"Too much coffee makes me anxious." She poured a cup for Pierre. "Is your cold gone? You can't drive the boat if you're sick."

"I'm much better." He accepted the cup. "But there might not be a boat. Guy called, and he's still in Marseille."

"He was supposed to be on his way back." She sat opposite him.

"He discovered a new trouble with the engine. He stopped at the repair shop in Marseille, but they don't have the right part. I could hear Guy swearing at the guy in charge from the other end of the phone." Pierre chuckled.

"It has to be ready!" Lana panicked. "We can't do anything without a boat."

"He wanted me to come and tell you myself.

He's afraid the phone in the villa might be bugged."

She was about to tell Pierre about Odette but changed her mind. The fewer people who knew Odette was hidden in the attic, the safer for everyone. Pierre would meet Odette when Lana brought her to the boat.

She remembered something Giselle said the day they met.

"I have an idea." She stood up. "Meet me at the dock tomorrow night at nine p.m."

"But what good will that do without a boat?" Pierre was puzzled.

For the first time since Sylvie's death, she felt in control. She put down her teacup and smiled.

"Who said there wouldn't be a boat?"

Pierre left and Lana finished her tea. She was clearing the tea tray when she heard a knock on the door. She thought Pierre had forgotten something and opened it.

Charles Langford stood outside, his car parked in the driveway. He carried a basket.

"Charles! This is a surprise."

"A good one, I hope." He handed her the basket. "I brought you some lemons from the market in Menton."

Charles followed her inside. She remembered their last phone conversation, when he invited them to his Christmas party, his mention that

Raoul Gunsbourg had disappeared, and she tried to hide her nervousness.

"I hope you didn't come all the way to Cap Ferrat to bring me lemons," she said lightly.

"It's not that far." Charles shrugged and looked around the living room. "What a lovely room. Do you mind if I sit down?"

Lana gulped. If Charles sat down that meant he would stay for a while. But if she was rude he might get suspicious.

"Of course." She nodded. "I was having tea."

He sat on the sofa and his expression turned serious.

"I didn't come only to deliver lemons, I came to thank you."

"For what?" she asked as she poured another cup of tea.

"Raoul Gunsbourg is safely in Switzerland, and I have a fairly good idea how he got there."

The teaspoon she was using clattered to the floor. Lana picked it up, ignoring Charles's gaze.

"I'd been trying to get Raoul across the border for weeks," he explained. "A man his age couldn't even consider going over the Alps. The Monte Carlo opera owes you a big debt of gratitude."

Lana walked to the window. What if this was a trick? Maybe Guy was right and Charles was a German spy trying to discover how Raoul escaped.

“I don’t know what you’re talking about.” She turned around.

Charles eyed her appreciatively. “When we met on the train I thought you were simply a pretty girl on holiday. Then you showed up at the casino with Guy and I asked myself if I was wrong. I’ve often wondered what Guy is really doing on the Riviera.” He was silent for a moment. “It’s only when I saw you get into Pierre’s taxi that I knew I was right.”

“Pierre?” Lana repeated.

“I was friends with Pierre’s father years ago. Louis was one of the first people I met when my parents started coming to the Riviera.” Charles warned, “Louis knew what Hitler was capable of and what was happening to the Jews.

“We thought up a plan. He’d hide Jews in the trunk to get them to my villa. Then I’d form groups to smuggle them over the Alps to Italy. Then Louis was killed and Pierre took over the operation. It worked until last September. The Germans cracked down and all the escape routes were cut off.”

Lana was about to say something but Guy’s warning reverberated in her head.

“You have your information wrong.” Lana’s cheeks were hot. “I met Guy in Switzerland years ago. He’s a successful businessman who bought a villa on the Riviera. Your parents bought a house here: you must understand the attraction. Why shouldn't I live with him? I'm not the first young woman to fall for an older man. And I met Pierre at the train station. He's a good tour guide, and he doesn't try to cheat me by charging outrageous fares."

Charles smoothed the crease in his slacks and looked at Lana pleasantly.

"You wouldn't be as smart as I think you are if you didn't say that. But you can ask Pierre himself. I didn't come to accuse you of anything, I came to help."

"What do you mean?" Lana asked.

"Lana, you know how ruthless the Gestapo can be. You saw what it was like in Paris; Parisians live in terror. Now the Riviera is crawling with Gestapo officers, they're at the casino and at parties." Charles reflected. "Please be careful. And if you ever need a place to stay, my villa is open to you."

"That's very kind." Lana walked back toward the sofa to indicate that it was time to part. "But the only thing I'm guilty of is enjoying the beautiful scenery and mild climate."

She stopped herself from saying anything else. It wasn't a good idea to let Charles leave angry. It was better that they remain on good terms.

"Your company included," she said warmly. "You've been so kind since we met on the train."

Charles followed her to the entry.

"I feel the same about you." He held out his

hand. “Take care of yourself and remember, you can trust me.”

Charles left, and Lana took the tea tray into the kitchen. Why hadn’t Pierre mentioned that he had worked with Charles? But wasn’t that the point of the Resistance? The only way to keep others safe was by not saying anything at all.

She placed the tray on the counter and locked the door behind her. There was no time to think about Charles now. She had to find a boat. Odette and Pierre and all the innocent Jews in Old Town depended on her.

“Lana, it’s nice to see you,” Giselle said when Lana turned up at her door. “I was painting. It feels good to hold a paintbrush instead of a cigarette.”

Lana followed Giselle into the living room. The curtains were open, and the room was flooded with winter sun.

“I won’t stay long,” Lana began. “The other day you said you wanted to do something that was important.”

“I meant it.” Giselle nodded.

“What if I needed your help with something but couldn’t tell you why?” Lana asked.

“It would sound like the plot of an espionage movie.” Giselle laughed. Her face grew serious, and she lowered her voice. “I’ll do anything you say without asking questions.”

"Do you remember when we met, you said everyone in Cap Ferrat is so friendly they leave their spare keys where their neighbors could find them?"

"You want to break into someone's house?" Giselle asked incredulously.

Lana sat on the sofa and crossed her legs. She looked at Giselle thoughtfully.

"I don't want to steal anything. I need to borrow a boat."

Giselle sat across from her. She wiped her hands on her smock. Her eyebrows shot up and she leaned against the cushions.

"What kind of boat?" she asked curiously.

A smile played around Lana's mouth. She sat forward and said conspiratorially, "One that could squeeze a few dozen people aboard. I thought maybe you'd know someone who had one."

"You want to enter someone's house and take the keys to their boat?" Giselle repeated.

"It sounds even crazier than it did in my head." Lana stood up and walked to the entry. "Never mind, I should go."

"Lana, wait." Giselle stopped her. "I know where we can find keys to a boat."

"Where?" Lana asked.

Giselle pulled off her smock and picked up her car keys. "I'll show you."

Lana couldn't have been more surprised when they approached the Petrikoffs' villa. It looked even more imposing in the daytime. The marble fountain bubbled, and the lawn glinted in the afternoon light.

"We can't come here," Lana hissed. "Natalia knows Hans was hanged for the assassination attempt. She could have you arrested."

"She's not going to see me." Giselle stopped the car. "While you pay her a visit, I'm going to sneak into the garage. That's where they keep the key to the yacht."

"What if someone sees you?" Lana hesitated.

"It's five o'clock. The cook will be preparing dinner, and the maid will be turning down the beds," Giselle said. "If we're lucky, Boris will be at the casino. He loves to gamble, he's almost never at home except for their parties."

"And if we're not lucky?"

Giselle slouched down so she couldn't be seen. "Then we'll both be in a lot of trouble."

Lana walked up the steps and knocked on the door. Water trickled through the fountain, and the air smelled of damp grass.

"Lana! What are you doing here?" Natalia stood in the entry. She wore a turban around her head and a silk hostess gown.

"I should have called." Lana handed her a bunch of flowers. "I was out for a drive and thought I'd see if you were home."

"These are lovely, thank you." Natalia accepted the flowers and peered outside. "Is Guy with you?"

"Guy is out of town; I borrowed a friend's car," Lana answered. "Guy is why I'm here. I need your advice."

"Please come in. I just finished getting a massage." Natalia opened the door wider. "Getting older is so depressing. These days, a massage is the most satisfying thing I do lying down."

Lana followed her into the living room. The space seemed even grander without party guests. Paintings in gold frames hung on the walls, and two borzois slept with their noses buried in the rug.

"Tell me what's wrong." Natalia sunk onto an armchair. "You both looked so happy at the party."

"We are happy." Lana sat opposite her. "Guy is kind and considerate. It's just . . ." She pretended to blush.

"You want him to marry you." Natalia finished her sentence. "Independence for a young woman is fine, but one day you'll notice the lines under your eyes and wonder how to keep his interest."

"That's it exactly." Lana nodded, following Natalia's lead. "Guy hasn't mentioned marriage, and I don't know what to do."

Natalia tapped her cigarette holder on the coffee table.

"Let me tell you a story. Once there was a young woman in Saint Petersburg. She was so beautiful she could have any man she wanted, but there was only one who caught her eye. He was different from the young men at parties with their fair good looks and expensive wardrobes. This man had dark curly hair and large brown eyes. And he always wore the same frayed sweater and slacks.

"A winter went by, and they fell in love." Natalia paused. "She pretended that she sprained her ankle so her parents wouldn't force her to attend balls. They spent their time in his university room. By the spring she was sure he was going to propose. She invited him to her family's dacha on the Baltic Sea that summer. He said he'd follow her.

"She waited for weeks, and he never came." Natalia inhaled her cigarette. "In autumn, she returned to Saint Petersburg and he was gone. His room had been let, and there was no forwarding address.

"She was so devastated that she married the next man who proposed: a cousin of the czar named Boris Petrikoff. But she never forgot the dark-haired student."

"What happened to him?" Lana asked curiously.

Natalia started as if she had forgotten Lana was there.

"I ran into him years later in Paris. He didn't ask me to marry him because he was Jewish."

"Did you know?" Lana wondered.

"I knew, but it never bothered me." She shrugged. "If only I had told him it didn't matter to me. Perhaps there's a reason Guy hasn't asked you to marry him."

"I don't know what it could be." Lana frowned.

"Tell him how you feel," Natalia instructed. "Love can conquer many obstacles, but you have to be honest. You don't want to end up with a head full of memories when you can have the real thing."

Lana said goodbye and hurried to the car, where Giselle was crouched on the floor of the passenger seat. Lana drove away.

"Did you get it?" she asked as they turned onto the road.

Giselle sat up and produced the key.

"You did!" Lana exclaimed as relief flooded through her. She pressed harder on the gas pedal, and the car sailed along the road.

"You're going to steal a yacht," Giselle said gaily. Her scarf blew in the breeze and she held on to her hat.

"I'm not stealing it; I'm borrowing it," Lana corrected.

"Whatever you're doing, you made me feel as if I'm part of something," Giselle said.

Giselle seemed young and carefree, as if a weight had been lifted from her shoulders.

"You can't know how happy that makes me."

Lana walked back from Giselle's to the villa. Guy still hadn't returned, and she was growing anxious. What if it wasn't just a new engine for the boat that was keeping him away; what if something happened to him?

She couldn't put it off any longer. She had decided she was going to tell Odette about the boat that would take her to England. The door to the attic was slightly open, and Lana hurried up the stairs.

Odette was crouched in front of the little table. The lamp was on, and there was a stack of envelopes.

"Lana, you're here." Odette glanced up. "I didn't hear you come up the stairs."

"It looks like you're busy." Lana waved at the notepaper.

"I'm writing to Bernadette. I didn't think I'd have anything to say, but I can't stop writing."

"What are you writing about?" Lana asked.

"Lots of things. Mainly about being afraid."

"Afraid of what?" Lana asked.

"People say that war makes you brave, but they're wrong. My mother was afraid of everything—of my father getting arrested at work, of German soldiers knocking at our door, of me getting shot in the street."

"Your mother was afraid because she loved you and your father," Lana corrected. "She couldn't bear the idea of anything happening to you."

"Don't you see, that makes it worse." Odette

pulled at her braids. “I can’t love anyone, because then I’ll be afraid of losing them.”

“That’s not how life works,” Lana said. “Many things last forever. My neighbor in Paris and her husband have been married for forty years. They start each day the same way. Lisette makes omelets while Victor reads the newspaper out loud.”

“It’s different during war. Everyone I love is gone.” Odette’s eyes filled with tears. “I’m only twelve years old. My parents will never know anything about the rest of my life; it will be as if they never existed.”

Lana remembered her mother saying that she had kept Nicolai in her life by eating his favorite cakes at the Russian tearoom. Would it help Odette to tell her that she lost her own father?

“My father died before I was born,” Lana said. “He was killed by the Bolsheviks during the Russian Civil War.”

Odette was quiet, letting the revelation sink in.

“You never had a father?” She looked at Lana.

“My mother escaped to Paris when she was pregnant. But she talked about him and showed me pictures,” Lana answered. “I always felt he was part of my life. My mother is married again now, but she still does things to remember him. His presence never goes away.”

Odette seemed to look at Lana with a new respect.

"My father and I did everything together. Every Sunday before the occupation, we'd go to a patisserie and try a different dessert. He always made me take the first bite so I could give him my opinion." She rolled her eyes. "As if it mattered. He was a pastry chef, and I was a child."

"Sylvie and Jacob will always be with you." Lana hugged her.

"I was feeling sorry for myself," Odette said thoughtfully. "But I had years with my parents; you didn't have any time with your father."

"I knew he would have loved me, and I loved him back," Lana said. "You can't be afraid of love. Whether it lasts a few hours or decades, it's the greatest part of life."

Lana's mind drifted to her wedding with Frederic: her bouquet of lilies and the wedding lunch with her mother and Jacques. For a moment she thought about Guy—not his easy charm or even his body on top of hers, but the way he made her feel bright and alive. It almost came as a shock. Could she be falling in love with Guy?

Odette looked up at Lana. Her eyes were clear, and her skin didn't seem so pale.

"Thank you for bringing me here," Odette said. "Guy says he has a phonograph with lots of records. Maybe he will bring it to the attic so I can listen to my mother's favorite songs. And one day if the Germans leave, I can go downstairs and see the kitchen. The kitchen was my father's favorite room; he said that's where people were happiest."

Lana couldn't tell Odette about the boat now. Odette was just learning how to live without her parents. Guy was being kind to her, and she felt safe and secure in the attic. It would make her feel as if she was losing everything. Lana couldn't bear seeing Odette unhappy again so soon. It wouldn't do any harm to tell her tomorrow.

"Why don't I prepare a snack while you finish your letter?" Lana waved at Odette's writing utensils. "All the talk about cakes made me hungry."

Lana and Odette ate fruit and cheese, and then Lana went to her room. Odette had given her the latest letter and she unfolded it.

> Dear Bernadette,
>
> I have some terrible news. A few days ago, my mother was shot and killed. I'm an orphan now. When I was younger sometimes I'd see orphans from the convent shopping with the nuns in the outdoor market. I thought it must be fun, to sleep in a dormitory with all your friends, to eat meals around a big noisy table. But I've only been an orphan for a few days, and I already know I was wrong.
>
> Being an orphan means there is no one to love you. Do you think that's why

Hitler keeps killing the Jews? So that the children left behind become starved of love? You need love to survive. The plants in the living room died when I forgot to water them, and my father said they need love and attention to thrive. I said I wasn't afraid of dying, but I was wrong. There's so much I want to see and do, and being dead is forever.

For now I'm staying with Lana, but I can't live here because the Germans might find me. I suppose I'll go to an orphanage, but I bet it won't be the fun that I imagined. I hope I can write to you from there. You're one of the few people I'm still in contact with who knew me before the war. From now on I'll be poor Odette Wasserstein, whose parents were shot by the Germans.

Your friend, Odette

Lana folded the letter. She wished Frederic were here to tell her how to ease Odette's pain.

"I'm doing the best I can, Frederic," she said out loud.

She thought again of Odette arriving in England all alone. But there was nothing else Lana could do. She slipped the letter into the envelope.

"I'm afraid it's not enough."

Chapter Nineteen

NICE, DECEMBER 1943

Lana stared at the bowl of soup she made for herself, and knew she wouldn't be able to eat. She remembered the morning of the last escape when Guy prepared eggs and toast. How did he have an appetite when her stomach felt like lead? She ate one spoonful and pushed the bowl away.

Pierre had been shocked when she delivered the key to the *Natalia*. The yacht was so big, she was afraid he wouldn't be able to handle it. But Pierre had puffed out his chest and insisted that he could drive any boat.

After she left Pierre's flat, she walked through Old Town. The streets were waking up, and the smell of coffee and warm bread drifted from a bakery. It all looked so peaceful and calm; for a moment she forgot about the night's escape. Then she heard heavy footsteps and quickened her steps. Brunner's men could be lurking at any corner. She got back into Giselle's car and drove to the villa.

She glanced around the kitchen and felt a catch in her throat. Guy's newspaper was folded on the counter next to a bowl of fruit. It would all be here the next day but it might not be the same. At best, the mission would be successful, which meant Odette would be gone. At worst, they would all be captured or killed.

She moved into the living room and glanced at the flowers she had arranged in a vase. An empty glass and Guy's jazz album sat on the phonograph. It looked like the living room of an ordinary family instead of that of three strangers thrown together by war.

Now she understood why Guy said working in the Resistance was lonely. She and Guy never talked about the future. She had grown so close to Odette, but in a few hours she would deliver her to the dock and wave goodbye.

It wasn't fair to put off telling Odette any longer. She dreaded breaking the news after their conversation the day before. But time was running out. She walked upstairs to the attic and found Odette curled on a cushion. She had a small book and a piece of writing paper open in front of her.

"What are you doing?"

"It's an English dictionary. I found it on the bookshelf." Odette pointed to a dusty shelf. "I'm teaching myself English so I can write to Bernadette. She'll be surprised because I told her I'm not going to school anymore."

Lana crouched down beside her and inspected the book.

"What if you could go to school and learn English at the same time?" she asked.

"What are you talking about?" Odette wondered.

"A good friend drives a boat that takes refugees to Algiers, and from there they get to England. Families in England are waiting for children like you. They want to take care of them."

Odette closed the book and crossed her arms.

"You mean Jewish children who don't have anyone," she said stiffly.

"Well, yes." Lana wavered. "Guy has a contact in England, and he's made some inquiries. He found a family with a house in the countryside. You could sleep in a proper bedroom and attend school. You need a home and to be around other children; you can't stay in the attic forever."

"You want to send me away to live with strangers." Odette's voice was cold. "I told you I was going to ask Guy to bring up a phonograph yesterday, and you didn't say a word."

"I came to tell you, but we started talking and it didn't seem the right time." Lana felt guilty. "A new family wouldn't be strangers for long; I was a stranger only a month ago. You'll meet new friends."

"Then come with me," Odette challenged.

"I can't, I have responsibilities here." Lana shook her head.

Odette's bottom lip wobbled, and she pulled on her braids.

"My mother said you cared about us, but you want to get rid of me."

"I'd do anything to keep you here, but it's too dangerous," Lana pleaded. "After the war, you can come back to France."

"And live with you?"

Lana studied Odette's thin shoulders. Odette had lost so much; she had to give her something to cling to. And who knew what the future held?

"Yes, live with me," she answered.

Odette seemed to consider it.

"Why can't I write to Bernadette and ask if I can live with her?"

"There isn't time for that. A letter could take weeks to arrive." She shook her head. "And we don't know Bernadette's situation."

"But I could write to Bernadette from England?" Odette said hopefully. "Maybe we could meet."

"You could definitely write to her," Lana agreed.

"It would be nice to meet; I'm sure we'd be friends. And I suppose it would be better than an orphanage." Odette fiddled with the pages of the dictionary. "If the war ever ends, I'm not going to become a silly teenager who only cares about clothes and boys. My father wanted me to go to university, so I have to start preparing now." She looked at Lana. "Do schools in England really accept Jewish children?"

"I'm sure they do." Lana gulped. "And they'd be lucky to have you."

"Good." Odette nodded her head. "Because wherever I go I'll still be Jewish. No matter what, I'll always be Jacob and Sylvie Wasserstein's daughter."

Lana was preparing lunch for Odette when she heard the front door open. She glanced up and saw Guy standing in the hallway. His clothes were rumpled, and he hadn't shaved, but his eyes danced when he saw her.

"You're the prettiest sight I've seen in days." He kissed her. "That sandwich looks good too. What do I have to do to get a bite?"

"You can kiss me again." Lana laughed and realized how much she'd missed him.

Guy kissed her deeply and pulled out a chair.

"I couldn't wait in Marseille forever." He bit into the sandwich. "I'll go back for the engine part when it's ready. Right now I'd do anything for a hot bath, followed by a comfortable bed."

"What about the escape?" Lana asked.

"Didn't Pierre tell you? There's nothing we can do without a boat."

"There is a boat." Lana sat opposite him. "I delivered the key to Pierre this morning."

"What are you talking about?" Guy asked.

Lana told him about Giselle's help getting the key to Natalia's yacht.

"Pierre couldn't have been more surprised if I told him he was going to drive a yacht owned by the prince of Monaco," she finished.

"I leave for two days and you become a high-class thief!" Guy said appreciatively.

"We're only borrowing the yacht. I'll put the key back as soon as Pierre returns."

"I don't care how you accomplished it, you saved our mission." Guy jumped up. "I have to go."

"What about your sandwich?" Lana's heart clenched. She didn't want him to leave so soon. "And that hot bath."

Guy glanced at his watch. "You can run the bath in exactly nine hours and thirty-two minutes."

Guy turned around, and he had never looked so handsome.

"Could you do one more thing?" he asked.

"What is it?"

"There's a bottle of champagne in the cupboard that I saved for special occasions. Could you put it next to the bath?"

"Of course." She bit her lip. Lana wasn't normally superstitious, but what if Guy was caught?

"I forgot the most important part. Could you be waiting in the bath for me?"

“Should I take off my clothes first?” She tried to laugh.

Guy’s eyes traveled over her body as if he was remembering every curve.

“You should definitely take off your clothes.”

Four hours later Lana hurried along the dock with Odette beside her. Guy was in Old Town, knocking on the doors of the houses. Guy hadn’t wanted them to leave the villa together in case they were being followed. And she didn’t want to wait for him. It would be safer to deliver Odette to Pierre before Guy and the refugees arrived. But the closer they came to the yacht, the more she dreaded letting Odette go.

They stopped in front of a royal-blue yacht.

“Is that the boat?” Odette gasped. Even in the dark, Lana could tell it was stunning. The yacht was the length of two fishing boats, and there was a wooden staircase that led to the lower level.

“It’s pretty, isn’t it?” Lana said, glad that Odette was excited.

“It’s as big as a house.” Odette stared up at the boat. “Wait until I write and tell Bernadette, she won’t believe me.”

“Odette, this is Pierre.” Lana introduced them when they climbed aboard. “Pierre is going to drive the boat.”

“It’s nice to meet you, Odette.” Pierre held out his hand. “I’m glad you’re joining us.”

"I've seen you before." Odette scrunched her nose. "You drive a yellow taxi. It has a meter on the dashboard," she gushed. "I've always wanted to take a taxi."

"Perhaps after the war, I'll take you for a ride."

Odette's eyes widened. She disappeared down the staircase, and Lana set the suitcase on the floor. The sky and the sea were the same inky black and the yacht swayed gently on the water.

"Guy told me about Odette's parents when he came to see me earlier," Pierre said. "I promise I'll take good care of her."

"I know you will, but I can't help but worry about everything. What if someone sees the yacht leave with the refugees on board?" Lana asked anxiously. "Or if Guy is followed here?"

"The dock is quiet as a tomb, and Guy knows what he's doing," Pierre answered. "There's nothing to worry about."

"Besides the German patrol boats and the soldiers who shoot anything that moves." Lana shuddered.

"You're doing the right thing," Pierre assured her. "It wasn't safe for Odette on the Riviera."

Lana nodded, even as her eyes filled with tears.

"I know, it's just . . . since Odette arrived we have all been happy: Odette and Guy playing backgammon and eating sandwiches together. It's as if we were a family. And you were right;

Guy is so good with children. He gave Odette his full attention."

Pierre looked at Lana curiously.

"You're falling in love with Guy, aren't you?"

The sound of Odette's footsteps drifted up the staircase, and Lana's heart felt as heavy as the thick ropes that tied the boat to the shore.

"I'm falling in love with both of them."

Lana sat up sleepily and glanced at the clock in the villa's living room. She had fallen asleep on the sofa, and it was past midnight. Guy was supposed to be back by now. She wondered if the yacht had left the harbor yet.

She was about to get up when there was a sound in the entry. Guy appeared in the doorway. He looked suddenly older. His shoulder sagged, and his movements were stiff. He unwound his scarf and walked straight to the sideboard.

"It's so late, did something happen?" she asked.

"It all went smoothly." Guy poured a shot of vodka. "The *Natalia* is on its way to Algiers."

"Thank God." Lana felt as if she hadn't breathed properly in days.

"I'm getting too old for this kind of thing." Guy groaned. "I can't run as fast as I used to, and my back aches. I tripped over a refugee's prayer shawl and almost sprained my ankle. I wouldn't be much use on the next escape if I'm limping."

Lana sat beside him and rested her head on his shoulder.

"You're not old at all! And the mission was a success."

Guy turned and stroked the fabric of her blouse. He put his thumb on her mouth and kissed her.

"I don't feel old now."

Her body melted against his, and she kissed him back.

"I'm sorry. I fell asleep and forgot to run the bath," she said when they parted.

Guy rose and pulled her up. He drew her close and they walked to the staircase.

"I'm glad you forgot the bath," he said when they reached his bedroom. "That's one less thing that stands in the way of getting you into bed."

Their lovemaking was tender and urgent. Afterward, Guy slept and Lana slipped on a robe and stood on the balcony. Guy's cologne lingered on her skin. She wondered what Odette was thinking. Did she miss Lana, or was she imagining her life in England?

Frederic would say that she had done the right thing. Because of Lana, Odette would be safe and well cared for. But what if Odette was miserable? She hoped she made the right decision. She remembered standing outside the convent and watching Frederic lift Esther Cohen out of the piano. At least Odette was on her way to England, away from Brunner and his men. She had to content herself with that. Because thinking about anything else—when she would see Odette again and what the future held for her and Guy—filled her with despair.

She pulled the robe tighter and leaned against the railing. How could her heart could be so full and feel like it was breaking at the same time?

Chapter Twenty

NICE, DECEMBER 1943

Three days later, Lana sat at her dressing table. It was almost noon. The villa had never been so quiet. Odette was in Algiers by now, and Guy had driven into Nice to see if Pierre had returned with the boat.

Guy and Lana woke early and sat in bed, talking about the war. In the last month, the Allies and Russians had claimed several victories. An RAF bombing raid over Berlin had resulted in one thousand German casualties, and the Nazis had lost 140 fighter planes in a dogfight near Emden. The Soviet Union and Czechoslovakia signed a mutual assistance treaty, and the Italians and Allies were fighting together along Germany's Winter Line.

She was glad that the war was turning, but at the same time it filled her with dread. She feared Brunner would only step up the raids and they could only thwart so many before they were discovered.

At least Odette was safe. Lana brought to mind Odette's dark hair and the freckles on her nose and already missed her. But it was better that Odette was far away than hidden in the attic.

The front door opened, and she ran to the top of the staircase to see who was there. Guy entered the living room and walked to the sideboard.

"Did you see Pierre?" She descended the stairs and joined him.

"He wasn't home, but his boots were there, so he made it back from Algiers," Guy answered. "The escape was a great success, over fifty Jews were saved. I heard a rumor that the next raid will be on the Cimiez neighborhood. It has some of the finest houses in Nice. It will be a nice bonus for Brunner that the Jews leave behind oriental rugs and crystal chandeliers. He's probably figuring out how to dispose of them on the black market."

Just thinking about Brunner made Lana anxious.

"It's almost Christmas," Lana urged. "I thought we could take a break."

Guy glanced up and his eyes softened.

"You're right, we both deserve a holiday." He walked over and kissed her. "Why don't we spend a couple of nights at the Hôtel de Paris in Monte Carlo?"

"Monte Carlo!" Lana repeated. "But I don't like to gamble."

"The hotel has a spa and an indoor swimming pool," Guy said. "Or we don't have to leave our room at all. We'll lie in bed without worrying whether the phone is bugged or Gestapo officers will rap at our front door."

"That does sound good." Lana leaned into his arms. "The other night I dreamed that a German soldier was inside my bedroom. In the morning I checked the closet and under the bed. I don't remember what it's like to fall asleep without wanting to keep one eye open."

"The concierge is a friend, I'm sure he'll give us his best suite," Guy said, and poured Lana a glass of water. She was about to take it when the front door opened.

Pierre appeared in the doorway with a small figure beside him. It took a moment for Lana to realize it was Odette.

"Odette!" Lana and Guy said at once. "What are you doing here?"

"Odette decided she didn't want to go to England after all," Pierre announced. "I found her in a closet on the yacht long after I'd left Algiers."

"You hid in a closet!" Lana exclaimed. "You could have suffocated. And what if Pierre left the boat when he reached Nice and you were trapped inside?"

"It wasn't closed all the way, there was space to breathe," Odette replied. "I could have stayed in there for a while."

"But why?" Lana asked. "You're supposed to be in England."

"I was cold, and there was a fur coat inside." Odette twisted her braid. "Then I decided I'd rather stay in France than go to a new country. Don't you see? If all the Jews ran away, the Germans would succeed at what Hitler is trying to accomplish. I'm French. This is where I belong."

"You're twelve years old, you can't fight the Germans," Lana spluttered.

Odette's eyes filled with tears. She looked like a young child rather than a brave twelve-year-old. Odette hadn't hidden in the closet because she wanted to fight Hitler. She hid because she was terrified of being far away and alone.

Guy put down his glass and turned to Lana. His expression was serious. He took a long breath and pointed to the staircase.

"Why don't you take Odette up to the attic," he suggested. "Let me talk to Pierre."

Lana and Odette walked silently up the stairs. The blankets were still folded in a corner next to the little table.

"Don't make me go back on the boat," Odette pleaded. "I tried to be brave, but I couldn't do it. I don't care what happens, I can't be so far from home. My mother said staying together was the most important thing. As long as you're with the people you love, everything will be all right."

Lana hugged her tightly. Odette's heart beat rapidly, and her shoulders were shaking.

"Don't worry," Lana soothed her. "We'll think of something."

She descended the stairs and found Guy sipping a drink in the living room. Pierre had gone.

"I didn't think I'd need one of these so early." He raised his glass. "If we survive this war, I'm going to take a year off from drinking Scotch. I used to enjoy it, but now it tastes like misery."

"We can't force Odette to go to England. She was terrified. She'll run away again." Lana sat beside him. "But how will we keep her safe?"

"We'll take Odette to Monte Carlo. I have a connection there who can get her to Italy."

"Italy!" Lana exclaimed. "But she doesn't want to go. She wants to stay here with us."

"She can't," Guy said firmly. "Either she goes to Italy, or she has to go to an orphanage."

They couldn't send her to an orphanage. She might get deported to a camp. Lana would have to explain to Odette that there wasn't any choice.

"But how would she get to Italy?"

"My friend Renato has a way. It will take longer, and it might cost a few hundred francs, but she'll get there safely."

"I don't believe it," Lana said stubbornly, thinking about what Charles had told her. "All the escape routes to Italy have been cut off."

"There are always new routes." Guy ran his fingers over the rim of his glass. "That's what the Resistance does."

"Why can't you take her to Switzerland like you did Raoul?" Lana persisted.

"I've been to the border too many times, someone will get suspicious." Guy shook his head. "You have to trust me; in a few days Odette will be eating pasta and sleeping in a warm bed."

"That isn't good enough." Lana's voice was choked. How could she send Odette away without knowing what was going to happen to her? And what if Odette refused to go? But Lana was the adult, and Odette was a child. She had to make Odette see this was the only way for all of them to stay alive.

"I wish things were different." Lana said stubbornly. "I wish she could stay in Cap Ferrat."

Guy looked at Lana for a long time. He picked up a strand of her hair and tucked it behind her ear.

"You've done as much as you can. Odette has a good head on her shoulders; she'll adjust. First, we'll all have a few days in Monte Carlo." He reached forward and kissed her. "I'm going to spoil you from morning to night."

Guy's kiss tasted sweet, and she laughed.

"I don't know what you mean."

Guy refilled his glass and leaned against the sideboard.

"I want to do what any man does when he is with a beautiful woman," he offered. "Have candlelight dinners and buy her pretty things and tell her he's so lucky to have her. We've been so busy making sure no one gets killed, there isn't time."

Lana's voice choked. She hadn't seen Guy get so emotional.

"I don't need pretty things, and just being with you is enough."

He walked over to her and pulled her close. The kiss was long and tender. When they parted his face held a serious expression.

"Is it enough?" he wondered out loud. "I thought it was too. But lately I've felt something different." He paused. "I'm falling in love with you."

Lana caught her breath. Why would Guy say that now? Was it simply the tension of the morning, or was it because he just realized his feelings for her? She studied his emerald-green eyes and the shape of his chin and knew it didn't matter. She felt exactly the same.

She leaned forward and kissed him again. "I'm falling in love with you too."

The Hôtel de Paris was the most glamorous hotel Lana had ever seen. Grand balconies overlooked the harbor, and there was a rooftop restaurant. The wine cellar held more bottles than any hotel in the world. Fragrant orchids dotted the public spaces.

They told the concierge that Odette was Guy's niece visiting from Switzerland. For two days they ate room service breakfasts of omelets and swam in the pool. Guy and Odette had backgammon matches that lasted for hours, and in the evenings Lana and Guy listened to jazz in the Bar Américain.

Lana's happiness frightened her. That evening, Guy's contact, Renato, would arrive and take Odette away. The thought of anything happening to Odette made her stomach turn.

The hotel's dining room reminded Lana of the lobby at the Paris Opera. Red velvet banquettes were scattered atop marble floors. French doors opened onto a balcony. Lana sat across from Odette and tried to look relaxed. Guy had slipped away before dinner and still hadn't returned.

"Would you like a wine with dinner?" the maître d' asked. "The Hôtel de Paris maintains the finest wine cellar in Europe."

"I'm waiting for someone, thank you," Lana said absently.

Two German officers passed their table, and an icy chill crept down Lana's spine. But they kept walking, and she let out her breath.

Guy appeared in the doorway. Their eyes met, and he joined them at the table.

"Where's Renato?" she asked quietly.

"Renato isn't coming," he replied, placing his napkin in his lap.

"Why not?" Lana inquired. She sipped her water and pretended they were having a normal conversation.

Guy glanced around to see if anyone could

hear them. His eyes returned to his plate and he lowered his voice.

"Because he's dead."

Lana opened her mouth and closed it. She couldn't ask questions while German officers smoked cigars nearby. She picked up her soup-spoon, but her hand trembled.

Odette was telling a story about the history of the hotel, and Lana tried to listen to what she was saying. But she couldn't stop thinking about Renato, wondering what had happened.

"When the Empress Sisi of Austria stayed here they suspended a trapeze from the ceiling of her room so she could exercise," Odette announced. "A grand duke used to bring his own gardeners."

"How do you know these things?" Lana asked.

"I made friends with the concierge," Odette said, leaning forward. "You can't imagine what goes on in a hotel. It makes my mother's old romance novels seem like children's books."

"I'd better have a word with the concierge." Guy chuckled, and Lana wondered how he could seem so relaxed. "I've had a similar experience, the concierge has been very helpful. I asked for a razor and shaving cream, and the hotel barber came to the suite and personally gave me a shave." Guy touched his cheeks. "I feel like a new man."

Lana was about to say something when two Gestapo officers approached their table.

"Good evening." The blond officer nodded. "We couldn't help but notice your beautiful family. I'm Captain Von Buren and this is Captain Heinemann."

"Good evening, gentlemen," Guy said in a clipped tone. His eyes roamed over the red armbands and medals on their chests.

"Your wife can't be old enough to have such a charming daughter." Captain Von Buren tipped his head at Lana. "She's almost a girl herself."

"Odette is my niece from Switzerland," Guy said briskly. "And this is Countess Antanova."

"Ah, a Russian countess. No wonder she outshines every woman in the room." He turned to Lana. "I had a grandmother in Saint Petersburg. She used to send me fur hats before the revolution."

"My mother left Russia during the civil war," Lana answered, wondering what the officers wanted. "We hope one day to return to Russia." She smiled flirtatiously. "That is, when Hitler wins the war and gets rid of the communists."

"Well informed and beautiful too." Captain Von Buren smirked. "Don't worry. Hitler will defeat Stalin and his army so brutally they'll wish they were run over by their own horses."

Guy busied himself sprinkling salt on his plate of vegetables. He looked up, and his expression was calm but firm.

"Chatting about the war is fascinating, but perhaps not in front of my niece," Guy said pointedly. "I hope you don't mind if we get back to our dinner."

"Of course, our apologies." Captain Von Buren turned to Guy. "If we could see your papers."

"We're in Monaco, it's a neutral country," Guy remarked.

"Technically, yes. But the casino is losing customers because no one wants to gamble among Jews." He noticed Guy's dinner jacket and gold cuff links. "You're a successful businessman. You can understand the owner's concern."

Guy reached into his pocket and produced his papers. Lana took hers out of her purse and handed them to the officer.

"Thank you, Monsieur Pascal and Countess Antanova." He returned them. "And for your niece."

Lana's stomach dropped, and she glanced at Guy.

"I told you, she's my niece from Switzerland. Her mother sent her to the Riviera for the sunshine."

"She's very pretty, but she still needs papers," Captain Von Buren countered.

Guy picked up his knife and buttered his bread. His expression turned contrite, and he looked at the Gestapo officers.

"I haven't been completely honest with you,"

Guy admitted. “My niece isn’t here on holiday. My sister’s husband left her for some damn RAF nurse. She can’t afford to raise her alone and asked me to care for her.”

“My condolences to your sister.” Captain Von Buren nodded. “If the papers are in your room we’re happy to wait while you retrieve them.”

Guy stood up, and Lana wondered where he was going. She was afraid of being alone with the officers and Odette. Then Guy walked around the table and stopped in front of her.

“Of course, gentlemen. But first I would be honored if you witness my proposal.” He dropped to his knee and took out a velvet box from his pocket. “You didn’t just interrupt our dinner. I was about to ask the countess to marry me.”

Guy snapped open the box and displayed a yellow diamond ring.

Lana put her hand to her mouth and gasped. What was Guy doing? They’d known each other for only a month, and she was still grieving for Frederic.

“Lana, I have loved you since the moment we met, and I want to spend my life making you happy,” Guy continued as if they were alone. “Will you marry me?”

Lana tried to answer but her throat closed up.

She couldn’t possibly have an answer. There was so much she still didn’t know about Guy.

Did he miss Marie the way she missed Frederic? They had never talked about life after the war. Would he go back to Switzerland?

Then Odette clapped, and she remembered why they were in Monte Carlo. It didn't matter what Guy's intentions were. The important thing was to distract the Gestapo officers from demanding Odette's papers.

"Of course I'll marry you." She held out her hand so Guy could slip the ring on her finger. Then she kissed him for so long the officers shifted uncomfortably.

"I asked the maître d' to bring a bottle of Château Lafite Rothschild from the wine cellar." Guy rose and turned to Captain Von Buren. "It's Hitler's favorite champagne. He took a case back to Berlin after his visit to Paris last summer. Would you join us in celebrating?"

Lana and Guy sat in the living room of their suite. Odette was asleep in the adjoining room, and the maid had drawn the curtains.

"I don't know about you, but I could use another drink after that." Guy filled a glass with Scotch. He had removed his tie and his cuff links lay on the coffee table.

"No, thank you." She shook her head. "I was so nervous, I drank too much champagne and I have a headache. You were very brave, you saved Odette's life."

Lana slipped the diamond ring off her finger and placed it in the jewelry box.

"Here." She handed it to him. "You were quite convincing. Even Odette believes we're engaged."

Guy looked up, but he didn't take the box. He sat back against the cushions and sipped his drink.

"You think I asked you to marry me to fool the Gestapo?"

"Why else would you have given me the ring?" she asked.

Guy took the box and turned it over in his hands. "Maybe I was wrong."

"Wrong about what? I did wonder why you had a diamond ring in your pocket, but you're always prepared for anything." She pondered. "Perhaps it isn't real, though it's certainly lovely."

"Of course it's real!" Guy's cheeks burned. "It's a two-carat yellow diamond that cost three hundred thousand francs. I've been carrying it around for days." He stopped and placed his glass on the table. "Waiting for the perfect moment to propose to you."

Lana's heart thudded. She was afraid to move. She raised her eyes to meet his, and there was a lump in her throat.

"You were really asking me to marry you?"

"I'll admit it wasn't the most romantic setting." He laughed lightly. "I was planning to do it over dessert or after dinner at the Bar Américain. But it stopped those bastards from making me get Odette's papers. By the time they helped us finish off the bottle of champagne, they forgot all about it."

"We never talk about the future." Her forehead puckered. "Why would you propose?"

"Why does any man propose?" He shrugged. "Because I love you."

The three words touched her like a pinprick when she was putting on a brooch.

"But it's so soon." She gulped. "We haven't known each other long."

She couldn't help but think about Frederic. He had been dead for only five months. It was too early to hear a proposal from another man. And yet she loved Guy.

"I told you earlier that I'm falling in love with you," Guy continued. "You shouldn't be surprised."

"Falling in love is different. It's heady and romantic and makes your heart beat faster. Marriage is . . ."

"Permanent?" Guy finished her sentence.

"Yes," she whispered, afraid to break the spell.

"Well that's a good thing." He grunted.

She waved at the box. "I still don't understand, when did you decide to buy the ring?"

Guy picked up his glass and ran his fingers over the rim.

“It was after the first escape. You arrived back at the villa, and you looked so strong and beautiful. Like a modern-day Joan of Arc.”

“Joan of Arc?” Lana asked curiously.

“From the moment you arrived on the Riviera, you never hesitated to put yourself in danger. You flirted with Alois Brunner and got close to Captain Von Harmon without worrying about being discovered. But you rushed inside after thinking I’d been shot at the dock and you were so disturbed. You cared about my safety more than your own.” He looked at Lana, and his eyes had changed from their usual clear green to a warm hazel. “That’s when I knew I loved you.”

For a moment Lana remembered when Frederic first said “I love you.” So much had happened since then. But refusing Guy wouldn’t bring Frederic back. She was young, and her whole life was ahead of her.

“The saleswoman at Van Cleef and Arpels tried to convince me to buy something even more extravagant with matching earrings, but that didn’t seem right. You aren’t the kind of woman I want to give flashy jewelry; you are the woman I want to spend the rest of my life with.”

“I’ve never seen a more beautiful ring,” Lana breathed.

Guy took it out of the box and slipped it on Lana’s finger. He put his arms around her, and their lips met. His hands traveled down her back, and she leaned into his touch.

She wanted to say they must be crazy; there were still so many Jews to save on the Riviera. And what about Odette? If they couldn't get her to Italy, how would they keep her safe?

But she could barely think. All she wanted was for Guy's hands to press against her skin and for his mouth to travel from her neck to her breasts.

Guy led her to the bedroom and unzipped her dress. He unsnapped the buttons of his shirt and laid it on a chair.

"God, you're beautiful," he said hoarsely.

She lay on the bedspread and waited for him to join her. He pulled off his socks and turned to her.

"You didn't say yes," he said.

"What do you mean?" She sat up against the headboard.

"You said yes in front of the Gestapo officers when you thought it was a ruse." He pulled off the other sock. "You're wearing the engagement ring, but you didn't actually agree to marry me."

Lana started laughing. She laughed until the laughter turned to tears and then she couldn't stop crying. She cried for Frederic and for the life they would have had. Five months ago she was hurrying to tell him the news about the baby. She would always miss Frederic, but that couldn't stop her from loving Guy. She cried for

Esther Cohen, and for Sylvie and Jacob, and for Giselle and Hans. She cried for Guy's wife and daughter and all the Jews who would never know happiness like she felt at that moment.

"Yes." She wiped her eyes and pulled him on top of her. "Yes, I'll marry you."

Chapter Twenty-One

NICE, JANUARY 1944

The afternoon of Brunner's party at the Hôtel Excelsior, Lana sat in the living room trying to concentrate on a book.

The first few days after they returned from the Hôtel de Paris had been magical. Guy's engagement ring twinkled on her finger, and everything seemed brighter. Then the war intruded again as the newspapers carried frightening headlines: Count Ciano, Mussolini's son-in-law, was shot by a firing squad for voting to oust Mussolini from office; twenty-two civilians were murdered in Lyon in retaliation for the assassination of two German soldiers.

Her mother's reports from Paris offered little relief. Would the paintings by the great masters ever hang on the walls of the Louvre again? Would the store shelves be full?

Even life on the Riviera grew harder. There was no wheat, and bread was hard to find. Barbed wire fences went up on the boulevards. It became hard to see the ocean. Lana heard rumors that the beaches were scattered with mines in case any Allied boats came ashore. The outdoor markets were deserted and some of the food shops in Old

Town were closed. She found herself thinking nostalgically of when she arrived in Nice.

They moved Odette into a bedroom and gave Giselle the explanation that she was Guy's niece. But Lana couldn't help but worry. Guy had obtained false papers for Odette, but what if they were questioned by the Gestapo? Every time a car drove by, a chill ran down her spine.

A bright spot was Pierre's visits to the villa. Pierre taught Odette how to play cards. They sang Sylvie's favorite songs. Odette and Pierre prepared omelets, and they all ate at the dining room table. At night after Odette went to sleep, Guy and Lana and Pierre plotted the next mission.

It had been Guy's idea to search Brunner's hotel room during the New Year's party. It was the perfect opportunity to look for information about upcoming raids. Lana was terrified: if Brunner went up to his room and discovered them, they'd be shot. But Guy kissed her and said Brunner wouldn't think of leaving his own party. If Brunner asked Lana where Guy was, she would find a way to distract him.

Lana answered a knock at the door. Giselle stood outside. Her hair was wrapped in a scarf, and she carried a flat case.

"Giselle, please come in." Lana greeted her.

Giselle followed her into the living room. She looked more relaxed than she had in weeks. Her face was carefully made-up and she wore perfume.

"You look lovely," Lana commented. "Are you going out?"

"I decided if I mope around the villa I'll turn into one of those spinsters in Paris who look old when they're thirty. Every morning I do my exercises and put on powder and lipstick." Giselle smiled.

"You always look beautiful," Lana said.

"You asked to borrow a necklace for the party," Giselle said, and handed Lana the case. "I found just the thing. It was sitting in my drawer, and I thought someone should wear it."

Lana opened it and took out a diamond pendant and matching diamond earrings.

"These are stunning," Lana gushed. "But I didn't mean something so extravagant. What if I lose them?"

"I'm sure you'll be careful. It would make me happy for them to be admired," Giselle said thoughtfully. "Armand gave them to me."

Lana recalled that Armand was Giselle's lover in Paris.

"They were the closest things he gave me to a diamond engagement ring, and I couldn't bring myself to sell them," Giselle explained. She glanced at Lana's diamond ring and sighed. "I'm glad everything worked out for you and Guy. I had no idea Guy had a niece, it must be nice to have her staying with you. You're going to be so happy."

Lana glanced down at the case so Giselle couldn't see her expression. She hated to lie to her friend. But telling the truth about Odette and their work in the Resistance was too dangerous for all of them.

"I am happy." She nodded. "But sometimes I wonder if the war will ever end. Guy and I want to get married in Paris, I can't imagine not having my mother and Jacques there. But we can't go back to Paris while it's occupied by the Germans. We live in limbo."

"At least you and Guy have each other," Giselle reflected, and a secret smile crossed her face. "Being in love during wartime can be romantic. There's a sense of urgency that makes people act on their feelings in a way they wouldn't during peacetime."

"What are you saying?" Lana asked curiously.

"I met someone," Giselle confided. "His name is Philippe. He's from Paris, and he moved to the Riviera a few years ago. He owns an art gallery in Antibes. I told him I was an artist and he asked to see my work. We ended up sitting in his back room and talking for hours."

"I'm so pleased." Lana squeezed her hand.

"It's too early, but just thinking about Philippe makes me happy," Giselle mused. "I thought I was no longer interested in men, but love is the best cure. It's healthier than cigarettes, and it doesn't give you a hangover like too many martinis."

"You're right, love is the best thing in the world," Lana said, her mind drifting to the danger Guy was putting himself in that night. "But when you find it, how can you stop worrying it will be taken away?"

Lana saw Giselle out and went upstairs to get dressed. She stood in front of the mirror and heard footsteps in the hallway. Guy appeared behind her. His fingers caressed her back, and she shivered.

"Let me help you zip that up," he offered, kissing her neck.

"It's already zipped." She laughed, goose bumps forming on her skin.

"Then I'll unzip it and zip it again," he said. "I can't miss the opportunity of admiring my fiancée's naked back."

"You'll get the opportunity later. After the party is over and we've safely returned to the villa." Her voice wavered. "I wish you wouldn't go through with this. What if you and Pierre are caught?"

"We've gone over the plan a dozen times," Guy assured her. "You'll join Brunner for a glass of champagne. Then you'll ask him to dance, and I'll meet Pierre and slip up to Brunner's room. I'll be back before the dancing is over."

They decided that Pierre would wait in the hotel lobby. Lana couldn't help but worry. What if someone noticed him? The concierge might become suspicious.

"Does it have to be tonight? There will be other parties and nights at the casino," Lana urged. "Brunner and his men will let something slip about the next raid."

Guy's forehead knotted together, and his hands dropped to his sides.

"Hitler is getting anxious. The Russians invaded Poland two weeks ago and sent the German army into retreat. And there's a rumor that the Allies are getting ready to invade France. Hitler isn't going to give up without a fight. I received communication from Henri," Guy said pensively. "The Gestapo operations in Nice are to be escalated."

"Escalated?" Lana repeated.

"Eichmann wants all the Jews in Nice to be deported by the spring."

"How would that be possible? They'd be sending Jews to the train station every week."

"That's why we have to act now." Guy clenched his jaw. "Before Brunner sentences every Jew on the Riviera to death."

Guy put his arms around her and kissed her.

"Nothing can happen to me. There's still so much more to accomplish."

Guy went to take a bath, and Lana finished getting ready. Giselle's diamond pendant glittered against her neck, and she spritzed her décolletage with perfume. Guy had been successful in every mission so far; why should tonight be different? But she couldn't shake the feeling of dread. She had learned from the war: just because Guy had so much to live for didn't mean he would stay alive.

The ballroom of the Hôtel Excelsior was decorated with gold and silver balloons. There was a dessert station and a band played songs by Charles Trenet and Tino Rossi. Waiters in tuxedos passed around glasses of champagne, and guests milled around the dance floor.

The evening had gone perfectly. Brunner greeted them warmly. Guy made pleasant small talk, and Lana flirted with Brunner lightly. Cocktails were followed by a sit-down dinner of coq au vin and round potatoes. Lana wondered how Brunner could afford it. She nibbled the sorbet that was served between courses and tried to stop her heart from racing. All she could think about was Guy slipping up to Brunner's room.

The dancing had begun, and Lana searched the ballroom for Brunner.

"There you are," a male voice announced. Charles Langford approached her. She hadn't seen Charles since the day he came to the villa and revealed that he too was involved in the Resistance.

"Charles!" she exclaimed, and kissed him on

the cheek. "This is a surprise, I didn't know you were invited."

"I wasn't going to come, I haven't felt like going out." He cradled his champagne flute. "But I decided it wouldn't hurt to be around people enjoying themselves. News about the war gets worse every day. I almost threw my radio out the window, but I didn't want to crush the flowers."

Lana wondered what Charles was doing there. But she couldn't ask him. Their Resistance work put them both in danger.

"Guy and I felt the same way," she agreed. "Since your Christmas party, there haven't been any social events. Everyone is so gloomy; it's almost like being back in Paris."

"Just seeing you makes attending the party worthwhile." He took in Lana's black sheath with the see-through sleeves and white cuffs. "You look wonderful tonight."

"Thank you. It's one of my favorite dresses."

"It's not just the dress, your eyes are sparkling." He waved at her hand. "I take it congratulations are in order."

Lana glanced at the engagement ring and let out a little laugh.

"Guy proposed at Christmas." She nodded. "We're very happy."

"And all this time, you insisted you were on the Riviera to have fun." His eyes met Lana's. "I always felt you were deeper than that."

Lana wondered what he was trying to say. Her cheeks colored as she tried to think of a reply.

"You were right when you said everyone leaves a bit of their hearts on the Riviera," she answered finally. "I'm no exception."

"That's what you say when you're trying to make an impression on a pretty girl on a train," Charles reflected. "By the time you work up the courage to say what you really mean, it's too late."

Lana gulped and brought her champagne flute to her lips.

"You don't seem to be afraid of anything," she said playfully. "I can't imagine you lacking courage to talk to a woman."

"Whatever happens, I'll always be there for you, Lana." Charles touched her arm. "All you have to do is ask."

Charles drifted off, and Lana saw Alois Brunner across the dance floor.

"Captain Brunner." She joined him. "I want to compliment you on a wonderful party. Dinner was delicious and the band is playing my favorite songs."

"I've been waiting all night to dance with you," Captain Brunner replied. His eyes seemed even blacker than usual, and his hair was slick with oil. "May I say you've outdone yourself, Countess Antanova? You've never looked so lovely."

Lana blushed appropriately.

"I'm sure you say that to all the women here,"

she replied. She waved at the gold tablecloths and floral centerpieces. "You have exquisite taste."

"The hotel staff has been very accommodating," Brunner agreed. He paused and looked at her intently. "I'm afraid you haven't been honest with me. Your relationship with Guy isn't what you described."

Lana froze. What did Brunner mean? She and Guy had been affectionate with each other all night.

"I don't understand," she answered carefully. "Guy and I are very close."

"It's more than that." He pointed to her diamond ring. "It seems you are engaged."

Relief flooded through her and she tipped her head.

"You don't miss anything," she said coquettishly. "How did you know?"

"Captain Von Buren told me. He ran into you at the Hôtel de Paris. It was the most intimate family tableau." He raised his eyebrows. "I had no idea Guy had a niece."

"She's staying with us." Lana nodded.

"What did you say her name was?" Brunner asked innocently.

"I didn't," Lana answered. She looked up at Brunner, and her eyes were clear. "It's Odette."

"What a pretty name. It must be French. I've never heard it in Austria or Germany," he said.

Lana knew that the next words out of her mouth

could seal Odette's fate and put her and Guy and Pierre in prison. She shrugged her shoulders and replied. "You're correct. It's a common French-language name. Odette is from Geneva, in the French-speaking part of Switzerland."

Lana and Brunner danced, and the party slowly wound down. She kept glancing at the entrance, waiting for Guy to return. Finally, most of the guests had left, and Lana entered the lobby.

"Countess Antanova." Pierre approached her. He looked around to see if anyone was listening. "Monsieur Pascal was feeling ill and had to leave. He asked me to drive you to Cap Ferrat in my taxi."

"Why didn't he come and tell me?" she asked, trying to stay calm. That wasn't like Guy. Surely he would have told her himself before he left.

"It came on suddenly. He didn't want to disturb the other guests," Pierre offered.

The valet opened the hotel doors, and Lana followed Pierre to the taxi. She waited until they drove away and then she leaned forward.

"When did Guy leave?" she asked frantically. "Where was he going?"

"I didn't see him. I only said that in case anyone overheard us." Pierre darted through the traffic of Old Town. "He never showed up in the lobby."

"What do you mean he didn't show up?"

"I waited for ages. I even went up to Brunner's floor, but he wasn't there."

"I saw Guy leave the ballroom," Lana said desperately. "Where else would he have gone?"

"Maybe there was an emergency, and he was called away," Pierre suggested.

"Yes, of course." Lana leaned back in the seat. Perhaps something had happened to the boat. German soldiers might have discovered it at the dock and grown suspicious. He would be waiting for her in Cap Ferrat.

Pierre pulled up in front of the villa. The windows were dark, and Guy's car wasn't in the driveway.

"Would you like me to come in?" Pierre asked.

Lana shook her head.

"Go home and rest," she said gently. "It's been a long night."

The living room was empty, and the light in Guy's study was off. She climbed the stairs and peered into Odette's bedroom. Odette was asleep, a pile of books on the bedspread.

Perhaps Guy had arrived earlier and was now fast asleep. She opened his door, but the bed was untouched. His robe hung in the bathroom next to his razor and shaving cream.

She entered her bedroom and sat at the dressing table. Giselle's diamond pendant felt heavy around her neck, and she took it off. The feeling of dread that had been hovering over her all night squeezed her chest.

When Frederic died and she lost the baby she

thought she would never be happy again. Then she arrived in Nice and fell in love with Guy. This evening she told Charles she left a little part of her heart on the Riviera, but that was a lie. She had given her whole heart to Guy, and if anything had happened to him, she didn't know what she would do.

Chapter Twenty-Two

NICE, JANUARY 1944

Guy hadn't returned. Not that night, not that week, and not the next. Every day Lana drove into Nice to see if Pierre had any news. She read the newspaper and kept the radio on all day, but there was no mention of captured Resistance fighters. She'd even managed to call Henri, having left a message with the sisters at the convent, but he had nothing to report.

For the first week, Odette asked daily when Guy was coming back, but then she stopped. Odette chattered on about everything else: the letters she wrote to Bernadette and the eggs from Giselle's chickens, but Lana knew what was going through Odette's mind. None of the adults who left ever came back.

At night, when Odette was asleep, she moved from Guy's study to his bedroom, searching for some clue of where he had gone: a train ticket or a receipt in a coat pocket. But his desk held only the usual bills and his pockets were empty.

On Thursday a car pulled into the driveway, and Lana ran to the front door. Charles stepped out of a yellow Citroën and bounded up the steps.

"Charles?" She opened the door. "What are you doing here?"

"Can I come in?" he asked.

She led him to the living room, where he took off his hat and placed it on the coffee table.

"Guy has been gone since the night at the Hôtel Excelsior," Charles began.

Lana's heart beat quickly. Perhaps Charles had some information about Guy. She didn't want to show how worried she was. She liked Charles very much, but Guy's suspicions had taken root in her mind; she still didn't know if she could trust him completely.

"He had business to take care of." She sat on the couch in the living room.

Charles continued as if she hadn't spoken. "I've inquired all over France and no one has seen him." He sat opposite her. "But there's more. Alois Brunner isn't at the Hôtel Excelsior anymore."

Lana looked up sharply.

"What do you mean Brunner isn't at the hotel?" she asked.

Brunner hadn't said anything at the party about going away. Something must have happened. And it might involve Guy.

"Brunner vacated his rooms; he's gone back to Berlin. Eichmann gave the order himself."

Lana gripped the edge of the couch to steady herself. Eichmann wanted all the Jews to be deported by the end of April. Something drastic must have happened for him to send Brunner away. She could only guess Eichmann's command had something to do with Guy's disappearance.

Lana remembered Guy saying he wasn't going to leave the Riviera until he or Alois Brunner was dead. Guy went where Brunner went.

"Guy will show up," she said, trying to sound confident.

"What if he doesn't?" Charles rejoined. "Brunner is gone, but Nice is still crawling with Gestapo officers. It's not safe here for you and Odette. If Guy is in trouble, you could be too." He paused and looked at Lana. "Pierre told me about Odette."

Lana winced. Pierre shouldn't have discussed Odette without talking to Lana first.

"What did he tell you?" she asked.

"That she lost her parents and that she's quite attached to you."

"I feel the same way about Odette." Lana nodded. "She's the loveliest girl I've ever met."

"Lana, you have to listen to me." Charles picked up his hat and fiddled with the brim. "Hitler is feeling threatened by the Russians and the Allies, and it's only making things worse. Thousands of women and children are being sent to death camps in Austria and Germany, and it's not just Jews. It's members of the Resistance too. Come with me to England, I'll keep you and Odette safe."

"You're going back to England?" she asked in surprise. "I thought it wasn't safe to cross the channel."

"I wasn't planning to, but with the Allies approaching, I'm afraid of what the Germans will do to foreigners." He put down his hat. "I have my own house in the countryside. In Sussex, near my parents. You and Odette can live with me."

"Live with you!" she exclaimed.

"It's the best thing for everyone," he offered. "Odette will have a good home, and I'll take care of you." He looked at Lana, and there was a question in his eyes. "After the war we could get a place in London too."

Was Charles implying that they would be a couple? He knew she was engaged to Guy.

"You don't have to do that," Lana interjected. "You need a wife and family. How will you find one if we're living with you?"

Charles brought his hand up to Lana's cheek.

"I don't have to. I want to. There's no one I'd rather be with than you," he said quietly. "Surely you realize I've been in love with you since I saw you on the train. You were reading *Anna Karenina* and all I could think was Tolstoy never created a heroine as lovely as you."

Lana knew Charles was fond of her. But could he be in love? She wondered if it was her fault for allowing them to get close. Charles was a good person, and she had needed a friend.

"I don't know what to say," she replied awkwardly.

"I don't expect you to share my feelings now, but maybe they'll grow over time." He rubbed his chin. "I'll do my best to make you and Odette happy."

How could she go and live with Charles when she was in love with Guy? But Charles was right. Odette couldn't stay in the villa forever. And nowhere they went in France would be safe.

"It's a lot to take in." She stood up. "Can I give you my answer tomorrow?"

Charles rose and picked up his hat from the table.

"Of course. I'll come back in the morning."

Relief pulsed through her.

"Charles, thank you for everything." She walked him to the door. "You've been a very good friend."

Lana went to the kitchen to make a cup of tea. She yearned to call her mother and ask for advice. But Tatiana didn't know anything about Odette, and she couldn't risk explaining over the phone.

Footsteps sounded in the hallway, and Odette appeared in the kitchen.

Lana wondered whether Odette had heard their conversation.

"I didn't hear you come downstairs," Lana said, taking the kettle off the stove.

"I saw a car leave, I wondered who it was," Odette said. She put her book on the counter and climbed on a chair.

Lana poured tea into her cup. "It was Charles, a good friend."

"Was it about Guy?" Odette's eyes brightened. "Did he say when he's coming back?"

Lana wondered whether she should tell Odette Charles's news. In a few months, Odette would turn thirteen. She deserved the truth.

"No one knows where Guy is," Lana admitted. "Charles made a proposition. He'd like us to go with him to England."

"Why would he invite me?" Odette questioned. "I've never met him."

"Charles is very kind. He has a house in the English countryside. You could go to school," Lana said thoughtfully. "You wanted to go to England, but you were afraid to go alone. Now I would go with you."

Odette's brow furrowed.

"Things are different now." Odette sat on the stool. "You're engaged to Guy. We're almost a family."

"I know that, but Guy has been gone for two weeks. He might not come back. It isn't safe here. And we can't go to Paris. It's too dangerous while it's under German occupation. Someone might question your papers and discover that you're Jewish." Lana hesitated. "Charles would give us a home and take care of us. It would be a good life."

Odette was quiet, and Lana was afraid she had said too much.

"I remember when I was nine, I stood outside my parents' room and heard my mother sobbing," Odette said meditatively. "It was just after the Italians occupied the Riviera, and no one knew what was going to happen.

"My mother wasn't crying because she was afraid of the Italian soldiers. She was crying because my father found someone who would take us to Switzerland."

"Why didn't you go?" Lana asked, surprised.

"We didn't have enough money for all of us. My father would have had to stay behind until he could afford to join us," Odette continued.

"My mother said she'd rather die than go without him," Odette finished. "My father tried to convince her, but she wouldn't change her mind. If you love Guy, you can't desert him."

"This is different. Guy isn't here; we haven't heard from him, and we don't know if we'll ever see him again."

"Love is always the same," Odette said, and Lana thought she looked wise beyond her years. "Remember when you said that when you're a child things seem like they will last forever?

What if Guy returns after the war and we're living with Charles in England? He'll think you don't care about him anymore. And our lives would become so different. You might forget Guy and miss out on the great love of your life. Before the Germans arrived, my father used to say he didn't envy anyone on the Riviera: not the people who owned the villas in the hills above Nice or the elegant couples strolling on the promenade. He had everything he dreamed of: a beautiful wife and a lovely daughter and a job at Hôtel Negresco doing what he loved. I have similar dreams: to have a satisfying career and a wonderful husband and happy, noisy children," she said, and her eyes were bright. "Every Sunday, I'll look around the table at the faces I love and be so grateful. You have to marry for love; it's the most important thing of all."

Once in their conversations, Lana told Sylvie that children have to believe anything is possible and Sylvie answered that there were no more miracles. Sylvie was wrong; miracles were simply dreams that came true.

Lana pulled Odette close. Perhaps Lana hadn't saved all the Jewish children in Nice. But if she had given Odette a reason to dream, wasn't that something? If only Sylvie were alive to see how brave Odette had become.

"We won't go to England with Charles," she said. "We'll figure out something else."

Odette looked up at Lana and grinned.

"You can tell Charles it's my fault we don't go to England. I haven't made much progress with the English dictionary, and my English is terrible."

Odette went upstairs, and Lana puttered around the kitchen, wondering if she was being foolish. They couldn't stay at the villa. Guy's disappearance could have alerted the Gestapo to something amiss. But where could they go that would be safe?

There was a knock at the door, and Lana peered out the window. Giselle stood outside, holding a shopping bag.

"Giselle, come in." Lana opened the door. "I was having a cup of tea, would you like one?"

"Yes, please." Giselle followed her into the kitchen. She opened the bag and took out a basket of eggs and some fruit. "I'm going on a short trip and thought you'd like these."

"Another trip?" Lana frowned. "Is it to do with Hans?"

"It's nothing like that. I'm going with Philippe to look at a gallery he might buy," Giselle said, and there was a sparkle in her eye. "I spent the whole day choosing what negligee to bring. It's been so long since I slept with a man. I couldn't decide what to wear in bed."

"I'm glad for you." Lana smiled and handed

her a cup. "You'll have a wonderful time."

"Is there any news of Guy?" Giselle asked, sipping her tea.

"Nothing." Lana shook her head. "I'm afraid he isn't coming back."

"You can't know that," Giselle insisted. "He'll appear any moment with an explanation. He had to go to Switzerland on business and got stuck at the border."

Lana bit her tongue. In the past two weeks she had longed to tell Giselle the truth about Odette and their work in the Resistance. But now more than ever, it would be too risky.

"What if he got cold feet and doesn't want to get married?" Lana fretted.

"Men need women more than we think," Giselle said meditatively. "I've seen the change in Guy since you arrived. He's never looked so happy."

They drank their tea, and Giselle got up to leave.

"Don't worry about Guy," she said when she stood at the door. "War might take away many things but it has no hold on love. If it did, the human race would have died out long ago."

Early the next day, Lana stood by the door and waited for Charles to arrive. But instead of Charles's Citroën pulling into the driveway, there was Pierre's rusty Peugeot.

Pierre jumped out of the car.

"Pierre!" Lana greeted. Her heart beat with excitement. "What are you doing here?"

She hoped he had heard from Guy.

"I have something for you," he said. He reached into his pocket and took out an envelope.

Lana's heart soared. Guy had written to her! But inside was a swath of papers, none of them in Guy's handwriting. Lana read through them, her eyes were wide.

"Where did you get this?" she gasped.

"Guy ordered them a couple of weeks ago. He said to give them to you if anything happened to him," Pierre answered. "I picked them up yesterday."

Lana read them again. Her own photo stared back at her and underneath her name was written in black ink: *Countess Lana Pascal née Antanova.* Odette's photo was pasted to an official-looking form with the words: *Odette Pascal, birthplace Geneva, Switzerland.*

Guy had had papers made showing that they were already married. She and Odette had the last name, linking them directly. Suddenly she had an idea. She and Odette would be safe in Switzerland. She turned to Pierre and gave him a quick hug.

"Thank you for being such a good friend. I'm going to miss you more than you know."

"You're leaving the Riviera?" Pierre asked in surprise.

"It's too risky to stay here with Odette." Lana folded the papers. "I'd be putting you and anyone else in the Resistance in danger. It's best if we go away."

"Where will you go?" Pierre inquired.

Lana thought a minute and then smiled.

"To Switzerland! Don't you see? Guy had Swiss papers made for us; he must have known he was going away. He could be in Switzerland. I have to look for him."

Pierre's face broke into its boyish smile. "I don't know where Guy might be. But you're Countess Antanova. I'm sure you'll find him."

It was almost noon, and Charles still wasn't there. She would give him a few more minutes, and then she would have to think of something else.

A car turned into the driveway and she recognized Charles's yellow Citroën.

"Lana, you look lovely this morning," he said when she opened the front door. He noticed the suitcases, and his face brightened.

"You and Odette are coming?"

Lana led Charles into the living room and motioned for him to sit down.

"Your offer means so much to both of us; I don't deserve your generosity."

Charles cut her off. He looked at Lana, and his voice was hard.

"But you're not going to take it."

Lana shook her head.

"I'm sorry, Charles. I can't."

"Where are you going?" Charles waved at the suitcases.

"We're taking the train to Switzerland."

"But that's suicide!" he objected. "Odette is Jewish. If you're not killed by a bomb on a train, you'll be arrested at the border."

"We'll be all right," Lana said. "We have papers, and we'll take a route through the French Alps."

Charles's brow furrowed, and he leaned forward.

"You don't know that Guy is in Switzerland; he could be anywhere in Europe," he tried again. "You won't have anyone to take care of you. You'll be alone in a strange place."

"That's what we've been here, and we survived," she said with a smile. "I couldn't live with myself if I didn't try to find him."

"Are you sure?" he asked. "We could have a good life in England."

Lana thought about Odette saying you don't let go of the person you love. But she didn't have to explain that to Charles. Guy might be in Switzerland. She had to look for him.

"Odette will be safe there. I can attend university, and Odette will go to school," she said instead. "When the war ends, we'll go back to Paris so I can start my own cosmetics company."

Charles stood up and took her hand in his. He glanced at Lana, and she could see the admiration in his eyes.

A small smile crossed his face. "We all have our dreams. Maybe someday, mine will come true too."

Lana sat next to Odette on the train to Geneva and stared out the window. For the first six hours she had been so nervous, she couldn't stop fidgeting. Every time the train stopped, she was sure Gestapo officers would jump on board and arrest them.

They arrived in Annecy in the French Alps. Lana and Odette fell in love with the beautiful town from the window. The lake was bluer than the Mediterranean, and the mountains reminded Lana of her picnic with Guy in Villefranche. She wished they could spend the day in the high, clear air, but Annecy was occupied by the Germans. She couldn't take any chances.

It was only when they changed trains and crossed the border into Switzerland that she finally relaxed. Fields blanketed in snow flashed by the train's windows, and Mont Blanc loomed in the distance. Hills were dotted with wooden chalets with slanted roofs.

"What will we do when we get to Geneva?" Odette asked, pressing her face against the glass.

"You asked me three times; it's the same

answer." Lana laughed, looking up from her writing paper. She had written a letter to her mother that she would mail when they arrived.

"I want to hear it again," Odette said. "I don't know anything about Geneva."

"It's on a lake. There are mountains close by, so we can go skiing." Lana folded her paper. "We'll get an apartment in the old section of the city. I'll attend university, and you'll go to school."

Lana was going to sell her engagement ring when they arrived. And her mother would send money once Lana was settled. They would have enough to get by.

"Will I have my own room?" Odette asked, excitement lighting up her features.

"You will definitely have your own room," Lana agreed, although she didn't know for certain. "You can decorate it any way you like."

"I'll cover the walls with maps. And I'll get a phonograph so I can play my mother's favorite records," Odette mused.

Odette went back to her book, and Lana was lulled by the motion of the train. She remembered the train to Nice where she met Charles. She thought of seeing Pierre for the first time at the train station and slicing tomatoes in Guy's kitchen.

Maybe Guy was far away or even dead. Or perhaps the thought of marrying Lana and taking care of Odette was too much for him. But there was nothing she could do to change things. She had Odette and they were safely out of France.

"I remembered something else I'd like in my room." Odette interrupted her thoughts.

"What is it?" Lana asked.

"Could we get an extra bed for sleepovers?" Her eyes shone expectantly. "For when I meet new friends at school."

The sun streamed through the train window and illuminated Odette's face. There was a new confidence about her, and Lana imagined the lovely young woman she would become.

Lana reached forward and touched Odette's cheek.

"We can definitely get an extra bed."

Chapter Twenty-Three

PARIS, DECEMBER 24, 1954

Lana stood at the counter of her cosmetics boutique on Rue du Faubourg Saint-Honoré in the fashionable eighth arrondissement.

The week before Christmas was her favorite time of year at the store. Saleswomen in elegant black dresses slipped perfumes into bags decorated with a gold-lettered *LANA*, just like she had always imagined. The air smelled of her signature scent, and glass cases were filled with powders and tubes of lipsticks.

In the nearly ten years since the war, so much had happened. After the war, Lana and Odette had gone to Paris. Lana worked at the cosmetics counter at Le Bon Marché and mixed perfumes in her mother's kitchen at night. For a whole year, she and Odette had moved to New York while she apprenticed at Elizabeth Arden. Then they returned, and Lana opened her own boutique in Le Marais. Her boutique did better than she had imagined. Two years ago a space had opened up on Rue du Faubourg Saint-Honoré between Lanvin and Chanel. Every morning when she opened the store, she marveled that Lana's was wedged between two fashion icons. A store of her own, with its mirrored walls and pale blue carpet, as fashionable as the rest on the street.

For the first few years after the war, she looked for Guy. She hoped he would appear with an explanation or maybe just a smile. Sometimes she recognized his overcoat on the bus or a man with dark hair entering a shop. But it was always a stranger, and eventually, she gave up.

She dated men, but after a few months they'd complain that Lana spent too much time with Odette or at the boutique. She always felt a certain relief when they parted ways. Then loneliness would wash over and she would accept a dinner date or tickets to the ballet. She often wondered whether she would ever feel what she had with Frederic or later with Guy again.

After they left Geneva, Odette began attending a lycée in Paris. Her teenage years were filled with worries about grades and boys. Lana cherished that time together. Now Odette was a bright twenty-three-year-old, in her second year of medical school. Lana's mother and Jacques still lived on Avenue Montaigne.

Taking stock on Christmas Eve, Lana felt she had much to be thankful for.

"Yvette, why don't you go home?" Lana suggested, looking up from the box she was wrapping. "I'll stay and lock up."

Yvette had been the boutique manager for

six months. Lana had wooed her away from Lancôme. Yvette was warm and efficient. She remembered the names of their best customers and had a croissant waiting for Lana when she arrived each morning. Lana didn't know what she'd do without her.

"If you're sure you don't mind." Yvette accepted. She gathered her purse. "François said he has a surprise, and I've been dropping hints about that fabulous coat in the Chanel window."

Lana spent the next hour polishing the cases and going over the receipts. A light snow started to fall, and she walked outside to search for a taxi. She noticed a man in a black overcoat leaning into a taxi window and froze.

Under the lamplight, she made out the man's dark hair and angular cheekbones. It had been years since she'd believed she would recognize Guy again. Before she could stop herself, she approached the taxi.

"Is there a problem?" she asked.

"I haven't had a chance to change my money, and this guy won't accept traveler's checks," the man said, still staring down the taxi driver.

"I can lend you money." Lana took four hundred francs from her purse.

The man turned around and his mouth dropped open.

"Lana! What a surprise."

Lana's eyes widened and she gasped. This time she hadn't been mistaken. Guy was standing in front of her.

She gulped and wanted to look into those emerald-green eyes forever. After all these years, she couldn't believe it was really him.

"What are you doing in Paris?" she asked, trying to keep her voice steady.

Guy gave the notes to the taxi driver and closed the door. He opened his umbrella and held it over her.

"On second thought, there's nowhere I want to go. Let's stay here and go to a café instead."

"You act as if we saw each other yesterday! I haven't heard from you in ten years," she said, the blood coursing through her veins. "It's Christmas Eve! What if I had to go home to my husband?"

Guy glanced at her naked ring finger and grinned.

"Do you have a husband?" he asked.

"No." She shook her head. "I was going home to my apartment."

"Good, then we'll get a couple of brandies and some crêpes. Something must be open around here, people need to eat on Christmas Eve."

Guy led her to a restaurant, and they sat at a table by the window. Snow covered the sidewalk. She recalled the winters during the occupation when it was impossible to get warm. Now a fire crackled in the fireplace and candles flickered on the tablecloth.

"I forgot how cold Paris is in December," Guy said when the waiter brought two brandies. He sat back in his chair and gazed at her. "You look beautiful. I like your hair better now that it's long again."

She had cut her hair years ago when Christian Dior came out with his New Look. But the bob didn't suit her, and now it was the length it had been in Nice.

"How do you know I cut my hair?" Lana wondered, and her breath caught.

This wasn't Guy's first trip to Paris after the war.

"I squeezed in a few days in Paris in 1947," he admitted. "God, Paris was intoxicating in the springtime. Cherry blossoms lined the Champs-Élysées and the outdoor cafés were overflowing. I didn't want to leave."

Guy had seen her years ago, and she never knew.

"Why didn't you call?" she asked frantically.

"I looked up your mother's address. I tried calling, but there was no answer." He rubbed the rim of his glass. "I took a stroll along Avenue Montaigne and saw you arm in arm with a man. He was quite good-looking. Blue eyes and short blond hair."

"Alain," she said out loud. Alain was a banker

she met at a party. “It didn’t last long; he expected me to wait home every night with his cognac and a pair of slippers.”

“I couldn’t blame him.” Guy chuckled. “I would have wanted the same thing. If I was ever in one place long enough to own a pair of slippers.”

“Why didn’t you call after that? Moreover, why didn’t you ever call? You just disappeared.” She felt a prickle of tears as the pain from ten years ago came rushing back. “You left me and Odette. I had no idea where you’d gone.”

“I couldn’t tell you then; I shouldn’t really tell you now.”

Lana looked at Guy carefully and waited for him to continue. His hair was flecked with gray, and his shoulders were slightly hunched, but everything she had missed—the strong jaw, his voice that was smooth as butter, and his slightly cocky manner—was the same.

“But I’m tired of secrets, and I’ve discovered in this line of work there’s always someone trying to kill you.” He met Lana’s eyes. “I left for the same reason I haven’t been able to return. Because of Alois Brunner.”

Lana shuddered. She’d spent years trying to forget Alois Brunner. At first, in Geneva, she scanned the news for his whereabouts. Perhaps wherever Brunner was, Guy would be there too. She still believed that Guy’s disappearance was linked to Brunner's departure from the Riviera. But then the war ended, and Guy didn't appear, and she tried to put it all out of her mind.

"Brunner's alive?" she gasped.

"You didn't know?"

"I stopped listening to the news after the war ended and the camps were liberated." She recalled newsreels showing men and women lying on bunks, their bodies barely more than skeletons. There were newspaper photos of corpses piled into holes dug in the ground.

"Brunner evaded capture," Guy said. "We think he's in Egypt on his way to Syria."

"But the Nuremberg trials," Lana began. "Almost all the Gestapo were executed."

"They got him mixed up with another Gestapo officer named Anton Brunner. Anton was hanged for his crimes. Our Brunner didn't have the SS blood tattoo on his arm and escaped. I've been trailing him for a decade."

The waiter brought their crêpes, and Guy told her everything. In 1944, Brunner was called away from Nice to Czechoslovakia, where he sent another thirteen thousand Jews to Bergen-Belsen and Stutthof. After the war, he received false documents and escaped to West Germany. Every time Guy got close, Brunner changed his identity and slipped away.

"Henri called the day of Brunner's party. He didn't give me a choice. He didn't even let me go back to the villa to pack a bag," Guy finished, eating a bite of his crêpe. "He learned that Brunner was being sent to Prague the next day and insisted I leave that night. He wanted me to get to Czechoslovakia before Brunner."

"Henri said he hadn't heard from you," Lana reflected.

"Henri lied. Brunner had gotten close to you, and it was too dangerous. He was trying to keep you safe."

Lana remembered dancing with Brunner at the New Year's party, and her stomach turned over.

"Why didn't you tell me after the war?" she asked.

"I was on Brunner's tail and didn't want to get you involved," Guy said. "I followed him to Berlin, but he went underground. I almost gave up after the Nuremberg trials, but I got a call from an old friend in the Resistance." He sipped his brandy. "Apparently the CIA hired Brunner to be a driver in Germany."

"The CIA hired Brunner!" Lana recoiled.

"They wanted him to keep an eye on the Soviets. He was part of a secret organization." Guy grunted. "I've been chasing him ever since."

Guy started to say something and changed his mind.

"Let's not talk about Brunner anymore tonight," he offered. "I want to hear about you."

Lana told him about the year she and Odette

spent in Geneva, and then moving back to Paris and starting her cosmetics company.

"Odette is in medical school in London and staying with Charles."

"Don't tell me Charles is in the picture." Guy frowned. "I knew he'd make a move the minute I was gone."

Lana smiled to herself. There was no reason to tell Guy about Charles's proposition all those years ago.

"Charles is married with three boys," Lana said instead. "It's a perfect arrangement. Odette loves being part of a big family, and Charles's wife and Odette get along well."

Guy seemed satisfied, and Lana continued.

"Giselle married an art dealer, and they own galleries in Paris and Antibes. Pierre has a fleet of taxis in Nice," she said fondly. "The female tourists think Pierre resembles a French film star. He hasn't married, but he has lots of girlfriends."

"And your mother and Jacques?" Guy inquired.

"They spend half the year in Paris and the other half on the Riviera. They bought a villa in Villefranche-sur-Mer."

"Villefranche!" Guy exclaimed.

"I took them to the Riviera a few years ago, and my mother fell in love with the light," she said, remembering her picnic with Guy high above the Mediterranean.

Guy reached across the table and took her hand.

"Lana, tonight wasn't a coincidence. I had a few days, and I came to Paris hoping to run into you. I've thought about you every day for ten years. I used to keep your photo next to my bed, but I had to put it away. I'd hold it up to my bedside light and never fall asleep."

"I see," Lana whispered. She wanted Guy to keep talking. She wanted his words to blot out the loneliness of the last decade and all the losses of the war. The memory of Sylvie and her fears for Odette's safety. Her own baby, who would have been ten years old now, and Frederic, who sacrificed his life so that a Jewish child might survive. And all the nights since the war when she lay alone in bed and wished that Guy were beside her.

"But I couldn't offer you a normal life while I was on the hunt for Brunner. I still can't," he was saying. "In three days I have to be on a plane to Syria."

Outside the window, couples walked arm in arm along the sidewalk. Red bows were wrapped around lampposts, and the Arc de Triomphe was lit with a thousand lights.

"During the occupation, I would have given anything to see the lights of Paris on at night," she said absently. "Then the war ended, and I was quite happy. Odette was thriving, and my business grew, and I was grateful for everything I had. But I'd see someone who reminded me of you and wish we were back in the villa at Cap Ferrat." She looked at Guy and made a decision. "If you only have three days, we don't want to waste any time."

"What are you saying?" he asked.

"I have more money in my purse. We can take a taxi to my apartment."

Guy leaned forward and kissed her. His lips were warm despite the cold.

"It's Christmas, and I didn't know when I'd be in Paris again." He grinned. "I splurged and booked a suite at the George V. We'll go there instead."

Lana called her mother and Jacques in Villefranche and told them she was stuck in Paris and wouldn't be joining them for the week after Christmas as she had planned. They never knew that she and Guy had fallen in love and he proposed. There hadn't been any point in mentioning it when he was gone from her life. Then she called Odette in England and told her how much she missed her.

She bought a negligee and change of clothes at the hotel gift shop and for three days they barely left Guy's suite. They ate room-service soufflés and talked about Lana's plans for a second boutique on the Riviera and Guy's travels across Europe. One day they ventured out and visited the Louvre and explored the Christmas markets in the Place Vendôme. Afterward, they came back and made love on the poster bed. Lana felt drunk with passion and happiness.

On the evening of the third day, Lana stood in the suite as Guy packed his bags.

"You don't have to go with me to the airport," he said, zipping up his suitcase. "We can say goodbye now."

"I want to," Lana insisted. She brushed her hair in the mirror. Her reflection looked different than it had a mere three days ago: her eyes were slightly hooded, and her mouth seemed fuller.

"Are you sure?" Guy crossed the gold carpet and kissed her. "I'd rather remember you reclining against the velvet headboard eating macarons than waving goodbye at a lousy airport."

"You can still remember me here." She laughed and returned his kiss. "But I'm going to see you to the plane."

The taxi delivered them to the departure terminal at Paris Orly Airport and Guy took his bag from the trunk. Lana stepped out after him.

"That's not necessary, I have to hurry." He glanced at his watch. He wore his overcoat, and a scarf was wrapped around his neck. "We should say goodbye."

Lana swung the bag with her overnight things over her shoulder.

"I'm coming with you."

"What do you mean you're coming with me?" Guy asked.

"I'm coming to Syria. Nothing is keeping me in Paris right now. My mother and Jacques are on the Riviera for the winter, and Odette doesn't have a break from classes until June. Yvette is capable of handling the store for a few months. I wasn't planning on opening the second store until autumn."

"You can't come to Syria!" Guy exploded. "It's much too dangerous."

"I'm a thirty-five-year-old woman." She pursed her lips. "I didn't ask your permission."

"Lana, that's crazy." Guy changed his tone. "You don't know what it's like over there. There was a military coup last February, and there's great political unrest. Everyone carries guns, and there are bombs everywhere. You could get blown up sitting in a café."

"Is that different than the Riviera during the war?" she questioned. "I've been thinking about it for days. I'm not going to change my mind."

He ruffled his hair.

"But I told you, I can't offer you a normal life. Who knows how long I'll be in Syria and where I'll follow Brunner next."

"Nothing about our life together ten years ago was normal. I feel the same way about you now as I did then." She looked at Guy. "Unless you don't want me with you."

Guy's eyes traveled over her belted overcoat and knee-high boots.

"There's nothing I'd like more." He took her bag. His eyes danced, and a smile lit up his face. "We always were a good team. Come on, we'll miss our flight."

After the plane took off, the stewardesses moved through the cabin delivering pillows and blankets. The cabin smelled of cigarettes and perfume, and outside the window the lights of Paris fell away.

A stewardess in a blue-and-gold uniform stopped next to their seats. "Good evening, monsieur and madame. Can I bring you anything?"

Lana thought about the day long ago when she discovered she was pregnant with Frederic's child and was giddy with happiness. She recalled other happy moments: when she saw her name scrawled on a tube of lipstick for the first time; the day Odette got accepted to medical school. A weekend last summer with Odette and her mother and Jacques at their villa on the Riviera. Who knew what the following day would bring? They could get blown up by a bomb in Syria. She wasn't going to think about that. Guy was beside her, there wasn't any point in worrying about the future. It was the present that was important. At this moment, she was happy. How could she ask for anything else?

The plane nosed higher into the sky, and she smiled at the stewardess.

"No, thank you, I have everything I need."

Acknowledgments

I am so grateful for the two incredible women who made this book possible. Thank you to my agent, Johanna Castillo. You always know the right thing to say and do. I would be lost without you. Thank you to my editor, Kaitlin Olson. Your incredible eye gets to the heart of the story and makes it so much deeper. Thank you to everyone at Atria/Simon & Schuster, especially Isabel DaSilva in marketing and Gena Lanzi in publicity for shepherding my novels into the world. And a special thank-you to Libby McGuire and Lindsay Sagnette. I feel so lucky to have landed here.

Thank you to Fiona Henderson and the team at Simon & Schuster Australia for your expertise and enthusiasm. I couldn't be more pleased to have such an amazing team behind me in Australia.

I am fortunate to have lifelong friends: Traci Whitney, Sara Sullivan, Shannon Forman, Laura Narbutas, and Kelly Berke. And thank you to my children: Alex, Andrew, Heather, Madeleine, Thomas, and my daughter-in-law, Sarah. You are the reason for everything I do.

Topics & Questions for Discussion

1. Chapter 1 ends with Lana having lost her husband and unborn child, as "the abstract fear had become something that happened to her" (p. 21). Consider what she must have thought and felt having now been directly touched by the war. How does this set the tone of the novel?

2. Lana's grief over Frederic's death is so strong she spends most of her time at the convent in the months following his murder, taking only one class at university. Could her conviction over his death be representative of a greater sense of loss? Discuss her motivations in taking up Henri on his offer.

3. Henri gave Lana a list of instructions on how to behave when gathering information from German officers: "always accept a man's offer of a cigarette because it made a good conversation starter; wear perfume because it made men stand a little closer and become more inclined to share their secrets" (p. 47).

What are some other actions and ideas that would have been useful for Lana to use in these situations?

4. When Lana meets Guy, one of the first things he tells her is “I didn’t mean to miss the train, but sometimes things happen that I can’t control” (p. 60). How does this foreshadow the evolution of their relationship and the events that unfold?

5. Lana’s relationship with Sylvie and Odette goes directly against Guy’s orders to avoid emotional attachments. Do you think it is a natural maternal instinct that keeps Lana from staying away and has her bringing Odette presents? Is she filling the void of her own child by attempting to help these Jewish children?

6. When Lana bumps into Charles Langford after the noon cannon goes off, she remarks that the Riviera “feels like Paris before the war” (p. 183). Discuss the differences you’ve read about both settings and how the Riviera is changing for the worse.

7. Discuss how Lana’s encounter with Captain Von Harmon in chapter 13 is still relevant to women’s present-day experiences.

8. Guy finally reveals his past losses to Lana starting on page 256. How do each of their own experiences mirror the other's? Discuss their motivations for joining the Resistance. Why do you think Guy finally opens up to Lana?

9. After revealing her connection to Hans, Giselle tells Lana, "But think of something important I can do. You can't understand how I feel. I'm tired of this war, and I'm tired of hiding." Each of the characters involved in the Resistance is looking for "something important to do." How has this sentiment transcended history? What are some ways people are still looking for something important to do?

10. Discuss the difference between Lana's reaction to Frederic's death in the beginning of the novel and to Guy's disappearance later on. How does her reaction to Guy's disappearance show how her strength and ability in herself have grown?

11. Charles turns out to be an ally to the Resistance, offering to help Lana and Odette escape France. Discuss how Lana's choice not to escape to England shows her loyalty to Guy but also her newly discovered independence.

12. The novel ends ten years after the events on the Rivera with Lana living in the moment, choosing to go with Guy to Egypt. She has learned "there wasn't any point in worrying about the future. It was the present that was important" (p. 391). How is this sentiment representative of the world and the people at that time during and following World War II?

Enhance Your Book Club

1. Throughout the novel we see many examples of women not following the traditional social constructs of the time. Lana turns the traditional role of women upside down by moving in with an unmarried man as well as by going back to school and eventually owning her own business. Giselle is a single woman living alone in a villa, and Sylvie's and Lana's mothers were both single parents. Discuss how each of these women is an example of early feminism. How do they personify women's empowerment and a more progressive belief in social norms?

2. When Lana and Giselle visit Grasse in chapter 6, Lana almost forgets about the war until the close proximity of an internment camp is discussed. Many of these areas have since been designated historical sites—for example, the Museum of Jewish Heritage, A Living Memorial to the Holocaust at Auschwitz—with thousands of tourists visiting them yearly. Given that we've seen how

the world has moved on since, discuss the impact of today's internet culture on people's views: has it created an even greater gap in understanding this time in history due to what many deem disrespectful online posts of influencers at Holocaust remembrance sites, or has the internet helped to increase education and elevate the importance of these museums and sites?

A Conversation with Anita Abriel

Q: What was one of the more fascinating facts you learned from your research for this novel?

A: One of the most fascinating things I learned was what was going on in the French Riviera during this time period. One hears so much about the fate of Jews in other parts of Europe: Germany, Poland, Hungary. It was chilling to learn what happened in an area that had been a safe and beautiful haven for Jews.

Q: Throughout your writing process, what have you found to be the most resourceful way to research World War II history?

A: I often start with the location, digging up as many articles and photos of the area during the time period, and then I read everything I can get my hands on. The internet is a great resource, as is my library. The stories my mother told me about the war are also very helpful in my writing and research.

Q: How much of *Lana's War* is factual and how much is fiction?

A: Everything about Alois Brunner is factual—how Brunner was determined to exterminate all the Jews on the Riviera and how he avoided capture for years after the war. I invented Lana and Guy, but everything about the hotels being taken over by the Nazis and the raids on Jewish neighborhoods is factual.

Q: The mother/daughter relationship is threaded throughout *Lana's War* and seen most strongly between Lana and her own mother, but also in Sylvie and Odette. Why did you choose to focus on these relationships?

A: Mother-and-daughter relationships are so important to me. My own relationship with my mother shaped me, and I like to write about similar relationships in my books. Mothers often have so much wisdom to impart to their daughters, and I have found there is nothing quite like a mother's love.

Q: Why was it important to you to tell the story about the effects World War II had on children throughout Europe, specifically in France?

A: The horrific thing about World War II, or any war, is the effect on children. Children are innocent bystanders in a war, but their whole lives are upended. During World War II, so many European children not only lost their parents; they also lost their heritage. It's important to write these stories down so there is a record of these events, and hopefully they won't keep happening.

Q: Why do you think female spies were such an integral part of the Resistance and intelligence networks throughout World War II?

A: Female spies were crucial to the Resistance because their presence in many situations wasn't suspicious. They could integrate themselves into places that men couldn't without causing alarm. Women have always been good at adapting to new roles; it's part of their nature. And I think women are much braver than they are given credit for. Many women I know would do anything for their families without hesitation. That level of sacrifice was merely increased during World War II.

Q: While a large part of *Lana's War* is about the romance between Lana and Guy, the story is ultimately about Lana discovering her own independence. Did you set out to write a novel about women pushing boundaries during World War II?

A: The novel evolved as I learned more about Lana's character. Romance is always important to me: I believe that love is one of the greatest gifts in life. But at the end of the day, one has to live with oneself. To be fulfilled as a woman, it's important to always be pushing boundaries. I was raised to believe women could do anything, as long as they worked hard and didn't give up on the things they believed in.

Q: Do you have a next project in mind? And, if so, what is it?

A: My next project is also set during World War II. It is about women and family and loss. With a good dose of hope thrown in!

About the Author

ANITA ABRIEL was born in Sydney, Australia. She received a BA in English literature with a minor in creative writing from Bard College. She lives in California with her family.

Books are produced in the United States using U.S.-based materials

Books are printed using a revolutionary new process called THINKtech™ that lowers energy usage by 70% and increases overall quality

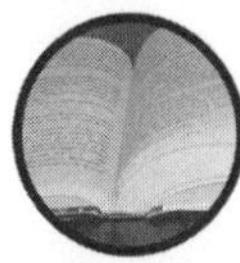

Books are durable and flexible because of Smyth-sewing

Paper is sourced using environmentally responsible foresting methods and the paper is acid-free

Center Point Large Print
600 Brooks Road / PO Box 1
Thorndike, ME 04986-0001 USA

(207) 568-3717

US & Canada:
1 800 929-9108
www.centerpointlargeprint.com